An Atlas of Bad Roads

An Atlas of Bad Roads

by Misha Burnett

First Printing: 2022

ISBN: 978-1-949313-93-2

Cover Design / Layout: Cirsova Publishing

Mystery Train originally published in *Wild Frontiers*, May 2019

The Summer of Love originally published in *Duel Visions*, February 2019

Dead Man's Chest originally published in *Milhaven's Tales of Terror*, September 2018

Black Dog originally published in *Sins of the Gods*, February 2018

227 Progress Loop originally published in *Occult Detective Quarterly #10*, Winter 2021

Epilogue previously published on-line

The Blacklight Ballet originally published in *Duel Visions*, February 2019

The Old Covenant originally published in *Planetary Anthology: Neptune*, December 2020

The Silk of Yesterday's Gown originally published in *All These Shiny Worlds II,* May 2017

What Lola Wants originally published in *Switchblade Magazine #11*, October 2019

A Cup of Kindness originally published in *Haunted Yuletide,* December 2020

We Pass From View originally published in *Sins Of The Past,* October 2014

The Lord of Slow Candles originally published in *Sins of the Fae,* November 2019

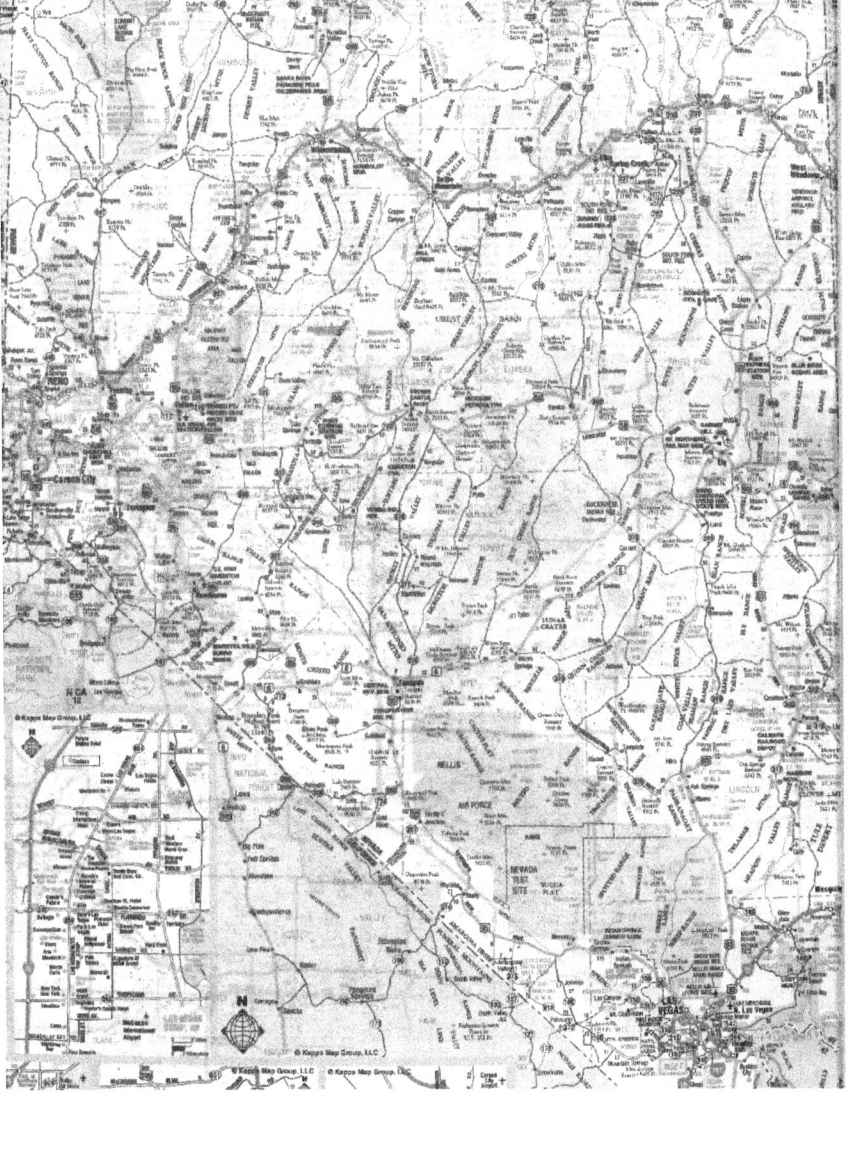

Other titles from Cirsova Publishing

From Misha Burnett
Misha Burnett's Endless Summer
Bad Dreams and Broken Hearts: The Case Files
of Erik Ruger

From Jim Breyfogle
The Paths of Cormanor
Tales of the Mongoose and Meerkat: Pursuit
Without Asking
Tales of the Mongoose and Meerkat: The Heat of
the Chase
Tales of the Mongoose and Meerkat: (Coming
2023)

Michael Tierney's Wild Stars®
The Book of Circles
Force Majeure
Time Warmageddon
Wild Star Rising
The Artomique Paradigm
Orphan of the Shadowy Moons (Coming 2023)

Cirsova Classics [Julian Hawthorne Collection]
The Cosmic Courtship
Absolute Evil & A Goth From Boston
Sara Was Judith
Doris Dances & Fires Rekindled

Table of Contents

Introduction: On the Subject of Wrong Turns

You know the scene.

EXT. HELICOPTER SHOT, DAY: A narrow, two lane blacktop road through autumn woods. A single car, older sedan, drives down the road.

SFX: Music plays as the opening credits. Gradually the music fades down to be replaced by the sound of arguing voices.

SLOW ZOOM ONTO THE CAR.

The voices grow clearer and the music fades out. Four young people, two male, two female, are arguing about which road to take. It's clear that they are lost.

The car approaches a fork in the road, unmarked. The car stops. The occupants of the car continue to argue. Angrily, the driver tells the others to be quiet, and drives to the left. As the car recedes, the camera pans down to show a fallen sign that reads, "ROAD CLOSED EXTREME DANGER NO ADMITTANCE."

You know this is a Horror movie. Because Horror movies start with wrong turns.

Horror is a genre difficult to classify, largely because it is by its nature transgressive. It breaks rules, usually starting with the rules of polite society and going on from there.

Lovecraft famously said that the oldest and strongest kind of fear was the fear of the unknown. As much as it pains me to disagree with such a luminary, I would say instead that the strongest kind of fear is fear of the *misapprehended*. It's not in encountering something completely alien that terrifies, it's encountering something that should be safe and familiar, but isn't.

A great many Horror movies begin with the metaphor of getting lost, and there is a reason for that. It's a classic opening because it works.

Most of the stories in this collection were conceived in that same spirit. I got lost.

Not the characters in the story, *me*. The author. I don't usually set out to write Horror fiction. I just make a wrong turn someplace and find myself in the haunted house, or haunted mall, or pizza factory,

Introduction

of convenience store on the graveyard shift, or... wherever. The October Country.

It's not a country that I am entirely comfortable with. I haven't made it my home, not in the way that Robert Bloch or Peter Straub have, and I don't consider myself worthy to even look upon the grim visage of its undisputed ruler, Ray Bradbury.

Nonetheless, my habit of heading off onto highway unprepared and my fondness for back roads takes me there from time to time. I slip over a border without meaning to, and there I am.

The end notes have my brief comments on the individual stories, but something for the reader to keep in mind is that most of these stories didn't start off as Horror stories, and I tend not to take the customary highways into that dark land. Like the poor teenagers who set off for a vacation and ended up being pursued through overgrown cornfields by something awful, I got there by accident.

And, like them, I spend a fair amount of time blundering around in the dark, I fear.

I do hope you'll enjoy the result, though. These stories were written over a period of about seven years. Some of them have been published before—five of them in Cirsova's *Duel Visions*, now out of print. Some of the rest were published in small press collections, and a few have never seen the light of day until now. All in all, I think they represent a particular cross section of my work to date. Most of them involve some sort of supernatural threat, although in true Weird Tales fashion, I usually don't explain the details. Details are hard to see in the dark.

And I suppose I should say something about the poetry. Well, it's poetry. I am a firm believer that formal verse—by which I mean that it rhymes and at least makes an effort toward metrical regularity— is the fiction writer's best friend. It teaches economy of phrasing and forces an expansion of the vocabulary. What elegance my prose possess was largely learned from hammering together poems.

Why did I choose to include the poems in this collection? I can't give a really logical answer, other than it *feels* right. The poems aren't directly connected to the story that follows, but I tried to match a unity of tone and theme. My advice is to read the poem first and take a moment to digest it (poetry is dense, and weighs heavily on the stomach of the mind) and try to take the mood with you when you move on to the story.

Of course, you can always choose to skip the poems and just read the stories. For that matter, you can skip the stories and just read the poems.

Or not read any of it. It's your book now, you can do with it as you like.

But I hope you'll read it all, and enjoy it. I enjoyed writing it, wrong turns and all.

Bon voyage.

Misha Burnett
19 November, 2021

The End of September

Down in the firefly weeds I remember
When the crickets chuckled of death in the grass
When I was a child at the end of September

Ambergris woodsmoke and lawnmower gas
Leaves in dead battalions of gold
When the crickets chuckled of death in the grass

A heartbeat between the heat and the cold
Sunset colors of charcoal and rust
Leaves in dead battalions of gold

Witches' eyes rimmed in skeleton dust
A time for stillness, a time for fear
Sunset colors of charcoal and rust

A voice on the wind that breathed in my ear
Run, child, run, for death's drawing nigh
A time for stillness, a time for fear

Run did I then, and run still do I
Down in the firefly weeds I remember
Run, child, run, for death's drawing nigh
When I was a child at the end of September

Mystery Train

Originally published in *Wild Frontiers*, May 2019

"**D**id you see much action during the war, Mr. Moriarty?" Isaiah Cotton, the Salt Lake City stationmaster asked.

Sean Moriarty frowned. "If you're referring to the War Between the States, sir, I was thirteen years old in '65."

The old man raised bushy white eyebrows. "Thirteen in '65... that would make you thirty-one today?"

"Yes, sir," Moriarty agreed.

"You look older than that," Mr. Cotton said. "Where are you from?"

"Illinois, sir. Town of Wood River."

"A Yankee, then."

"I prefer to think of myself as an American."

"So how does a man from the great state of Illinois end up as a federal marshal?"

Moriarty shrugged. "I needed a job. I went out west because I'd heard they needed cow hands. My father's a dairy farmer, I grew up working stock. I worked a ranch in New Mexico Territory for a couple of years. When it went bust, I needed work and the marshals were hiring."

"Work didn't agree with you?"

"I was with the marshals for six years. Then I heard of an opening with the railroad, so I applied."

"Been with us ever since?"

"That's right, sir."

"When you were with the marshals, did you ever kill a man, Mr. Moriarty?"

Moriarty kept his face impassive. "Yes, sir."

The old man waited. When it was obvious that Moriarty wouldn't volunteer any more information, he went on. "How'd you take to it?"

"It's a filthy business," Moriarty said. "Sometimes, though, the other fella doesn't leave you any choice. I never discharged a weapon that I did not have to."

"Ever shot a man for the railroad?"

"Yes, sir, on two occasions. One man died, one got away."

"Would you say," the old man paused, choosing his words with care, "that you are particularly disconcerted by the presence of the dead?"

"Disconcerted, sir?" Moriarty considered the question. "I don't believe so, no. I've attended funerals. And a few hangings. I didn't faint."

"Mr. Moriarty," the stationmaster said, seeming to come to a decision, "I've got a particularly ticklish piece of work to assign, and I believe that you are the man for the job."

"Thank you, sir," Moriarty said.

"You're familiar with the name Abraham Sutter, I presume?"

"Of course. I'm given to believe he owns a substantial interest in the railroad."

"Used to own," Mr. Cotton corrected. "He died this morning."

Moriarty nodded gravely. "I'd heard that he was ailing."

"A morbid infection of the bowels."

There didn't seem to be anything to say to that, so Moriarty just nodded.

"I have been charged with ensuring that Mr. Sutter's will is carried out," Cotton went on. "He has some rather specific instructions regarding the disposition of his remains. He is to be buried in Sacramento, and it was his will that his body be delivered there with all due speed. Overnight, if possible."

Moriarty considered that. "A good train and clear tracks could make that. Will we be leaving soon, sir? I take it that I am to accompany the remains?"

Cotton looked sour. "Mr. Sutter's will also specified certain... *rites* be performed before his body is placed in the casket."

"He was a Latter Day Saint?" Moriarty ventured.

"I would not call him a saint," Cotton opined flatly. "And I believe his wishes regarding his remains are, uh, somewhat in variance to local funerary customs as I understand them. I'll speak frankly, Mr. Moriarty, and trust to your discretion. Abraham Sutter has not been a healthy man for some time, in body *or* in mind. Quite distressing for those of us who knew him in his younger days. A formidable business intellect at one time, you understand."

Cotton fell silent for a moment, then sighed. "It is my considered opinion that his long history of ill-health adversely effected his brain. Of late he embraced odd ideas. Spiritualism. Theosophy. Oriental superstitions. He became convinced that he could escape the inevitable dissolution of his body—in the flesh, rather than trusting to a spiritual renewal through our Savior."

Moriarty nodded without comment.

"He also came to believe that he was the target of a peculiar secret society, a belief that was almost certainly true in the sense that his wealth was targeted by every charlatan and mountebank this side of the Rockies once it became known he was a devotee of the mystical."

Cotton came to an abrupt halt as if realizing that he had said more than he'd intended. In a more measured tone he added, "Your discretion in these matters is vital."

"Of course, sir," Moriarty said.

"In event, his will specified that he should travel with an escort, and that escort be armed against the possibility that parties would attempt to steal his remains, for... whatever reason," Cotton said. "You will be traveling in his private car, which should by now be hitched to Sacramento Overnight Express."

"The Death Valley Cannonball," Moriarty observed.

Cotton frowned at the nickname. "The Sacramento Overnight Express," Cotton said, emphasizing the company's official name for the run, "is being drawn by the railroad's newest Danforth-Cooke. The engineer and brakeman have been promised a substantial bonus to be in Sacramento by ten tomorrow morning."

Moriarty glanced out the window to the sky. Well after noon, but still some hours until sunset. He considered the route and nodded.

"One mail car, three freight, and Mr. Sutter's traveling car. The freight, I understand, is mixed sundries, clothing and light goods of that nature. A light train for such a mighty engine. Barring an impediment on the tracks, I anticipate that you will make the deadline handily."

Moriarty stood, feeling that the interview was at its end. Cotton stayed him with an upraised hand.

"Moriarty—that is in Irish name, I believe?"

"It is."

"Are you Catholic?"

"I am."

"I would consider it a great kindness if you would pray for Bram Sutter's soul, while on your journey. He was not a bad man, but I fear towards the end of his life he was... misled."

The intensity of Cotton's gaze was disconcerting. Moriarty

nodded slowly, realized that more was expected of him, and gravely said, "I will pray for Mr. Sutter's soul."

Then he picked up his traveling bag, slung it over his shoulder, and went out into the trainyard.

The engine was a beauty, all right, brand new and gleaming steel. Behind it was the tender, loaded with coal. Even it looked clean and new.

Next was the postal service car, clearly painted as such, the doors secured by ostentatiously large iron padlocks. Behind it was a single passenger car. Moriarty bent and glanced under the car to check the undercarriage and make sure the connections were sound.

When he looked back up he found himself nearly face to face with a woman in a black dress.

"Excuse me... miss," he said, stammering a bit. At first glance he thought her an old woman, but her face was smooth, girlish. It was only the severity of her gown that gave the impression of age. Her hair was covered by a dark scarf that was pulled back with such precision that it almost seemed a wimple and her vestments a habit. For a moment Moriarty considered amending his greeting to "Sister," so strong was this impression.

Then she smiled at him, and both the appearance of age and ecclesiastic garb faded. She was a lovely girl, too pale and unworn to be a native of the west. From back east, then, or maybe even Europe. Her gown was elegant in its simplicity, unadorned black. A mourner for the late Mr. Sutter, perhaps? Cotton hadn't mentioned any such among the passengers, but perhaps he didn't know.

"Is there a problem with the train?" she asked. Her English was clear, but her very lack of accent suggested that she'd grown up with another tongue.

"No, not at all," Moriarty reassured her quickly. "New engine, new tender. I'm just an old railroad man, checking the cars is second nature."

Her eyes flicked down his suit, registering his lack of uniform. "And what do you do for the railroad, sir?"

"Security, miss," he said automatically.

"I feel safer already," she said. Her smile dazzled him, and while he was dazzled, she turned in a whisper of skirts and was gone into the single passenger car.

Moriarty nodded after her and touched the brim of his hat. He saw several dark figures through the glass, already seated.

A wealthy foreigner, he decided, on a sightseeing trip through the American wilderness. Idly he hoped she had brought her own bodyguards. The Western territories weren't London or Paris, after all.

Then he checked the freight cars, making sure that they were latched.

Then at end, in lieu of a caboose, Mr. Sutter's own car. It was a lavish one, as befitted a part owner of the railroad. Moriarty wasn't impressed, though; he'd seen many such in his time with the company. Under the fine paneling and thick carpet, it was a standard passenger car—a long narrow box with a door at each end and windows along both sides. Much of the original furniture had been removed to make room for a long bier, although the coffin was not yet in evidence. The chairs that remained looked comfortable enough, and Moriarty considered that the job, once stripped of its macabre trappings, was one of the easiest ones he'd been assigned.

Sit in this fine car and stay awake through the night, watching for boogeymen. He'd been a bodyguard for rich men before, and this time he wouldn't even be expected to make conversation with his charge.

The walls were paneled below the windows, a fine polished rosewood. A moment's investigation revealed that the majority of the panels, when pressed, would open to reveal cabinets of a cunning space-saving design. A pocket library, mostly traveler's tales—the South Seas, Africa, India, the Orient. Interesting. Another panel revealed a small but well-stocked bar. A third held games, chessboard and pieces, a dartboard, several decks of cards and a rack of chips—

The door to the car opened, and Moriarty hastily closed the panel and stood. He turned to face the door.

Isaiah Cotton entered and guided four men, who were awkwardly maneuvering an ornate coffin up the steps and through the narrow door. The men wore the uniform of porters and were big men, experienced cargo handlers, no doubt. Still, the door was not designed for the task, and it took some sweating and grunting, directed by muttered instructions from Cotton. On the whole the performance had the air of a farce rather the the proper solemnity the occasion called for.

In due time, the coffin was settled onto the bier, and Cotton dismissed the porters with a curt nod.

"The Sacramento station master will be expecting you," Cotton said, "and it's my understanding that he will handle the paying of the behest."

Moriarty frowned. "Behest?" he asked.

Cotton raised bushy eyebrows in a feigned expression of surprise. "Oh, didn't I mention that? Mr. Sutter's will specifies a payment to his escort. Five hundred dollars, which is certainly a generous sum for one night's work." Cotton's tone made it clear that he felt that was another evidence of the tycoon's mental instability.

"It certainly is," Moriarty agreed, feeling a bit overwhelmed. That was more than he made in a year.

Cotton nodded, and turned to leave the car. At the door he paused and said, "You will remember to pray?"

"Yes, sir."

Two minutes later, the train was rolling westward along the track.

The setting sun painted the scenery outside the window in fantastic colors, the jagged bones of the Earth sticking out through the skin of the bleeding desert. It seemed impossible that this landscape could belong to the same world as the green hills of Illinois, much less the same country. No matter how long he lived in the West, the high desert never lost its power to astonish him with its savage beauty.

Moriarty turned to look at the coffin. The sides and lid were carved with patterns that struck him as more mathematical that theological, circles with triangles, triangles within circles, lines crossing and recrossing, but nowhere a human figure or even anything recognizable as script. The pattern was as intricate as a Navajo blanket, and as barren of meaning.

Feeling the weight of his promise to Mr. Cotton upon him, Moriarty retrieved his rosary from his bag and got to his knees, carefully due to the swaying of the train. He lowered his eyes, and beginning with the cross, he murmured, *"Credo in Deum Patrem omnipotentem, Creatorem caeli et terrae..."*

As he prayed, he felt himself relax. He was, his father would have said, an indifferent Catholic. Frequently, the railroad had him travel on Sundays, and his address was perpetually "in transit," which precluded any allegiance to a parish. Nonetheless, he did attend mass when he was able, often in tiny Mexican churches where his fair hair and complexion elicited curious looks. He confessed to a priest when time and circumstances allowed. At other times, he confessed to the vacant immensity of the night sky, feeling the weight of the heavens upon him, the weight of the glory of God, and cried to the stars, *"Miserere nobis!"*

As he prayed, small bead, large bead, in the old and comforting pattern, he felt the presence of the Holy Family, St. Joseph, the Blessed Virgin, Christ the Redeemer.

Lord, have mercy on me, a sinner.

When he had come to the end of his beads, he made the sign of the cross as he had seen Mexican peasants do it, a touch to forehead, abdomen, each shoulder, then a second pass to make a smaller cross at each spot, then a kiss to the rosary before stowing it carefully back in his bag.

Still on his knees, he addressed himself to the coffin and said, *"Réquiem ætérnam dona ei Dómine; et lux perpétua lúceat ei. Requiéscat in pace. Amen."*

In English he added, "I did not know this man, but I took his money while he lived, and I owe him my loyalty. I ask that his sins be forgiven in the name of Jesus. *In nómine Patris, et Fílii, et Spíritus Sancti. Amen.*"

If God answered, His answer was inaudible. Moriarty felt, at least, as if he had discharged his promise and his duty in good order. He chose a seat with a good view out the windows and sat back. The key to staying vigilant on a long trip, he'd found, was being comfortable.

The train picked up speed, and the miles rolled past.

As the sky grew darker, he lit the lamps that hung in a row down the center of the car. He'd started to wish he'd brought something to eat. There might be some kind of victuals stored in one of the cupboards, but Moriarty didn't much fancy the idea of eating a dead man's food.

In the game cabinet there was a slim volume entitled *101 Diverting Problems In The Game of Chess.* Moriarty took the book, the board, and the pieces. The board, he saw, had a small hole drilled in the center of each square and the each piece had a corresponding peg on their base, to prevent the game from upset due to the swaying of the train. He set up the board to match the first puzzle and studied it. He was no master of the game, but it should keep him awake for the hours it would take to reach California.

He'd solved two problems and was studying the third when the train began to slow. He pulled out his watch to check the time and was surprised to see how late it had gotten. Time to take on water. He went to the window and saw the lanterns of the engineer and brakeman. They were hurrying to fill the boiler and get moving again, mindful of the bonus Cotton had mentioned.

There was a knock on the door of the car.

It was the forward door, and Moriarty hurried to it. The only other railroad employees were at work on the siding, watering the boiler. But why would a passenger be at the door?

It was the woman in black whom he had seen at the Salt Lake Station.

"Miss?" Moriarty asked, confused.

"Heget," she said, stepping past him and into the car. "My name is Heget."

"Miss... Heget," Moriarty said hesitantly, intimidated by her manner, "you should return to your car. We won't be here long, and you won't be able to get back once we start rolling again."

She turned her gaze to him, a soft smile on her lips. "I'll be stuck in here with you? There are worse ways to spend the journey along the twelve hours of the night, I'll wager."

Moriarty frowned and fought to control his anger. There were always some passengers who thought they were above the rules, and it was not uncommon for them to be young, pretty women. No doubt she was accustomed to her smile making men do whatever she wished.

That didn't work on Sean Michael Moriarty.

"Miss Heget," he said sharply. "If you will read your ticket you will see that your passage is subject to conditions set by the railroad and among them is the stricture that you remain in the car to which you have been assigned. Failure to do so can result in your being put off the train."

Her eyes grew wide with an amused surprise. "Why, I do believe that you are serious, Mr. Moriarty. You would leave me in the wasteland to be beset by savages and wild beasts."

"Miss—" Moriarty began.

She held up one hand, graceful and slim, and his voice stilled.

She had an imperious manner, one that went beyond that of a simple wealth and privilege. She acted like royalty.

"One moment," she said, moving past him to the casket in the middle of the car. "I simply wish to pay my respects."

"You knew Abraham Sutter?" Moriarty asked. He glanced out the window. The lights were still moving around on the siding, evidence that the watering was in progress.

"Intimately," she breathed, gazing down at the patterns carved into the wooden box. "Oh, he was a clever boy, wasn't he?"

Outside the window the lanterns were moving back to the engine.

"Miss, for you own safety—" he began.

She raised her eyes to his. Those eyes were very large and startlingly blue. "We'll talk again," she said and was gone out the door into the night before Moriarty could react. He went to the door, but her dark clothes made her invisible in the night.

Serves her right if she gets left behind, he thought savagely.

A few minutes later the engine's whistle blew, and the train lurched into motion again.

It was only after he had seated himself and was setting up the chess pieces again that it occurred to him that he had never told her his name. Maybe the engineer had recognized him and mentioned his name to her. Whoever she, was it was clear that came from wealth. If she had known Mr. Sutter, it was possible—likely, even—that she was related to a shareholder of the railroad.

He sighed. Complications. Freight runs were the best, no one on board save fellow employees, nothing to worry about except track collapses, wild animals, and the occasional bandit gang. He'd take any combination of the three over rich, spoiled passengers any day.

He set up another chess problem and listened to the wheels running over the tracks and the wind rushing past the windows. They were making good time, the engine running smooth and swift as a silver fish cutting through an ocean of night. His eyes felt heavy and he realized all of sudden that both black bishops were on white squares and he couldn't figure out where he'd made a mistake. He tried to set up the pieces again, but the diagram in the book didn't make any sense. The black queen was threatening the white knight and the black queen looked like Miss Heget, smiling her enigmatic smile. The chessboard wasn't a chessboard anymore, that was the problem. He was trying to set up the pieces on the geometric patterns on the lid of Mr. Sutter's coffin, but that wouldn't work because there were too many pieces all of a sudden, dozens of them, pawns and kings and shapes he'd never seen before like twisted tree roots, and all the while the black queen kept laughing at him...

Then the whistle shrieked, and Moriarty's eyes snapped open. The train was stopped. He checked his watch. He'd been dozing over the chessboard while they crossed a hundred miles of desert—

Miss Heget was sitting on a chair across the car, on the other side of the casket from him. Two hulking men, also dressed in black from head to toe, stood behind her chair.

Heart hammering, Moriarty lurched to his feet, upsetting the chair. The three figures across the car reacted no more than a trio of waxworks. The scene was so uncanny that he was sure for a moment that he was still dreaming, and he scrubbed his eyes with his fists and looked again.

The young woman and her two bodyguards were still there, watching him.

Then Heget spoke, "Sit down, Mr. Moriarty. We have business to discuss."

"You're trespassing," Moriarty said, still standing. He felt in his pocket for his revolver. "I am going to have to ask you to leave."

"Please," she spoke with perfect calm, "sit. You have committed a grave injustice. I should like to give you the opportunity to make amends."

"What injustice?" Moriarty backed away clutching his revolver in his jacket pocket. The odds weren't good, with two men in the car who were probably also armed.

"Sit. I will explain."

Moriarty leaned against the window frame. The emergency cord ran along the window frame, inches from his hand. Even if the engineer and brakeman were assisting with the water and coal, they should hear the bell from the engine.

"All that you will accomplish by pulling that," Miss Heget said sharply, "is getting those men killed."

Moriarty was certain that he hadn't even glanced at the cord.

"My other retainers are at the front of the train," the woman continued. "They are constrained at the moment from taking action against mortals who are uninvolved with this affair. If you involve them, they become fair game. My patience is not inexhaustible."

22

There was no sign from the seated woman, but the two men behind her stepped forward.

Before they could cross the car, Moriarty reached behind him to right the chair he'd knocked over, then sat. "Who are you and what do you want?"

"I told you, I am Heget," the woman said. The two men moved back to stand behind her. Outside the window, the train's whistle blew. They'd finished refueling. "And I want what is mine."

Moriarty braced himself as the train lurched into motion again. He noticed that the others didn't, yet remained as still as if rooted to the spot. "All right," he said, "What is it that is yours, and how am I keeping you from getting it?"

Heget smiled. "Therein hangs a tale."

She gestured at the window. Moriarty glanced at it, then stared, open-mouthed. Instead of the desert landscape, beyond the window was a swamp, as seen from a boat on a slow moving river. On the bank of the river was a bonfire, surrounded by figures engaged in some sort of dance.

"Natchez," Heget said, "before the war. My... congregation. Young Abraham is there—he's in the owl mask."

Moriarty continued to stare. He could feel the wheels of the train below his feet, rushing through the night, but his eyes told him that they were drifting slowly. He could smell the smoke of the fire, the warm dampness of the mossy air. He heard music, too, a savage rhythm pounded on wooden drums. The figures, he saw, were masked, but wore nothing else except daubs of white mud tracing designs on their bare tanned skin.

"Abraham is thirteen, and he is being consecrated to my service. His mother is officiating the ceremony—she's on the far side of the fire, in the mask with the long horns. See her?"

Moriarty swallowed, his throat dry. He looked back to the woman in the car—if woman she was.

"How?" He couldn't complete the question.

Heget waved that away. "A minor trick. I simply want you to see that I tell you is true."

"*What* are you?"

"That's hardly important," she said. "I am sure that you can form your own opinions on the subject. Suffice to say that I am someone who makes deals, and I keep my bargains."

Mystery Train

"What kind of deals?"

She seemed exasperated by the question. "The usual kind of deal, Mr. Moriarty. *Everybody* wants *something*. I give it to them."

Another gesture at the window. The scene outside was now a sunlit square in some Eastern town, a large crowd milling around a courthouse. Moriarty was hit with a wave a vertigo because he could still feel the movement of the train, but the window seemed motionless, as if he were standing in a building facing the square.

"In Abraham's case, it was wealth," Heget went on. "Are you familiar with the North Georgia Gold Lottery? No? Well, it was in '32, before you were born. After the state removed the Cherokee, they held a drawing to assign mining rights to the land. I arranged for Abraham to win a rich lot, and in very short order his dreams of wealth were realized."

The scene changed again, and Moriarty gripped the windowsill. Whatever magic lantern trick this strange... person was doing, it was giving him vertigo. Now the window seemed to look down over the aisle of a church, as if the train car had been transported to the choir loft.

A wedding was in progress, the pews full of a well-dressed crowd. There were soft murmurs from the bride and groom. Moriarty noticed the church seemed strangely unadorned, lacking even a cross over the altar, and the priest—if priest he was—wore a simple black suit.

"Next he wanted love, and I gave him that, too." Heget went on. "Prudence was such a lovely girl, and from a fine family."

A sigh from Heget. Then, "Sadly, love did not thrive, despite the young couple's advantages. Abraham tired of his bride and sought to replace her with a woman more... in keeping with his tastes. He once again asked for my assistance, and I freely granted it."

The scene outside the window shifted again. It was a bedroom, richly appointed in what was obviously a mansion. A slim woman, moving with the slow, underwater motions of a sleepwalker, crossed the room to a chair. A rope hung from the ceiling beam above the chair. The woman mounted the chair and tied the rope into a crude noose.

Horrified, Moriarty tore his eyes away from the scene. Distantly he seemed to hear the sound of the chair falling, then the creaking of a laden rope swinging.

"Shall I continue?" Heget asked politely. "For three-score years and ten, as specified by the terms of our contract, I granted him many favors." An earthy chuckle. "Starting with his second wife."

A cry from the window startled Moriarty. It was wild and sensual, a cry of passion. Dark, animal passion. Moriarty refused to turn to look.

Heget gave a wry grin and inclined her head as if conceding the round. Then she continued, "His business thrived. Competitors had unexpected reversals. His own investments blossomed. He always invested in industries on the verge of success. His canny strategies were well known in banking world. People said that Abraham Sutter had 'the touch.' He seemed to know just when a penny could be spent to return a dollar." She paused, ironic eyes above a toothy grin. "As if by magic."

"Through his seventieth year, he maintained the physique of a young man." Heget waved a hand airily. "Not too obviously, of course. Nothing that would cause talk. Outwardly he aged just as other men, but he escaped the worse ravages of time. He had none of the annoyances of digestion or joints that bedevil other men of his age. His..." her pause was suggestive "*vitality* remained undiminished."

She glanced down, smiling sweetly as if indulging a memory both private and sweet. Then she lifted her head to meet Moriarty's eyes.

"At the appointed hour, I withdrew my protection, as we had agreed. And even then, I did nothing malicious, nothing to hasten his demise. I simply allowed nature to take its wonted course. It took two years, and he died a wealthy man, pampered by servants and drifting gently away on a warm sea of rum and morphine."

"What does any of this have to do with me?" Moriarty asked coldly.

Hegets's eyes flashed with anger. "I am coming to that, young man."

She stood fluidly, moving with an uncanny grace despite the swaying of the rushing train. She crossed to the ornate casket and held her hands above the carved wood, not touching it. "Abraham's lovely mother, Emmalou, was a conjure woman of no small skill. It was she who made the... initial overtures in our relationship. Naturally, she passed her knowledge to her son. Later in his life, as he felt his days slipping away, he strove to increase his mastery of the craft. He had the resources to purchase arcane knowledge from the ends of the Earth by that time." A shrug, a gently feminine gesture at odds with what Moriarty had come to know of the other. "Many of my clients do likewise, of course. They search for a way to break our compact before the payment comes due. I indulge such efforts, since they are invariably futile."

Comprehension dawned and Moriarty smiled. "Abraham Sutter found a way."

Heget looked down at the casket. "He found half a way, rather." Then back at Moriarty. "You provided the other half."

"Me?"

"You and..." Heget nearly snarled the words, "the Power you serve."

"The Power," Moriarty said. "You mean—"

"If you speak that Name in my presence, I will feed your eyes to my ravens," Heget's voice boomed through the car, and Moriarty flinched back.

The car swayed, and he risked a glance out the window. The desert night, stars swarming above black mountains. Back to his three strange companions. The two men were as still as granite pillars. If he hadn't seen them move earlier, he would suspect they were realistic manikins. Heget was as motionless, leaning over the casket, watching him.

"The Power I serve," he gave her words back to her. "You mean my prayer for Mr. Sutter's soul."

Animation returned to Heget. She nodded. "This construct, crude as it is, will not permit me to directly affect his mortal remains. Ordinarily that would prove only a minor obstacle, but your... *petition* complicates matters."

Moriarty nodded slowly, digesting that. "I see," he said at last.

"And you see why you must rescind your benediction," Heget said firmly.

"What?"

"You have taken what is mine," Heget said, rage showing now in her face and voice, "You and... the Other. Abraham had enough skill as a hedge wizard to build this box for his corpse, but that alone wouldn't have been enough to cheat me of my due. He could not petition for assistance from the Other on his own behalf, not after he had signed the compact with me. Only one who had shared the Feast of the Lamb could make invoke that protection."

"And now you expect me to..." Moriarty struggled for words. "To... what? Pray for his damnation?"

"Nothing so melodramatic!" Heget laughed. "Simply speaking aloud the intention will be enough."

"I... can't do that."

"Of course you can! It doesn't even have to be in Latin—you must know the language doesn't matter, it's just a silly affectation. Just admit that you were wrong to intercede on Abraham's behalf."

Moriarty shook his head. "But I wasn't wrong."

Heget laughed. "Not wrong? Praying for the soul of a black magician? If you had known what manner of man he was, would you have asked for his salvation?"

Moriarty considered that for a long moment, feeling the click of the rails under his feet. "Maybe not," he admitted. "But that doesn't mean I was wrong to... do what I did. It's not for me to decide who is worthy of salvation."

"But that is what you did," Heget said. "You took it upon yourself to intercede for Abraham."

"I made the petition," Moriarty replied. "I didn't grant it."

"*You had no right to make that petition!*"

Moriarty nodded. "No right at all," he agreed sadly. "It's not by right that we approach... that One."

"Abraham is *mine,*" Heget snarled. "He gave himself to me, freely, and I paid him all that I promised him and more. Justice demands that I get what is mine."

"Grace demands that you do not."

"You serve a cheat and a liar," Heget said. "A thief. That power turned against us—we who were once his most favored children. Do you think that you will receive better?"

"I can't say. I know I don't deserve better."

A sharp bark of laughter. "No, you don't, Sean Michael Moriarty. I can see your soul, and it is a small and ugly thing. You live your entire life from bloody birth to bloody death in the time it takes me to draw a breath. You have murdered. You have lain with whores. You have stolen—stolen from your own father. Your heart is as black as mine, and your crimes are less only because you are so weak."

Moriarty was silent.

"You think that you will be welcomed? What makes you think that? Why should some piece of meat like you be admitted into that eternal kingdom when I—I who was born there, who walked those fields in ages past—am cast out?"

"Because I asked for forgiveness."

Heget screamed with rage then and threw herself at Moriarty, and for a moment, all that he could see was her onrushing face, distorted into a thing of horror by blind imbecilic hate. In terror, he threw himself backwards and tumbled onto the floor of the car, her scream going on and on—

—and becoming the scream of the train whistle.

He was lying on the floor of the traveling car, the overturned chair beside him. The car was slowing. He lifted his head.

He was alone in the car, except for the oddly carved casket. To the east, the sky glowed red.

He got up and went to the window. Painted on the side of the water tank was *Roseville, California.*

"I slept the whole night away," Moriarty said softly to himself.

It was dawn.

When the train stopped, he got out onto the platform, stretching his stiff limbs. The engineer and brakeman were filling the boiler, the steam adding to the already considerable heat.

"How are we doing?" Moriarty asked.

"Great," the engineer said. "We'll have breakfast in Sacramento."

"How are the passengers?"

"Passengers?" the brakeman asked.

Moriarty turned to gesture at the car, then froze in place. There was no passenger car. The engine, a mail car, three freight cars, and then Abraham Sutter's traveling car. That was all.

"Didn't we..." Moriarty was suddenly sure of the answer, but asked it anyway, "have a passenger car when we left Salt Lake? Did we drop it somewhere along the way?"

The engineer and brakeman exchanged a look. The engineer answered. "Not this run. Heck, you know the Death Valley Cannonball is a mail run. We almost never have passengers."

"I must have been confused," Moriarty said.

"Must have been," the brakeman agreed. "They got some coffee boiling in the station office. Why don't you grab yourself a cup."

"I think I'll do that."

When the train got back underway, Moriarty collected the scattered chess pieces and board and set up another problem, but he found it hard to concentrate. Instead, he looked out the window at desert landscape, growing bright in the clean light of the morning sun. What a dream he'd had.

He looked back at the coffin containing Abraham Sutter's mortal remains.

"As I am," he said softly, "you once were. As you are, I must someday be."

He looked back at the chessboard. *White knight takes black queen*, he thought.

Mate.

Letters From the Front

"Pass your letters down the line, boys, pass your letters back"
The Quartermaster hefted the great and greasy sack
"We'll send them back to Base HQ and they'll send them home from
    there"
The Quartermaster's words were soft and scarce disturbed the air.

"If you don't know what to write," the Sargent's voice was also low
"Start out with 'I love you', that's always apropos
"You can say that we're advancing, but you can't say where to."
"Not that we know anyway," muttered someone in the crew.

"Is mail call finished?" asked the Captain, as he stood before the
    ranks.
"Seal your letters, send them off, we've an appointment with some
    tanks.
We want them safely on the train before the foe begins to shell
We're skipping lunch today, boys, tonight we feast in Hell."

The Summer of Love

Originally published in *Duel Visions*, February 2019

September 15th, 1968

You can watch the realization sink in, when they shuffle out of the darkness of the trucks and into the murderous Nevada sunlight. From the flat slab of bare rock we call the processing yard, you can see into The Pit, that vast multilevel excavation, spiraling down through the desert rock like Dante's Hell.

Technically, of course, it's the Silver State Cooperative Mine. But no one calls it that, except on official documents. By the time the men in the backs of the big black unmarked trucks get here, they've heard the stories. This is The Pit.

We take gypsum out of the ground and put men into it.

Beaten, starved, herded into containers and driven over miles of Godforsaken desert, the men know that they have been brought here to die. The average sentence of a prisoner is twenty-five years. The average life span is eight. They know that, but it's only when they see The Pit in all of its infernal glory that they understand in their hearts that they are walking dead men.

I've been assigned here for nine years. I've been on the upper perimeter for the last three. I've seen a lot of men brought in. The Pit, as they say, is always hungry.

Some men just give up and die as soon as they get here. They'll keep moving, but that's the body's reflexes, like a fish will flop around with its head cut off. You have to prod them to get them out of the way, and there's no point trying to get much work out of them. They look like they're standing up, but it's just a vertical grave.

There are fewer of that kind than you might think, though. Most men make some kind of bargain with The Pit, the work, the starvation, the killing heat and the strangling dust. *I'll die here,* they think, *but not today*. They put all of their energy into finding ways to survive one more day. They learn to read The Pit like a giant sundial, jealously guarding patches of shadow. They build dew catchers out of scraps of tent cloth and wire. They hoard their strength, plotting the paths of the ore carts for maximum efficiency and minimum effort.

The Summer of Love

In the end, of course, The Pit wins. Just like in Vegas, three hours by bus down the road, the game is designed to make the suckers think they've got a chance, but the house takes it all. Every single time.

Then there are those who gaze into the waiting abyss, understand that they have nothing to lose, and decide to take some of us with them on the way down.

Fortunately, they're rare. Most hero types get themselves killed long before they get to a sentencing hearing. You've got to watch for them, though. Sometimes the only thing that keeps a man from turning into a rabid dog is the hope that civilization still means something. You can get a lot of cooperation from people by holding out the promise that if they just behave and do what they're told, then everything will be okay. You know that the promise is a lie, and deep down inside, they know it's a lie, too, but they want to believe it so badly that they deceive themselves. That's the reason for all the rules and the uniforms and the whole big show. They make it easier for the prisoners to believe that places like The Pit are something other than a great big open grave.

With some men, when you take away the last hope, you also take the choke chain off that rabid dog that always knew you were lying.

All of which explains why I was watching the prisoners getting out of the truck instead of watching the guards.

My guards, technically. I was shift lead. Once upon a time, I'd been sergeant in the United States Army, and when the US joined the International League and the US Army became part of the League Peacekeeping Force, I kept my rank. It didn't mean much out here in a hole in the world, but on paper I was the guy in charge.

Kraus didn't pay any attention to who was in charge on paper. He was a Euro, an arrogant German son of a bitch who thought that since they won a war against Britain that anyone who spoke English was his inferior. Rumor had it that he had connections back in Berlin. What a guy like that was doing in The Pit was a mystery, although there were some theories. Some guys thought that he had gotten caught messing with some cabinet minister's wife or daughter and got sent here as a punishment. Others figured he had asked for the transfer—he was big and mean and liked hurting people.

The Pit was a good place for that. The desert could swallow any atrocity.

An Atlas of Bad Roads

I'd given up trying to tell Kraus what to do. He'd just give me this blank uncomprehending stare until I shut up, then went back to doing whatever he wanted. I'm not sure what that was—killing time with his Kraut buddies in the motor shop, probably—but it didn't involve being at his assigned duty station very often. Which was fine with me.

We logged the truck in at 14:00—middle of the afternoon and the heat of the day. The manifest said that there were 36 bodies inside. Creech Air Station at Indian Springs said that they were all alive when they left. On a day like today, we'd probably end up dragging half of them out, and half of those would go straight to the steep sided excavation that the troops called the Rose Garden.

I was in the gatehouse. Bucky and Turk would open the doors to the truck once the gate was secured. Those two would be unarmed, but they were my bruisers, both of them experienced at using their bulk to intimidate prisoners into compliance.

Hanging back by the gate was the rest of the squad, led by Negev. Six men with rifles pointed at the back of the truck. Absently I noticed that it was six men this time, not five, which meant that Kraus was in position. I didn't think much of it at the time; I was watching the truck.

Bucky and Turk trotted up, pulling their gloves on. The latches on the back of the truck were metal, and you could lose skin on any exposed metal that had been in the sun for more than a minute.

They looked to me in the gatehouse. I checked the board, and the three big lights were green, meaning that the magnetic locks that held the gate shut were all engaged.

I hit the intercom switch. "Tower one, tower two, are you ready?"

Stern and Peters gave me curt replies. They were on the 13mm guns in the towers, both set to cover the whole processing yard. They were good men. Tower duty was one of the best jobs on the gate, the towers were shaded and even had fans to keep the desiccated air moving—not for the comfort of the guards, of course. Too much heat could spoil the ammo.

I clicked over to the loudspeaker. "Go ahead and open her up," I said.

Bucky swung open one door and stepped back, then Turk pulled open the other.

Turk hollered, "Prisoners! Out!" in his funny high pitched voice,

33

and we waited to see how many would be able to crawl out of that reeking hell on their own power. I was counting moving bodies and had gotten up to eleven crouched in a ragged line—none able to stand upright yet—when I heard Stern shout from the tower.

"Kraus! Return to station! *Kehern Sie! Unmittelbar*!"

Only then did I see Kraus, walking towards the prisoners with his weapon slung. What the Hell was he thinking? I added my voice to Stern's.

"Kraus," I called over the loudspeaker, "Get back to the line. Do not approach the prisoners."

Rule number one—the ironclad rule that should be drummed into every officer long before he got anywhere near The Pit—is that no weapons are ever allowed within arm's length of the prisoners. Guards who had direct contact with the prisoners were unarmed.

Then Negev sung out, "Back now, Kraus!"

Kraus ignored all of us. Turk was pulling a prisoner out of the truck and Bucky stood over the ones who were already out. Neither of them looked back; they kept their focus on the ragged men at their feet.

Kraus trotted up and unslung his weapon. I just stared, uncomprehending. Kraus reached the first of the crouching figure and swung his weapon like a club, felling the prisoner.

Bucky looked around then, his face a mirror of the shock I felt.

Kraus, grinning like an idiot, swung his weapon at the next prisoner, and that man went down in a heap. He stepped on top of the second man to ready a swing at the third.

All of us were yelling now, and Bucky took a step toward Kraus. He looked like he was getting ready to manhandle Kraus back away from the prisoners, but he didn't get the chance.

Instead, the prisoner on the ground under Kraus's feet jerked and pulled, and Kraus went down, his weapon falling free. The next prisoner in line caught it. He must have had some military training, because he didn't hesitate, he swung it in an arc and opened up on the rest of the squad standing back by the gate.

I hit the ground in the gatehouse, and the towers opened up with their 13mms. I put my arms over my head. There was nothing I could do now except wait it out.

When the thunder finally stopped, we were able to take stock. All of the prisoners were dead—Peters had stitched the truck from end to end. The drivers were okay; they had both dropped to the floorboards when the shooting started, and Peters hadn't sprayed the cab.

Kraus was dead, the damned crazy bastard, and so were Turk and Bucky.

In Negev's squad, Vetch and Million had both been hit. Million got it in the gut; he'd get shipped back to Creech for a real doctor to work on. Vetch had a couple of through-and-throughs in his leg; we'd patch him up here and let him ride a desk for a while.

Pretty soon, everyone on the perimeter was running up, drawn by the noise. The big sirens were going off, too, alerting the whole Pit. Lockdown.

I put Negev in charge of cleaning up the mess and went to the Commandant. I figured it was better to put my head on the block than wait for them to drag me.

Commander Washington was a good man, and a top administrator. If he'd been white, he'd probably be a general, but there was no way that the Security Directorate would promote anyone who wasn't a racially pure European that high up the food chain. So he was stuck here, until he either died in office or retired. He didn't seem bitter about it, though. He had a reputation as a reasonable commander, and the men liked him.

I surrendered my sidearm to regimental secretary and asked him to tell the Commandant that I would await his pleasure. I took a seat in the outer office. I picked up a German photography magazine and leafed through it. Art shots in black and white of nude women in bird masks.

After about ten minutes, an orderly waved me into the Commandant's office.

"Okay," Commander Washington said, lighting a cigarette, "have a seat and tell me all about it."

I gave him the story, beginning to end. He didn't interrupt me, didn't ask any questions. When I was done, he told me to go have a seat in the outer office.

I went back to the birds. I knew a little German, but there were too many words that I didn't recognize to read the text. Probably art words.

I saw an orderly bring Negev in to see the Commandant, and after he was escorted out, Stern was brought in. They let me sit there without a guard. I waited.

Then the secretary told me to go back in to see the Commandant again. He had two sets of papers on his desk, typed neatly on official blue paper. He handed me the first one.

"Here," he said. "Four days in Vegas, next transport."

A little taken off guard, I looked down at it. It was a four day pass, sure enough, with the effective date as today. I looked back up, confused.

The commandant's weathered black face was impassive. "You've got accumulated leave and the rules state you can use it at my discretion. The bus is leaving at seventeen."

"Thank you, Sir," I said automatically.

He handed me the other neatly stapled set of papers. "Orders to report to Camp HQ for reassignment, effective 4 days hence. I'm relieving you of your command, effective immediately."

I nodded. "I see, Sir."

He closed his eyes and rubbed the bridge of his nose for a moment before replying. "I doubt seriously that you do, soldier," he said at last. "I have just received word that we will be hosting an inspection team from the Security Directorate. A team led by one General Horst Kraus."

Despite the heat, my gut felt cold all of sudden. "His father, Sir?"

"Uncle, I think," the commandant shrugged. "Look, there wasn't anything that you could have done differently. Everybody backs your story. Kraus brought it on himself, and he got two good men killed in the process. But... I'm thinking it would be better if you weren't here when General Kraus arrives."

"Yes, Sir," I said.

He went back to rubbing his face, then suddenly seemed to remember that I was still in the room. "Dismissed, soldier."

I saluted and left.

I went back to my quarters and changed clothes. I scrubbed my face and hands, then dug out my civilian suit. It was wrinkled, and I'd lost weight since the last time I'd worn it. I could take a shower in Vegas, I thought. A real shower, not just a sponge bath. Maybe I'd just get a cheap room off the strip and stand under running water for four days straight.

I packed my other suit and some socks in my weekend bag and put my papers on top. I tried to wipe the dust off the bag and just smeared it around. I couldn't remember the last time I'd been out on a pass. A year, maybe? Two? The days all ran together in The Pit. We didn't have seasons here, just unrelenting killing sunlight broken by a few flash floods a year.

Once I was dressed, I stopped by the PX and cashed a check. Then I headed for the fence. I showed my papers half a dozen times to get to the bus and got them stamped twice.

The bus was ancient, old enough that the grill said "Ford" instead of "National Motor Works". I flopped down on battered seat covered with what I guessed were tire patches and closed my eyes. The bus was only about a quarter full and nobody sat next to me.

I napped. Woke up briefly when we stopped in Indian Springs, then napped some more. It was getting dark when we got to Vegas and the neon was starting to paint the sky. I didn't bother trying to find a hotel with a military discount, I just grabbed a cab to Fremont Street and checked into a place at random. They had a bar and a pool; that was good enough for me.

I went straight up to the room and took a shower, a long shower. I scrubbed myself until my skin was raw and I finally felt really clean for the first time since...

Well, I couldn't remember the last time I had felt clean.

I put on my civilian suit and found myself looking in the mirror at an old man. An old, thin, man, growing bald, skin worn to leather by the desert sun, in a cheap suit ten years out of date.

I'm forty-seven, I thought. That's not old, not really old. Born in nineteen twenty-one, signed up in nineteen forty, when all the papers were sure that the US of A was going to join in the European War. Twenty-eight years in uniform, half of it in the US Army, half of it in the LPF. Two more years and I could retire.

If they didn't change the rules on us again.

You need a drink, I told the skinny old man in the mirror. A drink, some music, and maybe a girl who can make you feel young again in exchange for some cash. This was Vegas, after all. I had no idea how to find a working girl, even here, but I doubted that would be much of a problem. They were probably on lookout for soldiers on leave.

Damn, it had been a long time.

I walked past the waiting cabs at the curb and down Fremont, picked a casino at random without even noticing the name spelled out in blinking lights across the front.

I broke a couple of bills at the cashier's cage and went to the slot machines. Lots of flashing lights and ringing bells that clashed with the music coming from somewhere further inside. I took a stool and started feeding coins into the machine, more to have something to do with my hands than any real interest in gambling.

Now that I was here I was starting to feel distinctly uncomfortable. I didn't know what to do. I was so used to having every minute of my day planned out for me in advance. Relax. Have a good time. Did I even know how to do that anymore?

A waitress came by, leather boots and fishnet stockings and nothing at all above the waist. I stared at her. I must have looked like a rube, but she didn't seem to mind, she stood with one hip cocked forward and her hands on her hips and let me ogle her. After a moment, I recovered my composure and asked her for a shot of whiskey and a glass of beer, I didn't care about the brand.

She walked away, her hips rolling. Damn. It had been a *long* time.

When she came back with a tray and a broad smile, I handed her a couple of bills.

"Keep the change," I said, trying to meet her eyes.

"Drinks are complementary for players," she told me.

"In that case," I said, giving up and speaking directly to her chest. "Keep it all."

She went away again. For a moment I considered just hauling out the rest of my cash and seeing if she'd take it to go back to my room, but I restrained myself. It could get ugly, and I had no intention of spending my leave in the Clark County lockup. I was sure I'd get approached sooner or later. Probably sooner.

I threw back my shot and started coughing my lungs out. It had been a long time for that, too, and my chest felt like it was on fire. Through watering eyes, I found the beer and managed to drag the glass to my lips, spilling a generous measure down my shirt in the process. A couple of swallows and I had myself back under control.

That was smooth, I thought. Heck, at this rate I wouldn't have to proposition Bootsie to get myself bounced out of here. I fumbled some more coins into the one-armed bandit. See, fellows, I'm spending money. Leave me alone.

The waitress came back and I asked for a soda. One shot and one beer and I was feeling light headed. She got me a soda and unobtrusively left a stack of napkins. I tipped her outrageously again.

I ran out of change and decided that I needed food more than booze. I found the buffet line and loaded a plate, took it to a booth in the back and dug in. Good food, although it wouldn't take much to beat the mess hall at The Pit.

I was starting to feel ready to hit the bar again when somebody called my name.

"Blake?" an unfamiliar man's voice asked. "Roger Blake?"

I looked up. The man was big and beefy, dressed in shapeless worker's clothes, baggy corduroy pants and a gray shirt that might once have been white. I gave him a glower. "Do I know you?"

He slipped into the booth across from me. "No, you don't," he said. "But I know you. Roger Cheftwick Blake, am I right?"

I nodded, warily. "That's me. Who are you?"

He scrubbed his face with his hand. "Hell, I don't know anymore. Kevin Shelton, but I know that name doesn't mean anything to you. Not *this* you."

I looked him over. I still didn't recognize him. He looked like a military man, but I couldn't remember any Shelton that I had served with.

My plate was mostly empty. I started to get up, and he barred my way with a massive arm. In a near whisper he said, "You've got a scar on the back of your knee that you got by jumping out a hayloft when you were trying to impress a girl named Kathy... something. That was in Wood River, Illinois, where you grew up. Your first job was delivering eggs and milk for your uncle. Your mom made you take piano lessons for years and wouldn't ever believe that you're tone deaf. Your dad was a veterinarian, but he gave up his practice to work in a refinery because the money was better. Any of this sound familiar?"

I sagged back into the booth and stared at him. Yeah, it sounded familiar. He had just given me details of my life that no one who didn't know me well would know.

"Who are you?" I asked quietly, although I was sure I knew.

He sighed. "I told you. Kevin Shelton. We were in France together, then Germany. In the war. The war that never happened."

I glanced around. No one was close by. "First directorate?" I asked him softly.

He gave a harsh bark of laughter. "Yeah. Yeah, I guess you would think that—things being what they are. No, it's nothing like that," he paused. "But I guess if I were from the soviet secret police I'd claim that I wasn't."

This wasn't making any sense. If he was here to arrest me, he would have done it already. Was he trying to get information from me? About what? I didn't know anything worth going to this kind of charade for.

"Is this about Kraus?" I asked him. "I'll tell you everything I know, but it's not much?"

"Kraus?" he asked, then immediately waved that away. "Never mind, don't tell me. I don't care. Look, I don't want you to tell me anything. You don't have to say a word if you don't want to. But I have to tell somebody, and well, you're *almost* somebody I know. I don't know what's going to happen to me, but I figure it can't be good. Jesus, this isn't what I expected at all. I thought... well, I thought that I was making things better."

A waitress came by—this one topless as well—and the man who called himself Shelton ordered a whiskey sour. I told her to make it two.

He took a look around the bar, then looked back to me. "I'm guessing this isn't a good world to be a man without papers in?"

Before I could respond he said quickly, "And it's probably not a good world to know somebody without papers, right? Look, as far as you know I am a solid citizen of the New World Order or whatever the Hell you call it. I don't want to get you in any trouble. You saved my life once, even if you don't remember it. You tied a tourniquet around my leg when I took a round. Hell, never mind about that."

The waitress came back and dropped off the drinks. Both of us watched her go.

Shelton idly remarked, "They didn't have that in my world, well, not very many places. Topless waitresses, I mean. I guess it's the Weimar influence." He slugged down half of his drink.

I took a more cautious sip.

"Theoretically," he asked slowly, "what happens to somebody who doesn't have any identification—no, don't answer that. I can guess."

Crazy, I decided. He had to be crazy. But how did he know so much about me?

An Atlas of Bad Roads

He knocked back the other half of his drink. "Okay. I won't keep you any longer than I have to. What are you doing these days, anyway? Here and now, I mean."

"I'm a guard at the Silver State Cooperative Mine," I said. Whoever or whatever he was, there wasn't any reason not to say that much.

"The concentration camp?" he said. "Jesus, I'm sorry. Man, I never intended any of this."

I frowned. "I'm a non-commissioned officer in the League Peacekeeping Force."

"You would be," he said softly. "You were always loyal. Career man."

I looked around. I didn't see anybody watching us or standing around casually. I started to get up again.

"Please," he said. "Just hear me out. Then I'll go away. Someplace..."

I sat down and fixed him with a cold look. "Okay. Get to the point."

"Let's pretend," he said, "that the US got involved in what you call the European war. Let's pretend that Germany had a chancellor who didn't reach an accord with Russia. Suppose that Germany convinced Japan to bomb the US."

I looked at him. Drexler and Stalin had unified all of Europe. Roosevelt brought the US into the International League and made it more or less unanimous. Japan bombing the US? That was insane, Japan and China fought each other until the IL stepped in to bring them into the coalition by force.

He caught the meaning of my glance and said quickly, "Just stay with me for a moment, okay? Just... use your imagination."

I tried to humor him. "Why on Earth would Japan bomb the US? That doesn't make any sense."

"Because Germany was allied with Japan against Russia, and... the German Chancellor promised Japan the whole damned Pacific ocean. It doesn't matter exactly why. The point is that the European war got a whole lot bigger—Germany, Italy, and Japan on one side, Russia, Great Britain, France, and the US on the other."

I consider that. "Sounds like the end of the world," I suggested.

"Damn near was," Shelton agreed. "The US used atomic weapons... never mind, you don't have those here."

41

I shrugged. "Okay, I'm pretending," I said agreeably.

Shelton leaned forward. "It all came down to who was Chancellor of Germany. This man was a real firebrand. He had a gift for getting crowds riled up. He was the reason that the war got as big as it did. He drove the whole country crazy—convinced them that they had a destiny to rule the world."

I thought about the Germans I had known—men like Kraus. "That wouldn't be that hard," I suggested.

The waitress came by and Shelton ordered two more whiskey sours.

"Yeah," Shelton agreed. "He was in the right place at the right time. And I guess that was the point. Some people in... that other world, the one where the European War turned into the World War, figured that—"

The waitress returned with drinks. We both paused to watch her.

After she left, Shelton slugged down half of his second drink. I was still working on my first.

"Okay," he said softly, "this is the part that's going to sound really crazy. I don't expect you to believe it. But... just try, okay? Pretend that it could really happen."

I sipped my drink. I still couldn't figure his angle. There didn't seem to be any harm in listening to him, though. If he was trying to trap me into implicating myself, he was going about it in a damned strange way, and as long as I was careful about what I said back to him, I might as well sit here as elsewhere. It wasn't like I had any real plans.

"I'm pretending," I repeated.

"So," he began again, "after the second world war—"

"Second?" I asked him.

He looked irritated. "The big war—the European war. After it was over they started calling the Great War, the one in 1914, the First World War and the new one the Second World War."

I waved for him to go on. "Okay."

"After it was over," he went on, "the world was in pretty sad shape. America was looking good, and Russia came out okay, but Europe had been just about burned down to the ground. Japan was destroyed—there were two cities that were just gone. Those atomic bombs I mentioned—one bomb, one city, boom."

I nodded for him to go on.

An Atlas of Bad Roads

"The USA and the USSR divided the world between themselves. Literally, in the case of Germany. There was a... well, they called it the 'Cold War'. Both sides had the atomic weapons. Everybody was sure that sooner or later somebody was going to start using them. And then... that really would be the end of the world."

"Sounds pretty awful," I said, just to be agreeable.

He laughed. It wasn't a happy sound. "Yeah. Until I saw the alternative."

I frowned at him. "What do you mean?"

"This!" he hissed back at me, waving a hand to indicate the casino.

I glanced around, confused.

He shook his head angrily. "America. *Look at it*. Curfews, checkpoints, patrols. A third of the people in this country are starving, and the only reason it isn't more is that they're using slave labor to keep the farms operating. The only way to get ahead is to inform on your neighbors. The roads are falling to pieces, and the only traffic you see is military anyway. Christ, Blake, it took me three weeks to get here from Los Alamos."

I raised my eyebrows at that. I'd never heard of Los Alamos, but if he was telling the truth about not having travel papers, then he shouldn't have been able to move around at all.

He lowered his voice again. "I was trained in E&E. Escape and evasion. First by the OSS, then by the CIA, but never mind that. I ran black bag operations behind the Iron Curtain, but it's all iron curtain here. God damn it, this is not the America I thought I was going to come back to."

He seemed about to cry. "What happened here, Blake? What the Hell happened?"

I stared at him and shook my head. "I don't know what you want me to say," I began. "I heard about the crop failure, yeah, but I don't know what you expect us to do about it."

"Crop failure!" he said disgustedly. "Central planning failure. It was bad enough when it was just the Ukraine, but now you've got worldwide managed famines."

He let out a long shuddering breath just short of a sob. "And I did this. Me. I went back in time to 1895 and shot a little boy in the face. For this."

I sat back in the booth and stared at him. He had to be crazy. He

43

was a big guy, too, with what looked like serious muscle. I tried to think about what I could do if he got violent. Kick the table over on him and run for the casino floor. Security would be on us fast, and they could sort it out.

He seemed to get control of himself and offered me a little smile. It was kind of shaky, and not reassuring at all. "I'm going to hit the head," he said, and stood up, slowly, both hands on the table. "Be right back."

I watched him walk off to the bathrooms, thinking hard. He had to know me from the service, somebody that I had shared a barracks with sometime over the last thirty years. There had been a lot of faces, a lot of conversations killing time on long boring watches. But the fact that he remembered me in such detail while I had no memory of him at all was...

Creepy as hell, actually.

I decided to be gone before he came back. The buffet was pay-in-advance, there was no check to settle. I got up, and that's when I saw it.

It was on the seat where he had been, a small square of colored cardboard. The surface was glossy, not like a colored print, but some kind of photograph. I picked it up.

It showed four people, standing together in a group, smiling at the camera. The two in the center were young, a man and a woman. The man was in wide bottom dungarees of blue denim and a matching jacket, worn over a white shirt, half unbuttoned. His hair was long, and he had a thick mustache. The woman next to him was in a simple white dress, flowers in her flowing blond hair. A little behind the man was Shelton, in a black suit.

The man who stood beside the woman, smiling proudly, with a hand on her shoulder, was me.

I was heavier in that picture, and I had a small beard, but it was me. I had seen that face in the mirror every day for a half century.

Behind the four figures was the front of a little church, painted white. I could read part of the sign over the door: "Holy Pentecostal Tab—"

Tabernacle, probably, I thought dumbly.

I stood and stared at the picture for a long time. It had a white border that was smudged with dark stains, and a crease ran across the center, as if it had been hastily folded. I turned it over and looked at the back. Written on the back were the words, "Mickey & Veronica, 08/09/1968—The Summer Of Love!"

I put the picture back on the bench seat. Picked it up again. Held it for a moment more and finally stuck it in my pocket.

Shelton wasn't coming back, I realized. He'd used the bathroom as an excuse to get out. He probably thought that I would turn him over to authorities at my first opportunity. I'd never see him again.

But he'd left me the picture to prove that he had been telling the truth.

I spent the rest of my leave in my room, drunk. On the third day I went out looking for a woman, but I chickened out before I got out of the lobby and ordered another bottle from room service instead.

When it was time to get on the bus back to The Pit, I was hungover and depressed and felt like Hell. I was half convinced that I was going back to a court martial, maybe followed by a quick execution, and I didn't care.

Instead, I got a transfer to the mess hall. I lost my rank, but it was a better job, feeding the troops. I didn't know a damned thing about cooking, but I could unload the goods trucks and mop floors with the best of them. Evidently General Kraus was satisfied that being busted down to private and assigned to KP was punishment enough for the death of his nephew—I never had any official administrative punishment.

I decided not to put in for retirement. Talking to the truck drivers made me realize that the world outside wasn't a kind place for an old man. My retirement would be a simple white stone and a little patch of desert soil, my name on the wall of a hallway in the administration building. Until then, I had a cot and three squares a day, a broom to push and time to play checkers with the other old men at the enlisted men's club.

My place in the sun.

I still have the picture. I don't know if anything would happen if somebody found it. Nobody will—old soldiers know how to keep things hidden. I look at it sometimes, and I wonder what my life was like in that other world. They look happy, those four. Is that my daughter? Veronica? Veronica was my mother's sister's name. If so, I must have had a wife. Why wasn't she in the picture? Was I widower in that world? Or was she maybe just not in that picture, maybe somebody had wanted just the fathers of the bride and groom.

The Summer of Love

I wondered what she had been like. She was probably pretty. Our daughter was pretty.

The truck drivers like to talk. Quietly, around hand-rolled cigarettes. As we unload the trucks, they tell me about the world outside. The State of Emergency Regulations have become more or less permanent now, and the only traffic on the roads is official convoys. There are rumors of fighting, American Separatists shooting at troops in Georgia, or Missouri, or New Hampshire. Nothing is known for certain. There isn't any news any more.

Prisoners keep coming in. The troops like to talk, too. Nobody notices me pushing my broom between the mess hall tables to overhear the nervous whispers. I try to keep track of the scuttlebutt from the guards on the receiving yard, listening for someone talking about a big man with no papers or fingerprints on file, a prisoner who officially doesn't exist.

I don't think I will. Shelton won't be brought in here, I'm sure. He'd go down fighting, if it came to that.

But I hope he can stay free.

Tomorrow is Another Day

It's a small thing as these things go
Nothing to lose any sleep about
I don't know why it hurts me so
Not that much to go without

It's not as if God promised me
That what I want is what I'll earn
Or guaranteed my life would be
Fair, or that I'd get my turn

I sometimes have to wonder, though
If hunger is to be my lot
If I'd known then what there is to know
If I would have agreed or not

Breathe deep and look away
Tomorrow is another day

Burn Silent, Burn Bright
Previously unpublished

"I've been dreaming of the war again, doctor."

"Tell me about it."

"I'm watching it happen. I'm floating in space above the world, and I see the bombs falling. I watch the cities burn. I'm up high enough that I can see the curvature of the Earth, but I can see the impact. The cities falling, shock waves throwing buildings to the ground. I can't hear it—I think I'm above the atmosphere. I can see the flashes, the white light that makes everything else go dark. And the fires. Everything burns."

"While you're dreaming, do you think it's real?"

A long pause.

The doctor tried again. "In your dream, do you feel like this is a memory of something that actually happened?"

Another pause. Then, softly, "Yes."

"But when you wake, you know that it isn't, right? You wake and remember that there was no nuclear war. You know that it was all your parents' fantasy?"

"Yes." Too fast. The doctor would know he was lying.

"Michael, you know that these dreams are a symptom of stress. I think we should talk about what is going on in your life right now."

"Nothing."

"Your job? There haven't been any changes there? Any new policies? We've discussed how changes in routine affect you."

"No, nothing's changed." Michael worked in a plumbing supply warehouse, pulling pipe and fittings for customer orders, loading trucks for delivery. It was work that suited him, taking picking tickets and fetching everything listed on them, making sure that the numbers all matched. He was good at it, and his bosses relied on his attention to detail.

"Met anyone new? A new friend? Positive changes bring stress, too, you know."

"No." Michael didn't like to talk to strangers. He lived alone in a very neat room and always carried a book on the bus, pretending to read it to keep strangers away.

"Did you see something on the news that disturbed you?"

"I don't watch the news."

Michael looked past the doctor to the window. Outside, the sky was clear and the sun was bright, and for a moment, Michael could imagine the brightness was that of an atomic airburst and the silence that had fallen in the small office was the deathly silence of near-vacuum as the air was sucked into the firestorm.

"Michael, can you tell me what you are feeling right now?"

"I'm fine, doctor. It's almost time for me to go."

"Michael, I get the feeling that you're not being entirely honest with me."

Michael looked at the doctor, imagined his skin bubbling up like bacon, his eyes bursting as the humors boiled into steam, his clothes charring to ash and blowing away, the muscles underneath liquefying, and in the end, his blackened bones scattered among the millions of others, a carpet of charred skeletons covering this city, all cities.

"I'm fine, doctor," Michael repeated. "Can I go now?"

Michael stopped at the receptionist on the way out to confirm next week's appointment and took the stairs down from the doctor's fifth floor office. He didn't like elevators. The machinery could fail, and then where were you? Clawing at the walls of a steel box until you died of thirst.

Since it was Wednesday, and Wednesday was his day off, Michael planned on walking all the way home instead of taking the bus. He had time, the day was warm, and walking was good for you. There were sidewalks most of the way. That was important because walking in the street could be dangerous.

He was twenty-three years old. On average, he could expect to live another fifty-four and a half years. If something didn't kill him first.

His parents had died when they were forty-four and forty-one. But they were suicides. Suicide couldn't be predicted. One might say that killing yourself was a crime against statistical analysis.

Michael caught a glimpse of a police car headed down the street. He calmed himself with an automatic effort of will. He reminded himself that he was doing nothing wrong, and he had all of his identification with him, and there was no reason to be afraid of police. He still felt cold sweat on his back until the car reached the light ahead of him and turned right.

Burn Silent, Burn Bright

Michael's doctor told him that he should breathe deeply when he felt a panic attack coming on and to focus on his surroundings to try to calm his racing thoughts. Michael looked at the other pedestrians and the trees that grew up from their wrought iron cages along the sidewalk. He felt the sunlight—warm, rather than the killing hot of the desert where he grown up. He didn't live in New Mexico, anymore. His foster family had moved to Missouri when he was seventeen. Three years after his parents had died.

His foster parents still lived here. Michael saw them on holidays. They were very proud of him.

The walk went quickly, as it always did when the weather was good. He lived in an apartment building on a quiet street. Today there was a big truck double parked blocking the narrow street and two men in an argument with a pretty woman.

Michael slowed, assessing the situation. The woman was angry, gesturing at a large cardboard carton and then at the apartment. The men stood impassively, arms folded, shaking their heads.

Michael knew the woman by sight. She lived in the building, he thought. He had seen her in the stairwell from time to time, anyway, and exchanged greetings with her.

The back of the truck was full of other cartons, and there could be other men hiding in there, waiting. Not that the two men would need any help if they planned violence against the woman.

Of course there was no reason to suspect that they did plan violence, not here, not now. Threat analysis was just a habit for Michael. His parents had taught him to always be careful.

They had been insane, of course, but being careful was still a good idea. Not everything his parents had taught him had been wrong.

The woman was shouting. "I paid for delivery and setup!"

One of the men just shook his head. "We don't do stairs," he said, unsympathetically. "Insurance."

The woman used bad language then, and the men shared a look. One of them went to the back of the truck and pulled down the door. The other headed to the truck cab. They left the big box on the sidewalk.

The woman shouted after them. It didn't help. They got in the truck and drove away.

Michael headed down the sidewalk nervously. He didn't like

shouting.

"Hey!" the young woman said to him. She didn't shout, but her voice was loud and Michael flinched.

"Hey," she said, softer, "You live here, right?"

Michael nodded warily.

She gestured at the box. "Can you help me? Those dickheads were supposed to set it up, but they say they can't because I live on the third floor."

Michael looked at the box. It was awkwardly shaped, like the monolith in the movie 2001. His mother had a book with pictures from that movie.

"What is it?" he asked.

"It's an entertainment center," she said. "I bought it online."

Michael studied the box, then looked at the doorway and remembered the layout of the stairs. He touched the box, rocked it back to gauge its weight. Then he looked at the woman. She was young—his age, more or less—and slender, but looked to be in shape.

He spent a few moments considering the physics of the situation, then nodded. "I think we can do it," he said.

More than once on the journey up the stairs, he considered that he hadn't ever actually agreed to help, he just hadn't refused. The young woman—whose name Michael still didn't know—had taken his volunteering for granted once she had explained the problem to him. It wasn't easy, and she used bad language several more times before they reached the third floor.

Then she had to fumble for her keys, while Michael leaned the box against the wall and caught his breath. When she had the door open, they slid the box across the floor and inside the main room.

Her apartment was directly over his, and the floorplan—at least what he could see of it—was the same. This room was cluttered, though. He would never let his living space be so untidy.

There was a couch scattered with pillows and a pair of tables full of things—books and coffee cups and papers. Two mismatched pole lamps stood against the walls. A large television and a pair of speakers were set up on a collection of milk crates.

She caught him studying the layout and gestured. "You see why I need this." Then she sighed. "I hope I can get it put together."

"I can help," Michael heard himself saying. He didn't want to help her. He wanted to go home and take a shower and make his dinner.

"Would you?" she asked. "It's supposed to have all the tools we need in the box."

He nodded heavily. There didn't seem to be a polite way out of this situation.

"I don't even know your name," she said with an embarrassed little giggle.

"Michael Leibling," he said. Leibling was his foster parents name. With practice he had learned to say it naturally, even automatically.

"Pam Peronel," she said and stuck out her hand.

Michael shook it. "Pleased to meet you," he said formally.

She giggled again. "Thanks so much."

Michael turned to the box. In his pocket, he had a razor knife. At work he used it to open cartons. He carried it with him all the time, though. It made him feel comfortable to have a knife with him.

He flipped open the knife and slit open the carton, cutting the tape along one seam and carefully folding it open. Inside, there was a collection of boards. On top lay a sheet of instructions.

Michael spread the instruction sheet on the top board and studied it, then looked for and found the plastic bag that held all the hardware. The instructions were all pictures, without words, but they seemed fairly straightforward. He began laying out the parts in the order they would be assembled.

"You've done this before?" Pam asked.

He shook his head without looking up from the paper.

She watched him sorting the parts for a while, then asked, "Want a beer?"

"No, thank you."

"I'm going to get one," she said. Her tone was half a question, as if she expected him to object.

He said nothing.

Once he had the plans clear in his head, the actual assembly went quickly. There was only one part he needed her help with, holding one end of the longest board while he fitted the screws into the uprights. The screws were hex heads, to work with the included Allen wrench.

"You're good at this," Pam said admiringly.

"Thank you."

When the shelving unit was finished, Michael waited while Pam moved her television and then cleared away the milk crates and other clutter to make room to slide the unit against the wall. Then she put the speakers and the television and the other components on it, weaving a web of cables and cords behind the shelves to connect everything. While she was working, she finished her beer and got another.

Again she asked Michael if she could get him anything, and again he said no.

He just wanted to go back to his own apartment. The clutter of Pam's home was making him nervous.

Pam got the cables arranged to her satisfaction and clicked on the power. The screen came on, showing the logo of a streaming service that Michael had heard of but never seen. Michael didn't watch television.

She grinned and flopped down on the couch, then patted the cushions beside her.

Michael shook his head. "I don't think..." he began, then broke off. He couldn't find the words.

Pam frowned. "Come on," she said. She picked up her phone. "I'll order a pizza. I owe you that much."

This is normal, Michael told himself. People do these things. They help each other and eat pizza afterwards. It's okay.

He expected her to dial the phone and call the pizza place, but instead she started swiping around on the screen. "What do you like?"

"Anything," he said honestly.

She smiled at him. "There's a special on the chicken and bleu cheese," she said, then, as if confessing a fault, "That's my favorite."

"That's fine," Michael agreed. He couldn't seem to get comfortable on the couch but didn't want to draw attention to himself by squirming around.

As she ordered via the app, she said, "I'm going to get my money back on that delivery and setup charge."

"I think you should."

She looked at him with a half-frown, like she thought he was making fun of her.

"You paid for something you didn't get," he amplified. "You should get your money back."

Satisfied, she turned back to the TV and picked up her remote.

"What do you want to watch?"

He shrugged. "I don't know."

The half-frown returned.

Michael could tell that she was starting to sense his strangeness, the fact that he didn't fit in this world.

"I don't know anything about television," he said, and that sounded stupid, so he added, "I don't watch television," which sounded like he was some kind of snob, so he went on, "my parents didn't have a television when I was a kid," and he knew that he was talking too fast so he shut up, but she was still giving him that look so he finished with, "I just never got in the habit."

Her look softened a bit. He smiled and asked, "What's good?"

She smiled back.

Michael felt his pulse slow a bit. There were patches of sweat cooling on his back.

"So are you, uh, Amish or something?" she asked. Still smiling.

"Something like that," he nodded. "Out in New Mexico." *If I told her my parents' names would she recognize them*, he wondered. They had been on the national news for a while.

"Let's see," she said, picking up a remote control and turning to the television. She clicked around the menus for a while, and Michael watched. It was like the computer he used at work, not like the television that his foster parents had in their big dusty living room. Some of the other kids in his foster parents house had watched television a lot.

She shot him a sideways look, and for the first time he suspected that she might be feeling as uncomfortable as he was. That thought should have made him feel better, but it didn't.

She decided on a movie that he remembered from seeing posters at the bus stops. It was about a superhero. The movie had just started when Pam's phone rang and the pizza arrived. They went down the stairs together to get it.

The pizza was strangely sharp flavored, but Michael decided he liked it. Pam had another beer and got Michael a glass of ice water. She started the movie again and Michael relaxed a little. When the movie was playing, he didn't need to make conversation.

Quite suddenly, everything fell apart.

On the television was a scene of a line of cars waiting for a traffic light. There was nothing special about that scene, it was just a calm moment before other things happened. One of the cars had its window open, and a woman's arm was visible, just her arm. She was tanned and wore several bracelets of silver and turquoise. That's all.

Michael stood, too fast, and his head spun. His heart was hammering. He was going to be sick, violently sick.

"I have to go," he stammered out, and left. He managed not to run until he was out of Pam's apartment with the door shut behind him.

Then he did run, down the hall, down the stairs, getting out his keys as he ran to his door.

He almost made it.

At the door to his bathroom he fell to his knees, vomiting up all of the lovely pizza she had bought. Somehow that thought, that she had wanted to do something nice because he had helped her and now he was vomiting it up, was the saddest thought he'd ever had. He curled on the floor and wept, long and hard. He shivered with the force of his tears, feeling like he was floating in ice water, lost in an endless black sea.

In time it passed. It always passed.

Michael got up and cleaned up his mess. He took off his clothes and showered, standing under the hot water for as long as he could, making his mind as blank as he could make it.

In his bed, under the covers, he wept again. This is what happens when you want nice things. This is what happens when you forget that you're broken, too badly broken to ever be fixed. He would make up a story to tell Pam later, to let her know that she wasn't the problem, that Michael was the problem, and that he would always be the problem, forever and ever amen.

At long last he slept.

And dreamed of fire.

Perspicuity

The sign read: KEEP OUT TIGERS HERE
But the meaning was unclear
Was it safe to walk about
Because the tigers were kept out?
Or did it mean that I should stay
Extremely very far away?
The second meaning did I heed
In case the tigers couldn't read.

Dead Man's Chest

Originally published in *Milhaven's Tales Of Terror*, September 2018

"**M**ax, I gotta use your truck," Bennie said. "Right away."

Max sighed into his phone. "I'm at work, man."

"Ah, so tell 'em you're sick." He sounded high. He usually sounded high.

"My boss is your dad," Max pointed out. "And we got a deadline on this job. I should be out of here about six."

"You call me," Bennie insisted. "You call me as soon as you're free. It's got to be today."

"Sure, Bennie. I'll call you. Later."

Max put away his phone and went back to wiring, but he called Bennie back when he wrapped up for the day, and half an hour later was pulling up in front of Bennie's house. It was a dilapidated duplex owned by Bennie's father. The other half was never rented out. Max suspected that it didn't have an occupancy permit, and that's why Bennie's dad let him live there rent free.

Bennie's red Mercedes convertible, a hand-me-down from his stepmother, was parked at the curb. Max pulled into the driveway and parked before the closed garage door. A moment later Bennie came out and climbed into the truck. He looked sober enough.

"So what's this all about?" Max asked.

"Gotta pick something up," Bennie answered, mysteriously.

Max started the motor but didn't put the truck in gear. "You're going to have to tell me where we're going."

"Southtown," Bennie said. "Near Broadway and Chippewa."

"This place got an address?"

"Just head that way. I can find it."

Max sighed and backed out.

Bennie did find it, but it took over an hour and the streets were fully dark by the time Bennie pointed and said, "There! Down that alley. That's it!"

Max dutifully drove down the alley, crawling past the piles of trash that made the already narrow space into an obstacle course. The alley widened into a brick-lined cul-de-sac dominated by a loading dock.

"Back up to it!" Bennie said.

Max gave Bennie a sharp look and surveyed the cramped space. Trash and bits of discarded furniture littered the area. Still, he'd have to either turn around in here or back the whole way up the alley. Cautiously, he maneuvered his truck around, ignoring Bennie's suggestions.

Bennie hopped out of the truck as soon as Max set the parking brake, and he ran up to the dock, fumbling with a handful of keys. Max followed, watching his footing, and heard the roll-up door rattling on its track.

"You got a flashlight?" Max called.

"No," Bennie said. Then, "Do you? It was daytime when I was here before."

Max got the flashlight out of his toolbox. Clicking it on, he went up the stairs to the dock and shone it into the building.

"What is this place?"

"Mama Mia's Pizzeria," Bennie called back in a sing-song parody of an Italian accent. "Or some dumb Eye-talian name like that."

"This was a restaurant?" Max looked around. It looked like a factory. A dirty one.

"Naw..." Bennie said. There was a click and overhead lights came on, dim and flickering. "They made frozen food. It's been here forever. Old mob family, you know? Then Guido said something about Vito's sister and..." he raised his hand in a pistol shape, "...*pow, pow, pow*."

He laughed, then shrugged, "Anyway, it went into probate or some shit, and my dad bought it. Tomorrow he's gonna start tearing it down. That's why we had to come tonight, while the power's still on."

Max followed Bennie into an enormous commercial kitchen that looked like it had been last remodeled—or cleaned—in the 1960s. The shelves were empty, but the fixtures remained.

"What, do you need a new stove or something?" Max asked. The smallest of them would be a real bitch to move.

"Something like that." Bennie's voice was just ahead.

Max pushed aside a plastic curtain. Bennie waved to indicate a huge and ancient chest freezer, grinning like he'd just invented it.

"You're kidding," Max said.

Bennie shoved it, and it rolled a few squealing inches. "See, it's on wheels. No problem."

Max frowned at the filthy thing, estimating its size. Yeah, it would fit in the bed of his truck. Probably.

Experimentally, he gave it a shove. It weighed a ton. He lifted the lid.

"Oh, man," Max said, "it's full. Let's get all this crap out of it."

"No!" Bennie objected. "That's why I want it."

Max looked in. Under a sprinkling of ice crystals were stacks of frozen pizzas. The whole freezer was full of them. Dozens. Hell, maybe hundreds.

Max stared at Bennie, who grinned back at him.

"Free pizzas, man," Bennie said.

"Are you high?"

Bennie shrugged. "A little, yeah," he admitted sheepishly. "But it's still free food."

Max pulled the top pizza free from the stack. It was like the ones he saw in the supermarket, shrink-wrapped to a cardboard disk. A white sticker on the front read, 'Not Packaged For Individual Resale'. Nothing else, no list of ingredients or expiration date.

"How old are these?"

"The place was in business two weeks ago," Bennie assured him. "They're fresh. Freshish."

"And how come they don't have real labels on them?"

"They sold them to bars. Local places. Real cheap, too, I hear," Bennie said. "And then the bar turns around and gets ten bucks for them. What a ripoff."

Max looked behind the freezer and found the cord. He pulled it and was relieved to see that it was a common three prong plug. Something this old and big could have been 220.

"Okay, we'll give it a shot," Max said. *And if this screws up my truck, your old man is going to pay to get it fixed,* he added mentally.

With both of them shoving, the freezer rolled smoothly, if noisily. They got to the loading dock without too much trouble, but getting it onto Max's truck was a pain. When they were done, Max's tailgate was bent so that it didn't shut right.

Getting it out of the truck at Bennie's house was a nightmare. Bennie's idea was to use a ramp made from a sheet of plywood, which broke under the weight of the freezer and took Max's tailgate off entirely.

Max turned to yell at Bennie and then saw that his friend's arm was gashed and bleeding. Bennie looked at the blood running down his arm like he wasn't quite sure what it was.

"Shit.." Max bent to examine the wound. It was deep, and bleeding heavy. "You're gonna need stitches."

Bennie jerked his arm back, spattering blood on the floor, the freezer, and Max's shirt. "Naw, I'm fine. I'll just wrap it up. I got some medical shit in the kitchen."

"That's more than a Band-Aid," Max said. "Let's wash it off."

Bennie let Max hold his arm under cold water from the kitchen tap but refused to go to the hospital. Instead, he got out some gauze and had Max wrap it. Bennie's first aid kit was surprisingly complete, and after several layers of gauze and tape the bleeding seemed to be contained and Bennie went back into the garage.

The concrete of the garage floor had cracked, too, but the freezer itself suffered only a few dents. When they finally had the damned thing on the floor and shoved close enough to plug it in, the compressor started up right away.

"Rock on!" Bennie exclaimed. He opened the lid and pulled out a pizza. "Come on, let's eat."

Max shook his head. "I'll pass," he said. *At least until I find out if you end up with food poisoning. Or bleed out.* "I really think you ought to get to the ER."

"I can't, man, they'll test me for dope, and I'll go to jail."

"I'm pretty sure it doesn't work that way," Max said, "unless it's an on the job injury."

"I'm fine," Bennie said. "Lemme pop one of these in the oven real quick. You earned it."

"I've got to get home. I'm working tomorrow."

"You sure?" Bennie asked, disappointed. "I got beer."

"I'm sure."

It was a couple of weeks before Max saw Bennie again. Work kept him busy, and then his mom had her hip replaced. His dad wanted to visit her every night in the hospital but didn't like driving after dark, and Max got drafted as chauffeur.

The day after Max's mom went home—a nerve wracking affair involving finding a way to fit a wheelchair into the back of his dad's car, mom insisting loudly that she didn't need a wheelchair, and dad on the edge of nervous hysteria every time they hit a bump on the three mile drive—Max decided that a little of Bennie's honest craziness was just what he needed as an antidote for his parents' neuroses.

He dropped by the house in the early afternoon—late enough that Bennie would be awake, but too early for him to be totally trashed. The red Mercedes was in the driveway, and behind it was parked an older green Ford.

So Bennie had company. For a moment, Max continued just driving past, but then he went ahead and pulled to the curb. He slammed the door of his truck and walked slowly to the front door to make sure Bennie knew he was coming. He didn't want to interrupt anything.

The door was answered by a tall blonde in jeans and a T-shirt. She looked to be in her thirties, older than Max and Bennie by a comfortable margin, with a great body and tousled, just-got-out-of-bed hair. She glared at Max with cold, suspicious eyes.

"Yeah?"

"Is Bennie here?"

"Who are you?"

Bennie came up behind her, dressed only in a pair of cargo pants. "Sylvie, that's Max. Chill, he's one of the good guys. I've known Max since forever."

Sylvie shrugged and moved out of the way.

"Hey, Max, come on in," Bennie said. "What's up? Want a beer?"

Max flopped down on the couch. "I would love a beer."

And it was just like old times. Bennie told ridiculous stories about things that happened at the auto parts store where he worked part time, certainly made up, but funny as hell. He had a second job now, also part time, at the club where Sylvia worked. He was vague as to the details, and Max didn't push.

After a while, Sylvia warmed up to Max, but then she had to leave for work.

"You coming in tonight?" she asked Bennie.

"Yeah, in a couple of hours," Bennie assured her.

That answer seemed to satisfy Sylvia, and she left.

They had a few more beers. The gash on Bennie's arm was red and puffy, and Max asked about it.

"It doesn't hurt," Bennie said dismissively. "It just looks kind of

61

ugly. I'll have a badass battle scar." He went into a story about threatening some mook on a car lot with a windshield wiper because the mook had his car blocked in. Then he got up and went into the kitchen. "I'm hungry. You hungry?"

Max got up. "You want to go out someplace? I'm buying."

"Naw, man, I got this."

Bennie's kitchen was less of a mess than Max expected. There was an overflowing trash can, but it seemed mostly filled with beer bottles and cardboard. The counter-tops were fairly clear, and there were no dishes in the sink.

Bennie stepped out into the garage for a moment and returned with two plastic wrapped frozen pizzas.

Max stared. They were the unlabeled ones that had been in the freezer. "You're still eating those?"

"Yeah, there's like a million of them. And they're good."

Max looked into the trash can again. The cardboard he'd seen was all circles from the bottoms of frozen pizzas. "You eating anything else?"

Bennie was stripping the plastic and glanced back. "Sylvie ain't much of a cook, you know?"

The pizza isn't good, Max thought when Bennie put it in front of him. It smelled funny, and the meat looked unhealthy, a ragged strip of pink and gray. Max pulled it off and sniffed it, then set it on his plate.

"Dude," Bennie laughed, his mouth full, "you look like my mom. *Don't eat that, Bennie, it's treyf!"*

Max kept stripping the chunks of meat from his pizza. "This goes beyond *treyf.* Do you even know what it is?"

Bennie shrugged. "Canadian bacon?"

"Yeah," Max muttered. "Now we know what happens to a Mountie's horse when it gets old."

"You're missing out, Max," Bennie chided. "The meat's the best part."

Max offered his plate. Bennie scooped up the limp pink strips and popped them in his mouth. "Mmmmm... Made with real Canadians." And he laughed.

Max didn't.

Before Max left, Bennie invited him to The French Connection, the club where he and Sylvie worked.

"I'm tired, man. I just want to go home and get some sleep."

"Well, you should stop by sometime," Bennie insisted. He took a card out of his wallet and scrawled something on the back. "Give this to the doorman, they'll take care of you."

Max hadn't planned to go—strip clubs really weren't his thing—but on a Saturday night not long after he was feeling lonely and bored. He called Bennie, and Bennie said, "I'm about to go down to the club, meet me there, huh?"

The doorman—a hulking brute with a shaved head—glanced at Bennie's card and waved Max in without asking for the cover charge.

The club was a wide, dim room, broken up by a half-dozen small, round stages lit by colored spotlights. Women, mostly young and mostly pretty, danced on the stages to some 80s power ballad that Max vaguely recalled. A couple of dozen men with drinks sat in the shadows around the stages.

Max made his way to the bar. Sylvie was tending, in a T-shirt cut off high enough to show the bottom of her breasts.

"What can I get you?" she said flatly.

"Hey, is Bennie around?" Max asked.

For a moment she gave him a cold stare, then seemed to place him and nodded. "Back there," she gestured.

Bennie was in a corner booth, away from the stages but placed so that he could watch the whole club. He was wearing a polo shirt and had shaved recently. There was a laptop and a smart phone on the bar in front of him. He grinned and stuck out a hand.

"Have a seat. How you doing? Sylvia get you a drink?"

Max sat beside Bennie. "I'm good," he said.

"Let's get you a beer," Bennie said and gestured to one of the waitresses. "On the house."

Max shrugged. "Sure." Bennie, he noticed, had a glass of what looked like soda in front of him.

Bennie was sober and dressed in clean clothes. He was smiling and seemed genuinely pleased to see Max. Despite that, he didn't look good. He was pale and his eyes were red, like he wasn't sleeping well. There was a fresh bandage on his arm.

"That still bothering you?"

Bennie grimaced. "Fucker won't heal. Got some antibiotics, but they don't do bupkis."

A pretty girl in pretty underwear put a draft beer in front of Max, then left. Max took a drink. "So, what, are you managing this place or what?"

"Helping out," Bennie said. "Doing the liquor orders, shit like that." He shrugged. "How about you, still working for my old man?"

"It's a good job."

"Heck, yeah," Bennie agreed. "Now that you're in the union, you got it made. Put in your time, keep out of trouble, and wait to retire. You'll have that condo in Miami in no time."

He'd said it as a joke, but his tone was off and his eyes weren't smiling. He sounded mean, and that wasn't like him.

Max frowned. "Are you feeling okay, Bennie?"

Bennie slammed his fist on the table, making the laptop and drinks jump. Max scrambled to save his beer.

"God damn it!" Bennie shouted, then carefully lowered his voice. "Why does everyone keep asking me that?"

Max leaned away from him. "Relax, man," he said. This *really* wasn't like him, "I was just asking. This is me, remember? You just seem... different."

Bennie took a drink of his soda. He nodded slowly. "Sorry, man. It's just Sylvie, and Roman, and my old man... Shit, here I am, starting to straighten out my life, and everybody acts like I must be sick because I'm not a fuckup anymore."

Max raised his beer, took a swallow. "Here's to not being a fuckup anymore."

Bennie grinned at that, and for a moment seemed to be his old self again. "It's not easy, you know. I have to stop and think, *whoa, what would the old me do?* And then I do just the opposite. I mean, here I am in a place where they'll give me free drinks if I ask, full of girls who take off their clothes for money and all want to be my extra special bestest friend. The old me would have blown this whole gig inside a week. But look at me, being all responsible adult and shit."

"Nicely done." Max smiled.

He stuck around long enough to have another beer, and then he took off, feeling troubled. On the one hand, Bennie seemed to be more serious—about his job, about Sylvie, about turning his life around—than he had ever been before. On the other hand, Max wasn't sure that serious looked good on Bennie. There was something off about him. Something... cold. He'd always been funny, but now his humor had a dark streak. And he didn't look healthy. It was more than just the infected arm. He looked pale and drawn, like he was trying to shake off the flu.

Coke? Max wondered. Had Bennie switched from pot to coke or something stronger? They said that changes in personality could be a sign of drugs.

Or it could be a sign of having more stress than he was used to and a painful infected wound. Who could say? In the end Max decided that he was Bennie's friend, not his father, therapist, doctor, or rabbi. If Bennie asked for help, Max would be there for him. If it looked like he needed help but wouldn't ask, well, Max would deal with that when the time came. Until then, Bennie's life was his own business.

Max got in the habit of dropping by the French Connection on Saturday afternoons, when the place was slow. He'd find Bennie in the back corner booth and hang out with him for a couple of hours, drink a few beers and have a burger.

Bennie never let Max pay for anything. He still claimed that he was just helping out with the paperwork, but it was clear that the manager on duty deferred to him. Bennie himself never had anything but soda.

Privately, Max started wondering if Bennie was eating at all. He lost weight, and his skin was looking gray and unhealthy. The bandage was a permanent fixture now, and sometimes the wound would ooze and Bennie would have to go to the bathroom to change it.

Then one day Max showed up and Bennie wasn't there.

It was almost four.

Bennie was usually in his booth in the back by two. Feeling a little awkward, Max took a seat anyway. Inside a few minutes Sylvie came over to his table.

She spoke in a near whisper, even though no one was nearby. "What's up with Bennie?"

"I was going to ask you," Max said, surprised. "Aren't you..?" He wasn't sure how to finish the question.

Sylvie shook her head, a tiny gesture that barely disturber her hair. "Not any more. He started getting... spooky."

Spooky. That wasn't a word that Max could imagine being applied to Bennie.

"Think you could drop by his place?" Sylvie said so tonelessly that it almost wasn't a question. "Just to check?"

Max nodded. "Sure. I'll see if he's all right."

As he got to his feet, Sylvie said softly, "That boy ain't been all right for a while now."

The rundown duplex looked the same, brown dead yard, peeling paint, missing shingles. Except for the dusty red Mercedes sitting in the driveway, it looked abandoned, but it had always looked abandoned.

Max pulled up and parked, got out and went to the door. He knocked, loudly.

"Hey, Bennie!" he hollered. "You in there, Bennie?"

No answer. He waited, listened. Nothing moving around. He checked the door.

The smell hit him as soon as he pulled open the door. Meat gone bad, and a lot of it.

Max left the door open, then crossed the living room to the back door and opened it, too. The smell seemed to be coming from the kitchen.

Max glanced in there. It seemed even neater than the last time he'd seen it, but there was definitely something rotten in there. Something that should have been buried, or burned.

Max frowned and headed down to Bennie's bedroom. There were two bedrooms. The closer one was full of junk, furniture, boxes, all the random things that Bennie didn't want but refused to throw away. The hallway was dark, and Max clicked on the light. One dim bulb came on in the fixture, which didn't help much.

The door to Bennie's bedroom was ajar, but no light came from there. Max stuck his head in the room. There was some kind of black plastic over the windows. That was new.

Bennie lay sprawled across the bed in only a pair of blue jeans. He looked gaunt and pale in the dim light from the hallway. Max could see his ribs clearly. His right arm was flung out. The wound was crusted with dark dried blood, glued to the sheets.

"Bennie?" Max said softly, then reached to touch his arm. His skin felt cold and dry. Max turned away, feeling sick.

"What the fuck, man?" Bennie's voice was weak.

Max spun back. Bennie's eyes were open, but he hadn't moved.

"You want to get in here with me?" Bennie asked, his voice

rasping. Moving with a disturbing suddenness, his grabbed his crotch with his left hand. "You want some of this, huh? That why you're sneaking into my bedroom?"

Max fought to control his racing heart. "You didn't show up to club. Sylvie was worried, man. Wanted me to check on you."

"Sylvie is a selfish pig." Bennie sat up. The sheet clung to his oozing arm. "Seriously, she's a used rubber full of rat poison walking on platform heels."

"You look awful," Max said. "I thought you were dead."

Bennie peeled the sheet from his arm, frowned at it. "Obviously, I'm not dead, despite the best efforts of the fucking quack my dad makes me go to."

He glanced up. His eyes looked as dry as marbles lost in a playground. "I'm gonna take a shower, Maxie-boy. Want to join me?"

And he laughed. It was a sick sound, a death-rattle trying to tap dance.

Max fled into the living room.

Once there the smell from the kitchen was overwhelming. Taking a deep breath of the relatively clean air of the living room, Max went to investigate.

There was a dog in the trash can. A big dog, maybe a German shepherd, but it had been crammed into the can with its limbs twisted so it was hard to tell. Its fur was filthy and a large patch of it was peeled back, exposing torn muscle. Blood had leaked from the broken body and soaked a mass of crumpled cardboard and clear cellophane.

"Going through my trash now, Max?"

Max spun around. Bennie stood just behind him, still wet from the shower, again in just a pair of jeans, a shirt in his hands.

"Jesus, Bennie!" Max cried. "What the fuck is wrong with you?"

"Me?" Bennie's voice reasonable but his eyes were dead. "You break into my house and go through my trash can. You looking for my dope stash, maybe? Too bad, I gave that shit up."

"There's a dead dog—" Max began.

"Neighborhood stray," Bennie said. "It got hit by a car. Died right in front of my house. It didn't seem right to just leave him in the street."

"So you put him in your *kitchen trash can?*" Max sputtered. "Dude, that's..."

"It's my business, is what it is," Bennie said, and pulled his shirt on over his head.

Max stared at him, unable to process the changes in his friend. Is this what Sylvie meant by "spooky"? No wonder she bailed.

"Bennie, man..." Max searched for the words. "You worry me. You are starting to really worry me."

Bennie acted as if he hadn't heard. "You know, Max, I don't think I'm comfortable with you just inviting yourself into my house. If you want to visit, call first in the future. Okay?"

"Yeah," Max said. His back was wet with cold sweat. "I'll, uh, see you at the club, maybe? Later?"

"Headed over now, man." Bennie seemed, quite suddenly, to be his old self again. But as he was winding a fresh bandage around his arm, the blood that seeped through looked almost black.

As Max got into his truck he thought, *That dog didn't look like it was hit by a car. It looked like it was butchered.*

That night at the club Max didn't talk much. Instead he drank.

Bennie didn't seem to notice. He sat and chattered happily, told funny stories about the patrons, flirted with the waitresses. He looked and sounded so normal that Max wondered if he'd overreacted at Bennie's house and the kid was really just fine.

But then he'd remember the butchered dog and take another drink.

At the end of the night, he left his truck in the lot and Bennie drove him home. Max had a blurry memory of Bennie carrying him inside and then darkness.

In the morning—early, and feeling like hell—Max took a cab to pick up his truck.

After that, Max never saw Bennie again.

The next Saturday, he decided he didn't feel like going to The French Connection. He didn't want to think about how Bennie looked or what he'd seen in the kitchen. He didn't make any conscious decision to avoid Bennie, he just didn't feel like going out that week. Or the week after.

Or the week after that.

When the reports of the fire at The French Connection—and in the days after, what the authorities found in the ashes—began flooding the media, Max realized that, on some level, he wasn't at all surprised.

The early stories were confused. There had been a fire at what they euphemistically called a 'gentleman's club.' The loss of life was high—some reports put the number in the mid-thirties, but the final tally was twenty-four bodies.

Then the stories started getting weird.

There was evidence that the fire had been set. Evidence that exits had been nailed shut.

Some of the bodies, it seemed, hadn't died in the fire, but some time before—possibly days or even weeks earlier. Some of those bodies were partially dismembered, and there were pieces missing.

The name Benjamin "Bennie" Krantz began showing up as a person of interest. There were pictures on the news of Bennie's duplex shrouded in crime scene tape, with stern-faced deputies refusing to comment on what—if anything—they had found in the house.

Max watched the news reports with a growing sense of numb, sick horror, horror that didn't entirely fade as the stories did, the remaining unanswered questions being upstaged by fresher atrocities.

The red Mercedes convertible had been found at a truck stop a hundred miles away, parked neatly in the back of the lot. If the police found any evidence in it, they didn't release it to the press. Bennie was out there, somewhere.

Three months later, Max got a post card.

One side showed a cartoon of a grinning fisherman who had netted a busty mermaid under a banner announcing greetings from Myrtle Beach. The message on the other side was brief.

Don't worry, I'm OK.
Don't come after me and I won't come after you.
I'd hate to have to kill you.
Remember, you ARE what you EAT.
Arrivederci

It was unsigned, but Max knew who sent it.

That Front Porch

Westward facing, stone clad
Eight wide, four deep, six high
Room enough for a yellow dog
Couch, barbecue grill, and I

We bought the house in winter
A place for the kids to come home
That spring we hired a lawyer
We waited and we lived alone

For a while we were still a family
Her and I and the kids that weren't there
We furnished the rooms that the kids didn't live in
We trusted in waiting and prayer

That summer she'd sit on the porch with me
She'd play guitar and we'd sing
We'd talk about the plans we had
When we could still plan anything

I didn't smoke in the house itself
The couch was a good place to think
I'd sit and I'd smoke and I'd think and I'd read
And when bad turned to worse I would drink

The grill rusted out and the couch
Grew soft in the places I grew fat
Seasons changed and the grass turned brown
Leaves fell, snow fell, and I sat

I left that house in August
Took my books and some clothes in my van
Left the couch and the grill and the dog
And her, and her wonderful plan

I lived there five years, I've been away five

An Atlas of Bad Roads

In dreams I remember the scope
The size and the shape of a place that was mine
And the dog, and the feeling of hope.

Black Dog

Originally published in *Sins Of The Gods*, February 2018

"What's it like being a gravedigger?"

Andy had been painting the wrought iron fence that surrounded the River Street Cemetery, lost in thought and feeling sorry for himself. The sudden voice startled him.

"I don't know," he snapped. "I don't dig graves."

The questioner was a young woman, dressed in a neat black dress. "I thought you worked here," she said, indicating the graveyard.

"I do," Andy agreed. "But I don't dig graves. I just maintain the grounds. The funeral parlors dig the graves and fill them in."

She frowned. She was standing on the other side of the fence Andy was painting, in the narrow alley that led between the graveyard and the backs of a line of old red brick warehouses. She might have been at the funeral that had been held that morning, but Andy thought she had too much makeup for a funeral.

A large black dog sat on the sidewalk in front of her, no lead, no collar. It had sleek fur, night black from its sharp nose to its long black tail, and high, pointed, cat-like ears. Technically, all dogs on city streets were supposed to be leashed, but Andy liked dogs and it wasn't his job to write tickets.

He didn't have a dog now. His new apartment didn't allow pets. No pool, no phone, no pets, just like the old song said.

"So you didn't...?" the young woman gestured at the newly filled grave.

Andy shook his head. "No, that was Anderson and Sons. The city just maintains the grounds. The interments are performed by the funeral homes."

Andy had been surprised to learn that himself, when he first applied for the job. He had figured that Municipal Groundskeeper (River Street Cemetery) was a euphemism, but he'd had plenty of experience with a backhoe from running his own landscaping business and he'd really needed a job.

She cocked her head. "So what do you do?"

"I mow the grass, prune the trees, take care of the flower gardens, shovel the walks when it snows," Andy said, and pointed, "and paint the fences. I stay busy."

"This must be such a peaceful place to work," she said, looking wistfully around.

Andy nodded. It was a beautiful cemetery, and it was peaceful. His job was the best part of his new life, what he thought of as his "post-Lucy life".

The dog, which had been standing placidly beside the woman, gave a sharp little bark. Just one, a little yip. The young woman looked down, startled, as if she'd just realized the dog was there. Then she gave Andy a smile. "Nice talking to you," she said. "I've got to go."

Andy nodded. He glanced down at the dog. It was a beautiful animal. Andy didn't know much about dog breeds—he'd always had mutts—but this had to be some kind of expensive purebred. It had the sleek coat and thin body of a Doberman, but its face looked more like a borzoi. It looked back at him and he saw that its eyes were a pale brown, like amber.

Impulsively, Andy stuck his hand through the fence, fingers down, for the dog to sniff. "Nice meeting you, too," he said.

The dog gave him an appraising look then dutifully bent its head to sniff the back of Andy's hand. Then the dog trotted off down the sidewalk, and the young woman followed it, looking as if it were taking her for a walk instead of the other way around.

Andy bent back to his work. When he looked up again, they were out of sight.

That was the end of April, and he never saw the woman again.

It was the middle of June, and he was on the zero turn mower, running along the back fence. He saw a thin man with short gray hair and a neat beard, dressed in a blue suit and wearing a yarmulke, walking down the alley just outside the fence. Andy brought the mower to a stop. He didn't want to get grass clippings all over the man's suit.

That's when he saw the dog. The same strange breed, sleek black with that lean, pointed face, almost like a fox.

Andy shut off the mower and climbed off.

"What kind of dog is that?" he asked.

The man looked surprised. "Were you asking me?"

Andy came up closer to the fence. "I saw a dog like that a while back," he said. "I was just wondering what breed it is."

The man looked down. "I couldn't say," he mumbled.

Black Dog

The dog was looking at Andy. The light lay full across its face and its eyes were amber, with flecks of gold, and Andy was suddenly sure that it wasn't just the same breed, it was the same dog that had been walking with the young woman down this same alley.

Andy stepped back from the fence, feeling suddenly nervous in a way that he couldn't explain. The look in the dog's eyes was too cool and analytical, a look that didn't belong on an animal's face.

"Sorry to bother you," Andy said awkwardly, "I was... just curious."

"I'm sorry I can't help you," the man said without looking away from the dog. "I must go. I am late."

He started walking again, and the dog trotted along beside him.

Andy went back to the mower, got it started up, and looked back to the alley. It was empty.

Andy thought about the black dog as he finished the mowing and took the zero turn back to the shed. It was better than any of the other things he had to think about.

Probably it belonged to someone who lived in the area, and its owner had friends who walked it sometimes. Two different people just happened to pick the alley beside the cemetery for a walk. That wasn't out of the question. The River Street neighborhood was mostly commercial, but there were a few older apartment buildings among the warehouses. It was quiet, but hardly deserted.

He made a mental note to look up breeds of dogs when he got back to his apartment that evening, but there was another letter from his ex-wife's lawyer waiting for him, and he got distracted dealing with that instead.

July and August turned brutally hot that year, and Andy was busy fighting a war against the relentless sun. The city provided him with a small tractor equipped with a five hundred gallon tank for watering. Some days he filled the tank four times. Despite his best efforts, the trees suffered, the edges of the leaves turning brown and looking burned. The flower gardens fared better, but only because Andy lavished them with attention. He cut back on his mowing to avoid damaging the already over stressed lawns and made plans to reseed the worst patches once the heat broke.

He saw the black dog once in July and twice in August.

In July, Andy had been soaking down the sod that had just been rolled over a fresh interment. He had his doubts that it would take, but he wanted to give it every chance he could. It had been the first service in weeks and the crew from the funeral parlor had complained that digging the grave had been like drilling through concrete. The mourners had been soaked with sweat in their uncomfortable funeral suits. One young woman collapsed by the graveside. The family had refused Andy's discrete offer to call an ambulance.

After they had left, Andy rolled out the watering tractor, taking his time to let the water soak into the hard soil rather than roll off. He looked around the grounds while he held the hose, thinking about his latest meeting with his attorney. Lucy had been half owner of his grounds keeping business, and her lawyer had insisted that the business be sold and the assets split. That had hurt—he'd spent years building it—but what was worse was that the same lawyer was using the income they had from the business as the basis for Lucy's separate maintenance.

"They can't do that," Andy had argued. "They can't make me give up the business and then make me pay her what I would be making if I still had it."

His attorney had given him a sad frown and explained that, yes, they could do that. He left the meeting promising Andy that he would file a motion, but not holding out much hope.

Not fair, Andy thought, the whole thing isn't fair. My life isn't fair.

Then he saw the little boy by the fence.

And the black dog at the boy's feet.

The boy was blond, and his short cut hair gleamed in the sun. He was dressed in dark brown slacks and a blue jacket. Church clothes. He was walking slowly, looking down at the dog that paced him, an angular shadow, dark as midnight.

As Andy stared, the dog turned its head, and Andy saw the flash of amber eyes. Even across the expanse of cemetery grounds, Andy was certain that the dog was looking at him, directly at him. Despite the heat, he felt suddenly cold, and shivered.

He turned his attention back to the sprayer, moving the stream of water slowly back and forth over the small grave. *When I look back,* he thought, *they will be gone.*

And they were.

July became August with no respite from the heat.

Black Dog

Andy's own tiny apartment was stifling, and even though he ran the air conditioner as infrequently as he could stand, his electric bill was crippling. He was living on peanut butter sandwiches and canned soup. He started staying late at work, clocking out at the regular time and then spending the evening under the shade of the arbor with a book. At least there, he had occasional breezes.

One evening he looked up from his book, and the black dog was there, leading someone else down the sidewalk by the blank red brick walls of the warehouses. The woman was very thin, in a long green dress, and her hair was white, straight, and flowing down her back.

Andy set his book down and got to his feet, not taking his eyes off her. She looked old, but she wasn't walking like an old woman. She looked like someone who had just been let out of jail, seeming to bask in the sight of the blank brick walls and the blistering unmoving air.

"Nice day," Andy commented, although he didn't think so.

She turned a big smile on him. "A beautiful day," she agreed. "Oh, I've been waiting for this day... for such a long, long time."

Andy walked along the fence to keep pace with her. The black dog glanced up at him with its calm amber eyes, then looked forward again.

Andy stuck his hand through the fence. "I'm Andy," he said.

The woman stopped and stared at him for a moment. "Andy," she said slowly, as if she'd never heard the name before. Then, very gingerly, she took his hand. Hers was smooth and dry, cool, but not cold. "I'm Ruth."

"Pleased to meet you," Andy said.

Ruth gave him a grin. "Likewise, I'm sure."

She looked ahead at where the alley turned out of sight, and her expression became serious. "I think I should be getting along," she said. "Don't you?"

Andy looked down at the dog. It had stopped but not sat down. It looked to Andy, then resolutely forward again.

"Yes, I think you should," Andy said. "Have a nice night."

Then he turned away and walked slowly across the cemetery.

It won't mean anything, he thought to himself. *Even if I see what I think I'm going to see, it's not proof. It doesn't mean that she is... or that the dog is... or that I am...*

It doesn't mean anything.

He walked slowly up to the new grave, careful not to damage the saturated sod.

Ruth Katzman

June 17, 1935-Aug 5, 2017

The next time he saw the black dog, he wasn't at work.

Against his better judgment, he had accepted a dinner invitation from a couple of old friends. Friends from the old days, the pre-divorce days. When he'd been married, most of their friends had been her friends. Andy had never been very social. Since he'd been living alone, he hadn't gone out. He worked and he went home. Since he worked alone for the most part, only seeing his nominal supervisor every couple of weeks to file reports, Andy's interactions with other people were limited to clerks at the grocery store and the occasional conversation with a stranger at the cemetery.

He didn't think of himself as isolated, and he didn't feel lonely. It was just... easier not to go out of his way to seek people out. Seeing his old friends felt awkward, with conversations full of long pauses where no one could think of anything to say.

Craig and Shelia were different. Craig could always think of something to say. You didn't really talk to Craig; you listened to him jumping from subject to subject, following some map written on the inside of his skull. Craig and Shelia ran a company that built irrigation systems, which is how Andy knew him.

Lucy, naturally, had never liked Craig and Shelia.

Shelia had called earlier in the week to set up the dinner, choosing a new restaurant not far from Andy's apartment. Andy hadn't wanted to go, but Shelia handled the sales end of their business, and in the end, Andy agreed.

It had been a good evening, as it happened. The restaurant was good, Cajun food, which Andy had always liked. Shelia insisted on paying the bill—she also handled that end of the business—in a way that didn't come across as condescending. Craig had been his usual self, holding forth on everything from bird kills due to wind farms to his theory on why modern German literature was so damned depressing. He had an opinion on every subject, and while many of them were controversial or downright weird, they were always amusing.

Walking home, Andy felt better than he had in a long time. He'd had enough beer to make him tipsy but not drunk, his head buzzing more from Craig's manic energy than the alcohol.

He saw the lights of the ambulance when he was still a block away. It was parked in front of an apartment building, half blocking the street. The red and blue lights lazily rotated, transforming the scene into alternating vistas of ice and fire. A small crowd had gathered, standing in that embarrassed hush of spectators of a tragedy in the making.

Andy crossed the street to pass as far as possible from the ambulance and the onlookers. He just wanted to get home and get to bed while he still felt good.

Then he saw the dog. The black dog was standing on the sidewalk, and Andy noticed that none of the onlookers were standing close to it. No one was looking at it, but they all seemed to give it room. The dog was turned to the apartment building, watching the door and standing very, very still.

Andy's stride faltered, but he kept moving. He wasn't that far from the cemetery. Maybe the dog belonged to someone in the building, he thought, although he was well past believing it.

The dog turned to look across the street, directly at Andy. The calm amber eyes focused on him. *This is none of your concern,* they seemed to say. *Keep walking.* And then the dog turned back to the building.

Andy kept walking. He was cold sober when he reached his apartment.

The dog was Death.

Or something like that. A guide dog for ghosts. A service animal for the recently deceased. Somehow the dog was taking the spirits of the dead from the cemetery to... someplace else.

Andy didn't consider himself a religious man. His family had spent Sundays in the huge ancient stone structure of Grace Lutheran, and he'd attended Sunday school and Vacation Bible School. He'd been married at Grace Lutheran. The doctrines of Christianity had always seemed reasonable—or at least as reasonable as any other explanation for why the universe existed to begin with—but not very relevant to his life. Building a landscaping business didn't leave much room for Sundays off.

But let's just suppose it's all true, Andy thought. *Let's suppose that there is a God, and life after death, and all the rest.* Maybe not quite the way that they had explained in the Children's Church Lesson Bulletin—he certainly didn't remember any amber-eyed black dog standing next to the welcoming Jesus at the gates of Heaven—but the basic outline. We live and then we die, and after death we... move on.

And I can see this... Hound of Heaven. Why? Because I work at a cemetery? Because my job puts me at the right place at the right time? Because I take care of the grounds and clip the grass around the tombstones and that makes Death like me? If you look at it just right, I work for Death. I mow Death's front yard.

The thought made him grin. When he put together fliers for his business, he asked his clients for testimonials. When he'd gotten the contract to do the yard of a local hockey star, he'd given the player a nice discount in exchange for using the player's name in his advertising.

Death's Gardener. Now that would be something to put on a business card.

As summer cooled into autumn, Andy began taking a new interest in the graves themselves. He'd always seen them as obstacles to be avoided. Things to weed around. Carefully, of course, always with respect.

Now, respect became reverence. He began to feel the weight of history under the ground as he cared for the lawns and flowerbeds. River Street was an old cemetery, predating the Civil War, and many of the headstones were time-worn nearly blank. That didn't matter. The state of the bodies, gone to bones as brittle and pale as chalk, deep under his feet didn't matter. These people, men, women, children, had been as real as he was. They had lived, and their lives meant something. The cemetery wasn't full of death, it was full of lives, all these people who had been born and worked and loved and fought and cried and eaten and slept.

Some days, sitting on the stone bench under the rose arbor, he felt as if he were eating his cheap lunch in a crowded restaurant, surrounded by patrons who sat quietly, resting. Sleeping, but not dead.

He saw an inscription on one gravestone as he was carefully edging the weeds away from it that spoke to his soul.

As you are now, so once was I,
As I am now, so you must be,

Black Dog

He felt comforted by it. It was a promise, a promise of rest. A man could do much worse than to end up here, under the green trees in the still autumn daylight. This wasn't a bad place to spend eternity and Andy felt privileged to be its caretaker.

He saw the black dog nearly every time there was an interment now.

The black dog and the ghosts.

The ghosts didn't seem unhappy. They weren't frightening, and they weren't frightened. They were simply... on their way. Sometimes they would talk to him, never about anything important. Andy was careful not to refer to the fact that he knew they were dead. That seemed impolite, somehow.

They walked along the alley behind the graveyard, the black dog walking along beside them. They were dressed, Andy realized, in the clothes that they had been buried in. There was never any obvious sign of injury or deformity, although Andy supposed that some must have died in accidents. As ghosts, they were whole.

One day Andy drove around the cemetery, looking for the alley that ran along the back fence. He never found it, and that didn't surprise him. The little alley wasn't there, not in the world of the living.

Andy supposed that he could have climbed over the fence or squeezed through the bars to get into the alley and walked down it to see where it went, but he never seriously considered the idea. It wasn't that he was afraid of what he might find, it just seemed... wrong.

It wasn't his time. Not yet. He'd take that walk one day, and he could wait until then.

Halloween came and went. Andy had worried about Halloween. Not because of the dead but because of the living. Stupid kids with no respect. But there hadn't been any vandalism at his cemetery. Some damage at other ones, but nothing at River Street.

The air grew cold. Andy spread mulch on the flowerbeds and put the mowers away for the year, carefully draining the fuel tanks and removing the blades for sharpening. He put the snowplow blade on the little tractor and tested the snow blowers, while watching for the changing of the season.

Snow fell, and the beneath the snow the earth slept, dreaming of its buried secrets.

It was three days before Christmas when the black dog howled for him.

The air was crisp and cold, the shadows of the leafless trees sharp as razors in the clear winter light. Andy was in the tractor shed, sitting on a metal folding chair next to the space heater, reading a book on the Dutch Tulip Mania. He'd picked it up from the library on a whim and was finding it fascinating.

There wasn't much to do during the winter when it wasn't actually snowing.

The howl was long and piercing, a sound of loneliness and heartbreak. It seemed to come from a vast distance, from the end of the world. It was the cry of the last living thing on Earth, searching the blasted landscape for a companion and finding nothing. It was the siren of an ambulance responding to the death of God. It was the wail of the void.

It was a summons.

The sound pulled Andy to his feet and out the door, dragging him with chains of emptiness and shadow. The black dog was calling him, and nothing could ever resist that call. His book was forgotten on the floor of the shed. He left the door open and the space heater running. He ran, surefooted on the snow, so familiar with the grounds that he could have made the run in blackest midnight.

The black dog stood by the fence, silent now, as still as a shadow. Beside it stood a woman, shoulders hunched, looking down, wearing a black dress. Andy barely had time to think, *But there wasn't a funeral today*, when he recognized her.

"Lucy," he breathed, feeling gutshot.

She looked up. "Andy," she said. "How...?"

She didn't finish the question and Andy didn't try to answer it. Instead he asked, "What happened?"

She turned her head and looked past him, out to the pale blue emptiness of the sky. "It was so hopeless. *I* was hopeless."

"What happened?" Andy repeated.

"I just felt so worthless. Everything went wrong," Lucy sounded tired. Tired enough to sleep forever. "He left me. He just walked out and left me, and you were gone, and I had nobody."

Andy almost asked, *Who left you?* but stopped himself. It didn't matter now.

Lucy brought her eyes back to Andy's face, jerkily, as if she couldn't quite focus on him. "Do you forgive me?" she asked.

"Forgive you?" Andy asked. "How could I forgive you now?"

Lucy stared at him, pain on her face.

"Am I supposed to believe that you'll change now?" Andy continued. "That you'll make it up to me? That you'll promise to never let me down again?"

He took a deep breath and let it out slowly. "You're past my forgiveness. You're *dead*."

"I—" Lucy began.

Andy spoke louder. "I don't hate you. Not anymore. I did for a while, but I realized that it was just hurting me. I don't love you, either. That was hurting me worse."

Andy looked down to the black dog. It was looking up at him, its amber eyes shining in the winter light.

"But I can't forgive you," Andy said. "Because you're not around to forgive anymore. You're gone. This... this is just a glitch of some kind. You are going to walk away down that alley, and I won't see you again. Not in my lifetime. Maybe after, I don't know. Maybe in Heaven, or wherever that alley leads, we'll see each other again. Ask me then if I can forgive you."

"Andy..." Lucy gasped.

"Ask me then!" Andy repeated, feeling a sudden surge of bone-deep anger.

Lucy stared at him, and then turned away, walking down the alley. The black dog fell into step at her side. Andy watched them until they turned the corner, and then he stood at the fence, looking into the little brick lined alley that hung off the edge of the world.

After a time, a long time, the wind erased her footprints and the dog's pawprints, and Andy turned away and went back to work.

Our Cities Are Decorated

Our cities are decorated with the bones of the unquiet dead
Gaudy, glistening, gilded, silvered, hung with lights
You'd never know they were there hanging just above your head
Shadowed in the daytime, glowing faintly in the nights

This street a concrete canyon thirty stories deep
Built at the cost of perhaps a dozen slain
That's just the buy-in, not the upkeep
A few more every year, a few falls of crimson rain

You don't ever see the faces of the lost
You might read about them if the news is slow
You live a quiet cozy life while they have paid the cost
It's easier to relax at home because you'll never know

You sit in comfort surrounded by the things you've got
Not knowing you are safe because they're not

227 Progress Loop

Originally published in *Occult Detective Quarterly #10,* Winter 2021

A t two fifteen in the morning the phone woke Eddie, and blinking in the darkness, he took a moment to get oriented. *I'm at home, alone, and I'm on call, and this means I need to get up and go to work.*

That much sorted, he picked his phone from the bedside table, cleared his throat, and answered it.

"Yes?"

"This is Midwest Building Services, we have an emergency call."

"Right. Gimme a minute."

Bedside lamp—*ow, that's bright!*—glasses, notebook and pen.

"What have you got?"

"The address is two twenty-four Progress Loop Drive. Security is reporting that they have an alarm going off that they can't silence."

Eddie wrote the address automatically, then paused.

"An alarm? Shouldn't that be the alarm company?"

"Citywide Electronics has already been out. They say it's not their equipment, so there's nothing that they can do."

Eddie considered the address. He was pretty sure he'd never run a call out there before, but he had a vague idea of where Progress Loop Drive was. Up north, close to the airport.

He sighed. "They're sure it can't wait until morning?"

"County police has gotten complaints from the neighbors. I checked with the manager, and she said get somebody out tonight."

"Okay." Another sigh. "I'm on my way."

Pants, shirt, boots. Wallet, keys, multitool, flashlight, work ID on a lanyard. He ran on long habit and muscle memory, his hands picking things up and putting them in his pockets while his brain was still grappling with the transition from blissful sleep to a grudging wakefulness.

He checked his phone, wrote the time of the last call in his notebook, then stuck both in his jacket pocket and headed to his truck. On the way through the kitchen, he cast a longing look at his coffee maker, set up to start brewing at 5 am, but didn't stop. If county police has noise complaints logged, he'd best hurry.

He was fully awake by the time he'd turned on the radio in his truck and lit a cigarette. He found the call address in his map book—Eddie didn't like map apps, didn't trust them. He liked his old Utility Company Map Book, *damn it*, and it annoyed him that the new editions were getting tough to find these days.

One big EMP and half the country would starve while trying to find their way to the grocery store.

With the map open to the right page on the passenger seat beside him, he pulled out of his driveway. In two minutes he was on the highway. Ten minutes after that he was getting off the highway, and scanning the names of the side streets.

There was Progress Loop, and he took the left, obediently waiting for the light to change, even though his truck was the only vehicle on the road. A high cinder block wall ran beside the road for a while, once painted white but now a dirty gray. Tarnished metal letters on the wall advised him that he was entering Progress Estates.

It was a mixed use subdivision, commercial and residential, obscure company names vying with Move-In Special signs for his attention. 1100 block, 800 block, 500 block. As advertised Progress Loop was a big loop, and he'd entered on the wrong end of it.

200 block, and on one side of the street was a construction site, big equipment ranked around a sizable hole in the ground. Across from the site was his destination, an ungainly pile like a stack of Legos, in the style that was 1966's idea of the future.

He could hear the alarm as soon as he shut off his truck, an old style mechanical bell ringing continuously. Yeah, that's sure to annoy the neighbors. He grabbed his electrical kit—a repurposed laptop bag—out of the toolbox in the truck bed.

A big black girl—*young woman*, he corrected himself automatically, although she looked to be about half of his 41 years—in a security uniform was standing just outside the big glass doors. Unarmed, he saw.

"Eddie Rosten, Midwest Building Services," he said, extending a hand.

"I'm Glynis," she said. "Can you shut that thing off? It's been ringing since 12:30. Citywide couldn't do anything."

"Let's take a look."

Glynis opened the door to the lobby, and then the alarm got *loud*. Amazingly loud. No wonder she had been waiting outside.

Eddie scanned the modern fire panel beside the door. *All Systems*

Normal, it insisted.

Glynis didn't try to talk over the din. Instead, she pointed with an exaggerated gesture at a metal box mounted behind the lobby desk. A red light was flashing on it.

Eddie responded with a big nod and headed to the box. It was old, probably original with the building. A time faded label on it read, *227 P L.*

Eddie studied it for a minute. Two lengths of conduit ran from the box, both going up to disappear above the ceiling tiles. He got out a screwdriver and took off the front panel.

Inside the box, wires snaked from both conduits to meet at the light. He tested the connections—110 volt, which made sense, considering the probable age. Working carefully, he undid the hot leads and capped them.

The light stopped blinking.

The bell did not shut off.

Hollering to be heard over the bell, he asked, "Have you got a ladder?"

Glynis shrugged. "Around here someplace, I think."

"I'll get mine out of the truck."

A quick look above the ceiling tiles revealed a maze of pipes and wires but nothing that could house the alarm bell. The sound was impossible to locate, it seemed to come from everywhere.

So instead, Eddie traced the conduit from the box on the wall. They ran in parallel lines, up the wall, across the ceiling—Eddie moved the ladder, pulled another tile, moved the ladder again—to a big metal door.

"What's in here?"

"Stairs to the basement."

Glynis unlocked the door, and they headed down. Like most basements in commercial buildings, this one was a maze of abandoned furniture, all the crap that got left behind when businesses folded and the tenants slunk out in the middle of the night. Eddie shoved what he could out of the way and climbed over anything too big to move.

The conduits ran along the ceiling and then across the basement—no drop ceiling down here—and vanished into a wall.

No junction boxes and no sign of the bell. If anything, the ringing was louder down in the basement.

"What's past here?" Eddie had to shout above the bell.

"Nothing!" Glynis pointed. High on the wall was a row of tiny glass block windows. *"That's the outside wall!"*

Eddie examined the wall, thinking.

The box with the flashing light had been labeled *227 PL.*

227 Progress Loop. That had to be the construction site across the street. The conduit had once connected this building to whatever had been over there, and the workers had shorted something out.

"I think we'll have to..." Eddie broke off.

The wall of the basement was concrete, painted a faded white. Where the conduit vanished into the wall, though, a hole had been cut in wood. A sheet of plywood, maybe six feet by four feet, painted to match the concrete. The wall was filthy enough that it was hard to notice the change in material unless you were up against it.

Eddie found an edge of the plywood and slipped his screwdriver tip into the gap.

"There's something behind here," he explained in a shout.

He pried and the plywood budged enough that he could shine his flashlight behind it. *"There's a door,"* he announced.

"There's no door there," Glynis protested.

"I'm looking at a damned door," Eddie shot back. The bell was giving him a splitting headache.

He slid his screwdriver deeper in the gap and levered. Nails protested, and then suddenly the whole sheet gave way and slammed down like a drawbridge. Eddie just barely got out of the way.

Where the plywood sheet had been was a set of double doors, metal dark with rust.

Glynis stared in astonishment.

Eddie tried a handle and it turned. He pulled, then yanked, and the door came open. A dark space was revealed. The air coming out of it smelled like rust and mildew.

He shined his flashlight into the space. Glynis came up behind him and added her bigger light to his.

A tunnel stretched away under the street.

Eddie shined his light on the floor. It was thick with dirt, but at least it was dry. He looked up. The two lines of conduit headed down the tunnel. He followed.

Glynis followed him, scanning all around with her light.

"I never knew this was here!" she shouted. *"I don't think the*

manager even knows about this!"

Twenty feet or so down the tunnel, the conduit ended in a metal box. Another line ran from the far end of the box to a door in the wall of the tunnel.

Eddie started undoing the screws that held the cover on the box. Beside him, Glynis shown her light at the door, which stood a few inches ajar.

There wasn't any bell in the box, but wires ran to an ancient mass of relays. Eddie tested the circuits, found them live, and started unhooking wires.

The alarm bell stopped.

The silence that followed was a positive pleasure, like a drink of cool water on a scorching day. For a moment, Eddie closed his eyes to better enjoy the quiet.

Then Glynis yelled, *"Oh, Lord!"*

The door in the wall was wide open, and Glynis backed slowly out of it, her light trained on something inside.

There was a storeroom of some kind behind the door, a windowless concrete box. Inside, covered with dust, was a frame made from lengths of black-painted pipe, like some kind of exercise equipment. On the frame was something like a big doll or a...

"That's not a manikin, is it?" Eddie asked softly.

Glynis just shook her head.

They went back up the lobby, and Glynis made a call, speaking softly into her cell. Eddie filled out a work ticket then held it out for Glynis to sign once she ended her call.

"You can't leave," Glynis protested.

Eddie shrugged. "I'm done here."

"There's a dead body down there!" Glynis said.

Eddie bit back an acid comment—*what do you want me to do, fix it?*—and shrugged.

"Please," Glynis said, and Eddie saw that she was scared. Really scared. "Just stay until the cops get here."

Eddie sighed. The night was shot for sleeping anyway. "Okay," he agreed. "Have you got any coffee?"

The county police showed up, and then the building manager, who wore a black suit and a sour expression, as if she suspected Glynis of building the tunnel and stashing a corpse in it just to make her life difficult.

Eddie—whose ex-wife had been a big fan of *CSI*—expected a team of forensic investigators from the county to swarm in and photograph everything, picking up little bits of this and that to seal in tiny plastic envelopes.

Instead, the first cop on the scene took a look downstairs and wrote up some notes, and then a couple of men took the body away on a stretcher and loaded it into an ambulance.

And that was it. No one took Eddie's fingerprints or asked him what he had touched. They didn't even tape off the tunnel, just told the manager that the county building inspector would be called to check out the structure to see if it was safe.

After the cops were gone, the manager—Mrs. Park—said, "I need to look at this tunnel."

The command was directed at Glynis, but Eddie could tell that she was still pretty freaked out, so he stepped up.

"I want to see how far it goes, myself."

"It used to run under the street," Mrs. Park said. "When they built the complex, the idea was that workers in this building could live the apartments over there and commute by tunnel."

"But they tore down the apartments," Eddie said.

"There was a fire," Mrs. Park said. "Before my time. 1990, maybe? The apartments were condemned, and I thought they had filled in the tunnel. But I suppose they just walled it off."

Eddie led the way to the doors, Mrs. Park frowning at the collection of junk. "You know anyone who needs filing cabinets?"

"Sorry, no."

"Everyone's going paperless," she went on. "You can't give the damn things away. I'll have to see if I can have them hauled off for scrap."

At the tunnel door, she produced her own flashlight, a key-chain LED that gave out a surprisingly bright beam. "Storage units," she said, shining her light along the wall.

Eddie saw that the door that had been wired to the alarm was just one of a row of doors, the walls and the doors a uniform shade of dust gray. Mrs. Park tried handles as they passed them, frowning. "I'll need to get a locksmith and get these opened up," she fretted. "God knows what's in the rest of them."

Eddie shown his light down the tunnel. It went, he estimated, halfway across the street and ended in wall of concrete blocks. "I guess they filled in that half," he suggested.

"I'll check with the crew over there," Mrs. Parks waved to indicate the construction site. "They couldn't do anything with that place for the longest time—the owner died in the fire, and I guess the heirs wouldn't sell or something. I hear it finally got seized for taxes."

When they reached the one open door, the one that had held the body, Mrs. Park went in cautiously and Eddie followed her.

The room was a concrete box, about ten feet square and windowless.

The metal frame that the body had been draped across was against one wall. On the opposite wall were hung a dozen or so framed pictures.

Eddie peered at them, trying to see through the thick layer of dust.

Women. Or maybe just one woman, in a variety of outfits and poses. It was hard to tell, and Eddie didn't want to touch anything in here.

"Huh," Mrs. Park said behind him.

Eddie turned and saw what she was looking at. A row of hooks had been mounted on the wall. Long filthy things hung from the hooks.

"Somebody's sex dungeon, I guess." Her voice was flat, not condemning, just identifying the purpose of the room.

Eddie saw what she meant. The things hanging from the hooks were whips.

"And somebody just...died in here?" Eddie said, horrified. "And they left the body?"

Mrs. Park turned her attention to the pictures on the wall. After a long moment she said, "Maybe she died in the fire. The woman in the pictures. And maybe nobody else knew he was down here."

Eddie felt cold. "I've got to get going," he said.

"Yeah. Me, too."

It had gotten too late to try to go home and get some sleep, so Eddie got coffee and takeout breakfast sandwiches and drove to the shop. In the parking lot, he went through his toolbox while waiting for the shop to open and made a list of parts he needed to restock.

Midwest Building Services dealt primarily with small problems, changing lightbulbs and sink washers, fixing fans that wouldn't run and toilets that wouldn't stop running. Their clients tended to businesses small enough that they didn't have their own maintenance department.

It was a good job, and Eddie had been with them for fifteen years now. The work was varied enough to stay interesting, and he was off on his own most of the time, without a supervisor breathing down his neck. A few of the clients were jerks, but you'll get that anywhere.

When the office opened, he went in and turned in his ticket to the office manager who matched it up to the morning's report from the call center in Ohio. There was nothing pressing, so Eddie headed back home, promising to keep his phone on in case it got busy later.

Once home, Eddie heated up some leftovers and then crawled into bed.

Slept.

And dreamed.

He was lost, and he couldn't find Her. She had been right there a moment ago, and he had turned away, gone to the bar to get Her a drink, but the bar was far, far away, all the way across the room full of tables and people and there was no one behind the bar, so he went around to get Her the beer she liked, but it wasn't there, and so he went to the storeroom, looking for a cooler, but the hallways just stretched on and on and then he was in the basement, and the concrete corridor was miles long, all the doors locked, the lights dimming as he walked on and on, now just looking for the way out, the way to get back to Her, and the lights flickered, dimmed, and he was walking in darkness, hands outstretched to feel the cool concrete of the walls, walls all around him now, boxing him in, he was in a room, Their Room, and he was alone, and afraid, but still, through it all, he knew She needed him, and She missed him, and She would be so disappointed that he went away and never came back, and the thought of making Her cry woke him with tears on his cheeks.

It was dark when Eddie woke up, confused. He hadn't meant to sleep the whole day away. He automatically checked his phone, but there weren't any missed calls.

The dream was sticking with him, that feeling of fear and loss.

And... familiarity.

In the dream, he knew the room where the party was being held. A big open room, but with a curiously low ceiling. Rows of folding tables, all covered with cheap paper tablecloths. Drinks served in red plastic cups, or cans of beer.

It had all been incredibly vivid. He could hear the music—Depeche Mode—playing from somewhere behind the bar. One wall of the room had been covered with black paper, and he knew that it was taped over floor to ceiling windows.

It was nine thirty at night, and Eddie was wide awake. Worse, he knew he'd be wide awake for hours. He'd only meant to take a nap, not sleep the whole day away.

He drank the one beer in his fridge, considered going out for more, and decided it wasn't worth the drive. He tried to watch TV, but nothing held his attention.

He got on his computer and tried looking for news stories about the fire at 227 Progress Loop, but the old editions of the north county newspapers weren't digitized, and all he could find about that address was the announcement that a new urgent care clinic was going into that spot.

When the phone rang at quarter of one, he wasn't at all surprised. It was almost as if he'd been waiting for the call all evening.

"It's 227 Progress Loop. They say that alarm you worked on yesterday is going off again."

"I'm on my way."

When he pulled up outside the building, Glynis was standing outside again. Eddie got out of his truck and grabbed his toolbag, the alarm ringing all around him, and felt that, somehow, he was reliving the night before. As if it had been a level in a video game that he had failed, and now he needed to try it again and get it right this time.

"When did start?"

"Twelve-thirty. Just like last night."

She unlocked the door, and Eddie went through and into the horrible noise of the bell. He headed for the basement and had half-crossed the lobby before he realized that he was alone. He looked back and saw Glyinis standing outside, looking at him through the glass door.

He shrugged and went on.

The lights in the basement were on, and more of the junk furniture had been shoved out of the way, making a path of sorts the door to the tunnel. Both sides of the double doors were open, too, propped with doorstops.

Eddie pulled out his flashlight to supplement the light coming in through the open doors and headed into the tunnel. The other doors were still closed, but the one to... *their room* was standing open. Eddie paused to look into the alarm box and was not surprised to see that it was just like he'd left it the night before, all the wires disconnected and capped.

He went into the little room, shining his light all around. Whatever was making the alarm sound was in here, he was sure, and he was beginning to suspect that—somehow—it was not an electrical problem.

His booted foot hit something that rattled, and he bent down to examine it.

The moment his fingers touched the cool metal, the bell stopped.

It was a length of chain, maybe a foot long. Once chromed, now thick with dirt and rust. Like a chain collar for a big dog.

Eddie picked it up. His hands felt strange, distant from him, as he examined it. There was a tag on it, heart shaped, and he rubbed the dirt from the letters engraved on it, knowing, somehow, what it would read.

MY BOY.

This was your place. Your special room, a secret place for just the two of you. She could lock you up inside your special place. That was your game, wasn't it? A game that both of you enjoyed. You had a failsafe, an alarm you could use to call from help if anything ever happened to her and she couldn't come and let you out. But something went wrong. The fire. The fire cut off the power from the other building, and no one knew you were down here. You died, in the dark, alone. You died thinking that she had abandoned you.

"Is it going to stay fixed this time?"

Eddie jumped at the sound of Glynis's voice. Heart hammering, he turned and saw her standing in the doorway.

"Let me make sure," he said. "Give me a few minutes."

She nodded, then stood there, watching him.

"Can you go back upstairs?" Eddie asked her. "Keep an eye on that light and let me know if it's starts flashing again, okay?"

"Sure."

When she was gone, Eddie turned his attention to the pictures on the wall. Carefully, reverently, he wiped the dirt from glass and used his flashlight to study them.

It was the same woman. Straight hair, dyed black with the last few inches bright red. In most of them, her makeup was also black and red, with exaggerated eyes and lips, almost stage makeup. In one picture, she wore a corset that made her breasts bulge, spilling out enough to expose her nipples. In another, she wore a severe black suit with a very short skirt and very high boots.

She was heavyset, with broad shoulders and a thick waist. Her face was square and—in the shots without the dramatic makeup—rather plain. Not the usual pinup girl.

But one of the pictures was a framed page from a magazine, showing her standing, looking down at the camera. The photograph had been taken from almost floor level, looking up a pair of boots that stretched to her mid-thighs.

Lady Hecate, the caption read.

Eddie glanced down the tunnel nervously, then took that picture off the wall. After a moment's fumbling, he got the back off and slid out the magazine page. He rolled it very carefully and slid it into his jacket pocket. He put the chain into the other pocket.

He went out into the tunnel and then paused, glancing back into the room. He felt as if he should say something, but no words seemed to be the right ones so he just left.

"It didn't flash," Glynis said as Eddie came out of the door from the basement stairs.

"What?" Eddie asked, confused.

"The light," Glynis said. "It didn't flash."

"Oh, good," Eddie said, then held out his ticket book for a signature.

On the way home, he stopped for coffee at a gas station. He had work to do once he got home.

It took Eddie most of the night to find her.

The problem was that "Lady Hecate" turned out to be a very popular name. He had pages of results, but none of them were the *right* Lady Hecate.

He tried taking a picture of the magazine page and doing a reverse image search—which didn't come up with anything useful—and saw that there was an ad for Lady Hecate's website on the other side.

Without much hope, he typed the address into the search bar and was surprised when a weirdly formatted page of text came up. The left side of the page was jagged, like the blade of a saw, the paragraphs marching back and forth across the page, indented with varying numbers of spaces.

It was an archive of a newsgroup, Eddie realized. Ancient history, as the internet measured time.

The text was laid out on the page in reverse order, last response first, so he had to wade through pages of *[hugs]* and *[sending prayers]* and *[OMG-so sorry]* before he reached the posts that contained any real information.

It was further complicated by the use of abbreviations that Eddie didn't know, and a lot of words that seemed to have a different meaning than the common one.

Gradually, though, details emerged.

Lady Hecate and her partner—who used the name LHsboy—had held regular parties. The address was evidently kept confidential, but Eddie could figure it out.

227 Progress Loop.

The fire had taken place in August, on the night of the monthly party.

Three people were confirmed dead—Lady Hecate, someone called MasterKarl, and someone called BucketGirl. Several others were injured, a few seriously.

Lhsboy vanished after the fire.

It turned out that nobody knew—or would admit to knowing—his real name or address or workplace, nothing that would identify him. It's not hard to disappear when nobody knows who you really are.

The assumption was made that Lady Hecate's boy had withdrawn from group, stopped attending events, shut down that email address, gone back to his ordinary—what they called his vanilla—life.

Eddie took the length of chain out of his pocket and ran it through his fingers. *MY BOY*, read the tag.

You didn't go back to your vanilla life, Eddie thought. *You never left that room. Not until now.*

The newsgroup archive was on something called The Female Led Relationship Forum.

It was a poorly designed website, looking as if it had been assembled by copying parts of other sites. Navigating it was difficult; many of the links were dead or connected to something completely irrelevant.

One link that did work got Eddie to the Dungeon of Mistress Paradox, a slick professional site that offered video clips and online domination sessions.

There had been MsParadox on the newsgroup archive. She had been at the party on the night of the fire and had been one of the injured. She'd also been a close friend to Lady Hecate, judging from her posts.

Eddie found a contact link and sent her an email. "I'd like to talk to someone about the fire on Progress Loop" was all he said. After a moment's thought he included his phone number.

Eddie was surprised to see the sun was coming up. He called the office and left a message that he was calling in sick, then took a shower and changed his clothes, made a fresh pot of coffee.

At 8 am, he called the County Police and eventually was connected to a bored clerk who explained that unclaimed human remains would be cremated at the state's expense and the ashes held in storage for two years before interment. He couldn't say if the body found at Progress Loop had been cremated yet, but did say that it usually took a couple of weeks, so probably not.

While he was on the phone with the county his phone beeped to let him know he'd gotten a text message.

"You've got my attention," it read.

"Can we meet somewhere?" Eddie texted back. "I'd rather explain this in person."

There was no immediate response.

Eddie puttered around his house, straightening up, taking out the trash, cleaning the kitchen. He was just about to give up and go to bed when he received a text back from Mistress Paradox, suggesting a restaurant and a time.

"I'll be there." he texted back.

Mistress Paradox turned out to be a slim woman in jeans and a baggy sweater, with silver gray hair cut very short. In person she didn't look much like the pictures on her website.

"So," she said once they were seated, "what's your interest?

Eddie had prepared several different ways to start the conversation, but what came out of his mouth was, "I think I found Lady Hecate's boy."

"Oh?"

"I mean, I think I found his body," Eddie felt himself babbling but couldn't seem to stop. "That is, I was there when the body was found."

"What do you mean?" The woman leaned back in her seat and looked about to bolt.

Eddie reached into his pocket and pulled out the chain, laid it on the table.

"Did he have a necklace like this?"

She leaned forward and examined it without touching it.

"Tell me everything."

Eddie, much to his surprise, told her everything. The strange alarm and his inability to find the bells, the way it had come back the following night, his finding the chain and the magazine page, his long search to identify the right Lady Hecate. All he left out was the dream.

Mistress Paradox listened without any expression on her face until he had finished.

"What are you going to do with this information?" she asked softly.

Eddie shrugged. "Nothing. I just... felt like somebody who knew him ought to know what happened to him. That's all."

She looked out the window for a long moment before she spoke. "His name was Michael. His family was rich—I mean, 'let's take the family jet to our place in the Caribbean' rich. Manhattan private prep school, Ivy League business degree. He was terrified that his folks might find out about his kink. Kate made me promise not to even joke about it. Some men get off on the fantasy of being blackmailed, as long as they know it's not really going to happen. Not Michael. He made damned sure nobody in the lifestyle could find out anything about him."

Eddie assumed Kate was Lady Hecate's real name. He nodded.

"He bought her that building," she went on, shaking her head at the memory. "That just blew me away when I heard about it. 'Happy birthday, dear, I got you an apartment building—I hope you like it.' I think he probably could have bought her the whole damned block, if she'd asked for it."

"He was my first client, as a pro. Kate asked me to do a few scenes with the two of them." A shrug. "That's how I got my start."

"Did you know about the basement room?" Eddie asked.

She looked down at her hands. "Yes," she said in a small voice, then looked up. "But I swear to you, I thought he was out of town that night. That's what Kate told *everybody.* Even me. We were supposed to do a big scene with Michael—not just Kate and me, but three or four other women. Then a couple of days before the party, Kate calls it off. She says Michael had to go back east for the weekend for some family thing. We never questioned it."

"And I was in the hospital after the fire. My lungs got scarred from the smoke. By the time that I got back online and found out Michael had gone missing, it was too late. They'd sealed up the tunnel. Damn it, they should have searched it. They *said* they searched it."

Eddie nodded sadly. "But you suspected."

She was blinking back tears now. "Kate ran the wrong way. Everyone else was headed for the exits, but Kate was trying to get to the basement stairs. That's where they found her, halfway down the basement stairs. The ceiling fell on her."

Eddie pushed the chain across the table towards her. "I think you should take this," he said. "I think he'd want you to have it. I think... I think he wants you to know that it wasn't your fault. That he doesn't blame you."

Without looking up from the chain she said, "Thank you."

Eddie got up from the table and drove back home. It was time to get some sleep.

One Man's Highway

One man's highway is another man's maze
Our eyes don't always work the same
The problem that you've sweated for days
To someone else might seem quite tame

What I seek is out of reach
Though well within another's grasp
Different gifts are granted to each
A different lock adorns each hasp

No merit in hating those who can
No guilt in failing one small task
All pleasures are not allowed to man
Some things one cannot even ask

I really shouldn't be so tense
When giving up makes much more sense

Epilogue
Previously published on-line

"What kind of monster are you?" she asked
And I said, "What kind of monster would you like me to be?"

S o, anyway, I had just gotten out of the Duchy lockup—total
bullshit rap, the sheriff was looking for some good ink and
nabbed a bunch of us on a conspiracy beef. I didn't even know
most of the other guys. The public defender told us to just play cool,
and once the papers got done squawking about how safe the good
people of Forest Green felt now and how much they loved the sheriff,
la la la, we all plead down and got out with time served.

Except one of the guys I did know, Billy the G, decides he's
gonna make a constitutional issue out of it, pleads not guilty, and
gets sent up to the Big Rock. Which just goes to show, stupid can
strike at any moment.

Me, I know better. I kept my big mouth shut and my big eyes on
the floor and let the mouthpiece do the talking. "Yes, Your Honor,
my client used to be big and bad, but now he's repentant and
reformed, la, la la." I can do that innocent act in my sleep.

The only real change in my circumstance was I got me a new PO.
Well, it did so happen that some old business got settled while I was
in the Duchy, but the fat little bastard had it coming. He burned me
in a real estate deal, years back, but I got a long memory.

My new PO, he wasn't a new kid who thinks he can save me from
myself or one of those dried up old geezers who wants to bring back
the ax, he was reasonable. Practical, you know.

He got me a square job in a butcher shop. Never been much of a
nine-to-fiver, myself, but I do know my way around a good cut of
meat, and if you're going to be chasing a paycheck there are worse
things to do. Believe me, I've done most of them.

My new boss was one of those guys who was raised up in the
business, married his childhood sweetheart, junior chamber of
commerce, never took a step off the reservation in his life. He came
on real sympathetic-like, but I could tell he was just itching for some
tough talk, something to let him pretend for a while, relieve the
boredom. So in between customers, I'd talk about the old days—

100

pure fairy tales, what he wanted to hear. No way I was going to give him anything that might come back and bite me, you know?

I'm starting to think that there might be something to this rehabilitation business. I'm staying in this boarding house, and the old lady who runs the place doesn't keep track of when I come and go or snoop in my room, on account of she's got a sideline in the chemical trade she'd rather not get talked about. All in all, I'm—what's phrase? "Adjusting to non-institutional life."

Then one day, I'm carving up some stew meat—the secret to good stew meat? You make all the pieces the same size, so they're all done at the same time—and *she* walks in.

It had been fifteen years, but I knew her before she was all the way through the door.

She'd filled out a bit, rounded the curves and softened the edges, her fiery hair had streaks of ash, and there were lines on her face that I didn't remember being there, but, damn, she had grown up from a beautiful girl to a beautiful woman. I'd put on some weight myself, a few pounds here and there, some of it muscle, but more of it beer. Ah, well, nothing lasts forever.

I watched her, my hand on the knife going through the motions on pure reflex—I was damned lucky I didn't take my own thumb off. She walked with her basket through the sundries, picking up some bread fixings and a few spices, walking in that way that made you think about what a woman's hips are for.

She'd glanced at me when she came in and her eyes just slid over me without sticking—new guy behind the meat counter, so what—I was just furniture in a bloody apron. Then her eyes came back to me, all by themselves, and the rest of her figured out what they were looking at, and she stopped in her tracks. Those eyes—still such a bright green—got big.

"Hey, Red," I grinned at her, "been a while."

She shook her head, slow, and I saw her start to say something, then start to say something else, then finally settle on, "Yeah. It's been a while."

She started walking again, towards me.

"So, how you been?" I asked her. "You still with old what's his name?"

"Jack," she said, a little sharply. "Yes. We're still married."

I put down the knife, stripped off my gloves. "And kids? You've got kids, right?"

She nodded. "Yes, the twins. They'll be thirteen in September."

"Thirteen. Time flies, huh?" I didn't have anything to do with my hands, so I picked up a towel and started wiping down the counter, which didn't need it.

Another nod. She'd stopped a couple feet from the counter. Outside of arm's reach.

"So." I tried to think. "Jack still in the lumber business?"

"He's a area manager now. He's got six crews under him." Her eyes had recovered from the surprise of seeing me, and now they weren't giving anything away.

"Six crews, huh. Big man."

She folded her arms. "He's done very well for himself. And for me. And for our children."

I raised my hands. "Hey, I mean that. I'm glad you got yourself a good man."

She relaxed a little. "Look, I know you've got good reason not to like him, but ..." she trailed off into a sigh. "Let's just not have that conversation."

I nodded and smiled. I wasn't sure what conversation she thought we weren't having, but I was good with it. Instead, I waved to the front of the case. "So what can I get for you."

She looked down to check out the display. "So you're cutting meat now?"

"Learned it in Big Rock. Six years in the kitchen, and believe me, you don't want to run into unhappy customers in the yard."

She looked sharply back at my face then, and I felt like apologizing for bringing it up. Screw that, it was true.

She looked back down and said, "How are those hens?"

"Sweet," I told her, "plump as judges, and every one of them died happy. They'll roast up nice."

"Give me two."

I got a fresh pair of gloves and picked out the two plumpest ones, started wrapping them in crisp white paper. Even though they'd been hung to drain the blood, I double-wrapped them—paper's cheap, and it's the little things that impress the customers.

She was checking out the rest of the case and chewing on her knuckle a little while she thought. It was a gesture I remembered from the old days.

To fill the quiet, I tried a little sales talk. "We got some good sausage—we don't make it here, the boss buys it from some outfit just outside town."

"Golden's, yeah, I know," she said kind of distractedly. I guess it made sense she'd know that. She'd probably been shopping here for years. "I'll take a pound, and oh, two pounds of ground beef."

I got busy weighing and wrapping. I wasn't going to say anything, because there wasn't anything to say. Maybe make some small talk about shopping, talk her into buying pork chops, but that was all. I wasn't going to talk about the old days. There was no point to it.

I was folding the paper around the sausages—you make real sharp creases with your fingernail, and it'll stay closed up tight until it's time to fry them—and it just slipped out, like the words had a mind of their own and didn't care what I thought.

"Do you miss it?"

I looked down at my hands, still folding. I couldn't look at her. I don't know what she was looking at, but the quiet turned into silence.

She didn't say, "miss what?"—we'd never been any good at lying to each other. She didn't say, "let's not have that conversation," because it was pretty obvious that we were going to have that conversation, whether or not either one of us wanted to.

"Sometimes," in a very small voice.

My hands were finished with the sausages, and I watched them building a little wax paper box for the ground beef. "I guess Jack's... not that type."

"He's a good man," even smaller.

I nodded down at my hands, then glanced over at her, quickly, careful not to see anything I shouldn't. Her eyes were dry, and her face was serious. She looked young, almost as young as the last time I'd seen her.

"Good." I let out a breath that I hadn't realized I'd been holding. Louder, then. "Good, I'm glad. You deserve a good man."

Meaning, not one like me, but neither of us said that.

Her eyes met mine and held them for a long time before she smiled. I'd spent twelve years of my life, all told, locked up in stone hotels, and I'd dreamed of that smile every night. It was good as I remembered it.

"I don't blame you," I said, and regretted it right away. That smiled faded away, and her eyes got moist. Cursing myself, I turned

103

away to pick up her packages and slap them down on the counter.

"You want this delivered?" I asked, and then to make sure there wasn't any misunderstanding I added, "The boss's boy does the deliveries, you know."

She nodded, puffed out a long breath. "Yes, please. I'm in the delivery book."

I nodded back, and we just looked at each other for a while.

I really didn't blame her. What happened had happened a long time ago, to a couple of kids who didn't know what they were doing. What everybody had seen, what had been in the papers, that had been the truth.

It just hadn't been all of the truth.

I marked her name on the packages in grease pencil and had her sign the book.

She said, "I've got to…"

And I said, "Yeah…"

And just like that, she left again.

I put her packages in the walk-in for the boss's kid to deliver when he made the next day's rounds. I went back to making cubes of stew meat, but the blade didn't feel right, so I took down the steel and worked on the edge for a while. The boss had some good steel, I had to give him that.

I watched my hands working on the blade for a while, the steel sweeping back and forth, and I wished I had a drink. It'd be nice to sit back in a dark room and knock back shots of whiskey, one after another, until I didn't have to think any more.

Instead, I put a good edge on my boss's knife and went back to work. Life goes on, right?

The Listener

Not dead but somehow still a ghost
I through these haunted hallways pass
Unseen by all, unheard by most
A stranger's statue made of glass

And who was here? Not I, not me
Some other's feet disturbed this dust
Some other's shadow did you see
I moved the air, but only just

I'm nothing you will recollect
Nor block the light that meets your eye
The memories that you collect
Have no space for such as I

I from my mother's breast was torn
And buried alive when I was born

The Blacklight Ballet

Originally published in *Duel Visions*, February 2019

There were k-rails across all of the entrances to the mall parking lots, but the service entrance just had a chain, and Pete Ferris had come in that way. The firm he represented had expressed an interest in buying the mall, and the management company had given him a map and keys. They'd offered to send someone with him, but Ferris preferred to work alone and get his impressions without someone trying to sell him on the place.

His first impression wasn't good.

The service drive was a mess. Ferris did his best to avoid the biggest potholes, but the damned road was all potholes. Midwestern winters were Hell on asphalt. The mall had been failing for years before it finally went under, and fixing the service drive would have been a low priority. To make matters worse, the mall was built against the bluffs, which made the narrow drive into a canyon. The wall of the mall rose up on his left side and the hillside—nearly as steep—rose on his right. During a heavy rain, the drive probably became a creek.

He pulled into the loading area and stopped the car. Featureless cinder block walls, dirty and covered with creepers like random crayon scrawls. A couple of dumpsters—one that looked like it had been set on fire—and a scattering of trash.

Ferris got out the site plan and tried to find a way to spread it out. He was a big man, both tall and broad, and the rental car didn't really fit him. Spending so much time on the road made it hard for him to work out as much as he'd like and easy to eat more junk food than was good for him. He'd probably put on a good sixty pounds since he left the Army ten years earlier. He managed to fit the map on the seat beside him.

The layout of the place was a Y, three arms of about the same length, each ending in an anchor tenant, with a food court in the middle. Two levels throughout, but one arm of the Y—the one he was closest to—was higher, so that the upper level in the other two arms met up with the lower level on this one. The receiving docks were under this section.

It was quiet. The sound of the road was muffled. Atop the bluffs, he knew, was the interstate, but no sound of it filtered down here. It was also cool in the shadows. On the way from the airport, Ferris had run the air conditioning, but now he shut it off and opened the window. He got the camera out of the glove box and started taking pictures, driving slowly around the building.

When they'd shut down the mall, they'd run a ten foot chain-link fence around the entire perimeter, about a foot away from the building. That had kept the damage to a minimum. Ferris had been a structural engineer long enough to know that urban spelunkers will always find a way in, but the fence was a good way to discourage casual vandals.

Fewer broken windows than he'd expected, and most of those were just a spider web of cracks from a thrown rock. A couple looked like they had been broken out from the inside, evidence that the chain link wasn't an impenetrable barrier.

Most of the windows were spray painted opaque. Across one set of glass doors the words "Send Help" had been scratched in the paint on the inside of the glass. Somebody's idea of a joke, no doubt.

There was the usual garbage—beer cans and fast food wrappers, mostly—but less than he'd expected for a place that had been empty for five years, and most of what there was looked old. Maybe the local cops had cracked down on vagrants in this area. All in all, the exterior wasn't in that bad shape. Ferris had been surveying abandoned properties since he'd left the service, and he'd gotten a feel for the cycle of urban decay. This place didn't look its age.

That was just the outside of course. The condition of the interior was the real test.

Once he got back to the loading dock he parked and shut off the engine. He stretched, sighed, and took a look around, vowing to get back to hitting the gym three days a week as soon as he got back to LA.

He was dressed for a walk inside a possibly unstable structure— thick jeans, heavy work boots, a long sleeved shirt. He had a large multi-tool in a belt sheath and a ring to hold his heavy tactical flashlight. Lastly he pulled on a pair of thin but tough leather gloves.

Then up the concrete stairs to the loading dock. It was easy enough to see which door was still functional, since all of the others had sheets of plywood nailed over them. Someone had spray-painted, in thick black letters, half a man high and stretching the length of the loading dock, 'ALL HOPE ABADDON YE WHO ENTER HERE.'

Ferris tried three keys before he found the one that opened the remaining personnel door. It grated on the floor and squealed when he pulled it, but it opened. Flashlight in hand, he entered the mall.

There was more trash just inside the door, but most of it looked like debris left behind when the stores moved out. Stacks of broken pallets, wire racks and carts that hadn't been worth the trouble of hauling away, boxes of God knew what that were slowly turning into piles of mold. A wide hallway stretched away into the gloom, leading into the mall proper.

Down at the end of the hallway, a vertical line of dim light marked a pair of doors. Ferris moved slowly down the hallway. Some graffiti here, and a few bottles and cans. He ignored that—he was here to document things that couldn't be fixed with a broom and a coat of paint.

Once through the doors, he put away his flashlight. There were skylights running down the length of the broad corridor and the sunlight was bright enough to get a good look at the surroundings.

Someone had broken up the benches in the seating area and used them to build a bonfire. He got pictures of the damage, then went up the dead escalator to the upper level. Like most malls, the top level was an open gallery, railed spaces overlooking the lower level, which allowed him a good vantage for both concourses. There was a lot more graffiti on the inside. A colorful mural covered the fronts of a half dozen shops across the concourse. Ferris took a panorama shot of it. It looked like a circus scene, a big-top tent and clowns dancing. The artwork was pretty good. He moved on.

Nearly all shops were intact, the gates down over the entrances, the spaces empty. A few gates had been forced up, but even in those the damage from trespassers was minimal.

In one space, a half-dozen mannequins had been dressed and posed. Ferris paused to stare. Four of them stood in a semi-circle, two were on the ground in front of them. The four standing figures had all been painted, faces white with exaggerated red smiles and big round eyes. Clowns again, Ferris realized. Two were in harlequin costumes of red and black, one was dressed as a mime in black and white, and the center figure was draped in a comically over-sized purple suit.

The two figures in front of them were unclothed and lying flat, and both of them had been liberally doused with red paint, covering their bellies and chests.

Somebody's idea of art, Ferris decided, took pictures, and moved on.

About halfway down the arm of the Y he heard movement. He stopped dead, listening. Something bigger than a rat or a pigeon was moving through one of the stores. He clicked on his light at shone it through the nearest window. Nothing, an empty space with a single broken clothing rack sagging in the middle of the floor. A mirror at the far end of the space caught his light and threw it back in his eyes, momentarily dazzling him. He shone the light on the floor and waited.

Nothing. If anything was in here with him, it was quiet now. He'd run across large animals in abandoned structures a few times—coyotes, feral dogs, armadillos. They usually weren't a problem—urban wildlife tended to be very shy of humans.

There was extensive water damage in many of the units, evidence that the roof wasn't holding back the rain. Ferris was getting shots of a collapsed ceiling when he heard the sounds again.

Something big, something close. Ferris whirled around, hand on his light. Something was definitely out there, but the echoes made it impossible to tell where the sounds were coming from.

Footsteps. Not animal, but human.

"I'm not a cop," Ferris said, his voice loud and confident. "I'm not here to arrest anyone. I'm just getting pictures for an investment firm."

Silence.

Then someone laughed. It was an overblown, theatrical sound, like a supervillain in a comic book. "Eeeh, eeh, eeeeh, aah, aaah, ah!" The sound echoed throughout the big open structure.

Ferris took a deep breath and made himself relax. Whoever was out there was just playing games. Unpleasant and annoying, certainly, but probably not really dangerous.

"Thank you," Ferris muttered to himself as he moved to the next storefront. "I'll be here all week. Be sure to tip your bartender."

The first manic laugh was joined by a second, then a third. The sounds carried and seemed to be coming from everywhere, but Ferris was sure that there were three distinct voices. It was hard to tell, but there seemed to be two males and one female.

"Whatever," Ferris muttered.

He made sure his right hand was free and close to his mag light from then on, and watched for movement around him. Judging from the layers of graffiti, whoever had been laughing out there in the darkness considered the mall their personal domain. Ferris just wanted to do his job and get out. Squatters weren't his job. Just another kind of urban wildlife, louder than most, but basically harmless. Usually. Sometimes you ran across dangerous nuts in vacant buildings. Situational awareness, they had called it in the army. Watch your own back.

This slowed him somewhat, but eventually he reached the central court. It was a huge open space, three stories high, with the usual accumulation of fast food places at the bottom.

Ferris took pictures, most of his attention focused on listening for the squatters. He noticed that there was more smoke damage on the balconies around the food court, evidence of another big fire.

Several big fires, he realized as he headed down the stationary escalator, still taking pictures. There were smoke streaks all over the walls. He could smell the fires now, wood and something like burned grease. He looked down at the ground floor and tried to make sense of what he was seeing. The area had been extensively damaged. After another flight he decided that damaged wasn't a strong enough word. It had been destroyed.

In the center of the space had been a large round fountain. The mechanisms had been torn out and it had been used as a fire pit. Remains of smashed furniture lay in a thick layer of ash. Some kind of scaffolding had been built over the pit, heavy beams supporting a mass of dangling chains. The stores had all been torn down— possibly a source for some of the wood that had been used in the fire pit. Around the pit was a circle of metal structures. Ferris guessed they had been made from heavy shelving units looted from retail spaces.

Bizarrely, a single dining table remained intact, close to the edge of the old fountain. More than just intact, the plastic top and matching benches sparkled, as if they had been wiped down recently, in stark contrast to the filth and destruction around it.

The lowest level of stairs leading to the food court was had been torn out. There had been two sets of steps and two escalators. All of the steps had been cut away. Ferris took close-up pictures. What was left of the supports showed the bright clean edge left by an industrial chop saw.

One of the escalators had also been destroyed—an even more impressive feat of vandalism. They hadn't tried to haul away the wreckage though, it lay in a jagged heap of scrap twenty feet below the gap in the railing.

Ferris carefully examined the remaining escalator. It seemed intact. Ferris took careful pictures, he stood at the top and looked down. It was as filthy as everything else around the court. The hyenas who lived here had to have some way to get down there—they wouldn't sabotage the only way left, would they? But why destroy the others?

No guts, no glory, he thought and started slowly down the escalator. He wanted to get some closer shots of whatever had been done down there. The metal steps were solid underfoot, just like all the others. Because he was focusing on the steps, it wasn't until he reached the bottom that he got a good look around.

In a semi-circle around the old fountain were the metal structures that he had seen from above. They were made of heavy steel uprights welded together—cages, he suddenly realized.

Slowly, he stepped closer. This was above and beyond anything he'd seen before. Heavy steel cages, the fire pit with the scaffolding built over it, the table, cleaned and polished and waiting.

For what? Just what the fuck went on down here?

A motor coughed into life, somewhere above him, and Ferris nearly jumped out of his skin. He quickly scanned the high concourse. By the top of the remaining escalator, dimly silhouetted against the light filtering in from the distant skylights, stood a figure. It seemed to be a man in a dark-colored suit, and he was laughing. His face was a white smear in the dimness. Over the racket of the motor—a small gasoline engine, like a riding lawnmower—Ferris could hear the figure making the screeching theatrical laugh he had heard before.

Ferris headed to the escalator at a trot, then stopped dead. The stairs were in motion, moving jerkily, headed down. That wasn't what stopped him though. Each new step that came into view bristled with blades. Knives looted from the restaurant kitchens or from housewares departments were attached to the treads, handles broken off and blades welded to the steps.

The escalator was a deathtrap. Trying to get up that descending mass of blades would be suicide.

Ferris looked around. There were still two concourses that allowed an exit on this level. They led away from the exit, but he could go down one of them until he reached a stairwell, then go to an upper level and double back.

"Are you real?" a small voice behind him asked .

He spun, his heart hammering, his flashlight raised like a club. One of the cages was occupied.

She was filthy and her eyes were wide, close to madness. The fingers clutching the bars of the cage were slim, the remains of some glittery polish on her broken nails.

Ferris kept his eyes moving, trying to look all around him at once, as he stepped carefully to the cage. "Who are you?"

"You are, aren't you?" she responded, her voice a hoarse rasp. "Real. You're from the outside?"

"I'm from LA," he said. "I came here to get pictures. What the Hell's going on?"

"Get me out of here," she rasped. "When they come back they'll kill us."

Ferris examined the cage. The bars were thick steel, square stock looted from industrial shelving of some kind. A heavy padlock secured the door.

"He has the keys," she whispered. "You'll have to kill him. *Please!*"

"Who?" Ferris asked. He wasn't planning on killing anyone.

"They call him Jack," she said softly. "The one in the suit. He keeps all the keys."

Ferris examined the hinges on the door. They were welded to the door and the frame, but they were just standard hinges.

"Hang on a minute," he said and pulled out his tools.

"We don't have a minute," she said, then started crying.

Ferris looked around again, then said, "Sing out if anyone comes."

She nodded, her movements jerky, but seemed to understand and scanned the darkness.

Using his thinnest screwdriver and his flashlight, he popped the pin out of the bottom hinge, then the middle one.

She saw what he was doing and whispered, "Hurry."

"Hold the door up," he replied and popped the last pin. Swiftly, he slid the multi-tool back in its sheath then grabbed the door from her and swung it open, pivoting on the hasp for the padlock. "Let's get out of here."

She was shivering as she stepped from the cage, her mouth working, but nothing coming out. She reminded Ferris of descriptions he'd read of prisoners of war being liberated. She clung to his arm but she seemed to be able to walk. Just beaten and starved, probably raped, and scared to death. Time to shut this circus down. He pulled out his phone.

"That won't work in here," she hissed. "We have to go." She tugged his arm.

Ferris glanced at the screen as he let her lead him away. True to her prediction, there was no signal. Not surprising. Too much metal and concrete all around them.

Once outside the semi-circle of cages she stopped. "I don't know which way to go," she whispered.

"I don't think it matters," Ferris said and headed down the closest concourse. It was darker here, and he looked up. Two levels up, the skylights had been crudely spray-painted black. That must have been fun, he thought, and clicked on his flashlight.

She followed close behind him, close enough that he could feel her trembling.

"What's your name?" he asked.

"Rose."

"I'm Pete," he replied. "Relax, I don't know what kind of game they were playing, but it's over now. We'll get out of here and call the cops. It's over."

"It's never gonna be over," Rose whispered.

Ferris guided her along the darkened concourse. He was suddenly aware that she was warm and young and had once been very pretty—and could be again. Her hair was filthy and matted, but he could see the warm red under the filth. Her body was rounded, firm, under scraps of jeans and a sweatshirt. She should be in the sunlight, happy and carefree, not trapped in a cage like a rat. Whoever had done this would get no sympathy from him.

They passed empty shops with gates over the entrances. Then Ferris saw something glinting in the beam of his flashlight. Wire, across the concourse. Strands forming a grid. Ferris got closer.

Black Light Ballet

Barbed wire. Razor wire, actually. Ferris frowned. His wire cutters could snip it, but even with his gloves he was likely to get cut, maybe seriously. He flashed his light up ahead. There seemed to be another razor wire fence behind the first one. And maybe another past that one. Steel poles stuck up at random, supporting the razor wire. In places, the dusty white forms of manikins were used instead.

He looked to either side. Both shops were protected by steel shutters, but there was an open gate through the fence, an archway of painted wood. Obviously, whoever had set up the funhouse wanted him to go that way, which was a damn good reason not to. But what were his other options? Try to force his way into a store? Or go back to the food court and explore the other concourse?

Neither of those sounded like a good idea, either.

Rose was growing agitated as he stood there, considering. She tugged on his arm, making small noises of fear. She was right, the sooner they got out of this damned place the better.

"Stay behind me," Pete whispered. He went through the open archway. Once past the first fence, the arrangement was clearer. It was a maze of some kind, narrow aisles through rows of sharp wire. Funhouse had been the right word—it was a funhouse designed by homicidal perverts. Manikins were set up as part of the structure, like fence-posts, blank white figures wrapped in wire.

Pete walked slowly and deliberately, the flashlight held in front of him. It wasn't that dangerous, with a light and heavy clothes and taking it slow. He could imagine, though, someone rushing into it in a blind panic blundering into the tight strands and getting cut to ribbons.

Pete shook his head. "Who are these people?"

He didn't expect an answer, but Rose said softly, "They are neither man nor woman, they are neither brute nor human, they are ghouls, and it is their king who tolls, who so delights in rolling on the human heart a stone."

Pete stopped to look back at her. "What?"

Rose was looking down, not meeting his eyes. "Go," she whispered, "please keep going."

Right. Pete faced front and continued threading his way through the razor wire maze. He could see the passage split ahead, a T-intersection with each path leading to one of the darkened stores on

114

either side of the concourse. A manikin stood at the intersection, pointing in both directions.

Pete shone his light each way. Both of the stores had been broken open, the gates forced up and the doors smashed. There seemed to be no easy way to choose. Pete went to the left, and Rose followed close behind.

As he got closer, he pointed his light towards the open store. Something inside caught the light and threw it back, reflecting all around. Slowly, he moved forward, keeping his light low and trying to make sense of what was in there. Mirrors, it looked like.

There were standing mirrors, like the ones they used in dressing rooms, set up all through the space, held in place by some kind of frame built from 2x4s.

What the Hell, Ferris thought, *they built a goddamned mirror maze.* Cautiously he ducked and stepped into the store, flashlight held low. The floor under his feet sagged a fraction of an inch, and he heard a soft click.

The strobes that came on were so bright that he felt them as pain before it registered as light. He closed his tearing eyes and lifted his hand in front of his face. Behind him, Rose whimpered.

Ferris forced his eyes half-open, still shielding his face with his hand. He could see nothing but the blaze of light, flashing off and on. With his other hand he swung the flashlight, slowly, trying to feel his way ahead. His flashlight clicked against the glass of a mirror one way, then he felt empty space to the other. The light was becoming less painful, but the strobes and the mirrors made it impossible to get oriented. He shuffled forward, tapping with the flashlight. Rose stayed close behind him, almost touching.

With his next slow step, something brushed across his calf. Even as cautiously as he had been moving he nearly lost balance. It felt like a wire stretched between the mirrored partitions. He glanced down long enough to lift his boot and step on it. He put his weight down and felt it pull free from the partition. Then he slid forward another step. The next wire caught him across mid-thigh. In the crazy strobe light they were nearly invisible. Ferris paused.

"You know something," he said softly, then shouted, "*Screw this shit!*"

He turned and put his boot firmly against one partition, leaned back, and shoved hard. There was a splintering of wood, and then the wall gave way, the mirror breaking as it fell. Behind him Rose gave a little squeak of surprise.

The partition had fallen against the next one, and Ferris kept pressing forward until that one splintered and gave way as well. The mirrored walls weren't anchored at the top—the top had to be open for the strobe lights to cover the whole space. A little bit of leverage and a solid pair of boots could take the whole damn maze down.

Ferris could see where the lights were anchored to the ceiling. He hadn't heard the roar of a generator when they'd come on, so there had to be batteries around here someplace powering them. Shutting them down would be nice, but mostly he was concerned with smashing his way to the exit. If he could get into the service corridor, they could take that back to where he had come in.

Rose screamed, and Pete spun to see the clown with the knife coming up behind them.

He was all in white except for welder's goggles over his eyes. Thanks to Rose's warning, Pete was able to get his flashlight up in time to block the clown's knife—a machete, actually, with a long and viciously sharp blade.

Ferris didn't give the clown time for a second swing. He bulled forward and got inside the other man's arms, and both of them went down. Under them, glass shattered and wood splintered. Ferris didn't need to see the man under him, he just slammed what he felt under him into the concrete. The man smelled horrible, like meat gone bad. A thick layer of greasepaint covered his face and made his skin slick. Ferris grabbed a handful of hair and slammed the man's head into the floor.

One of his hands came free, still holding a greasy hunk of hair, and Ferris punched him. Ferris could hear his own harsh breathing, but not his foe's. He felt the skin split under the greasepaint, but the man still fought in total silence.

He felt the man go limp but kept pounding. He was probably giving the guy a concussion, if not worse, but he didn't care. He'd deal with the assault charge later, once they were out of this madhouse. He heard the machete drop from a flailing arm and clatter onto the floor.

That was probably enough. Slowly he got up. The man's face had been covered with white makeup, but most of it was on Ferris' gloves now. It was the manikin, Ferris realized, that they had passed at the intersection. This man had been made up to look like a manikin and had stood perfectly still, waiting for them to trigger the strobes.

Once Ferris was on his feet, he prodded the white-clad figure with the toe of his boot. It didn't move.

Rose did. Before he could react, she dropped to her knees beside the body and brought her arm down. She'd retrieved the machete and swung it in a vicious arc. Blood fountained, shockingly red in the brutal strobe light. She swung again and again, making harsh crying noises.

Moving very carefully, Ferris got behind her and grabbed her swinging arm.

"That's enough," he said. "Let's get moving."

Rose paused, with her arm upraised, then slowly lowered it, holding the blade in a tight grip. Ferris didn't try to take it from her. Instead, he helped her get to her feet. She was shaking but could stand. He put her arm gingerly around her shoulders. Her body was slim under her rags and her muscles were all taut as piano wires.

"It's okay," he whispered. "Take a deep breath. Stay with me now."

For a moment, it was as if she didn't even hear him, then he felt her slowly begin to relax slightly. "Okay, Rose? We're gonna do this, right? We're gonna get out of here, and we're going to do it together. Right?"

She nodded. Her eyes were wide and her knuckles white on the handle of the machete, but she looked only frightened, not crazy. She looked like, deep down inside, she was starting to have hope— maybe for the first time—that she might actually escape this terrible place.

Ferris leaned against the partition in front of him, felt it give, and stepped back. "Watch your eyes," he warned Rose and kicked it over. One more and he could see the store's exit.

He glanced back. The white clown was now a mess of red, his head and chest looking like a slab of meat. A concussion didn't seem like that big a deal anymore.

Once through the exit door, he stood very still, Rose beside him, and waited for his eyes to adjust. He could still see the strobes jittering across his vision, and his head ached. The door was sealed tight, though, no light escaped into the hallway.

He stood and listened. He could hear his own breathing and felt the warmth of Rose's skin next to his.

Nothing moved. After a while, he could see dim shapes and risked turning on his flashlight. The hallway was full of trash and dust. Nothing else. It looked like the inhabitants didn't use it—they probably had a path they had cut through the stores.

But where from here? Ferris pulled out the map and looked at it in the flashlight's glow. He could take the service hallway back to the emergency exit—no, that was blocked by the chain-link fence outside the wall. But there were fire stairs which would take him to the upper service hallway, and from there he could get into the upper concourse. Then around the food court and back into the section where he'd entered.

He looked at Rose. She was standing rigid, staring down at the bloody machete in her hand.

"Rose," he said softly.

She looked up, her eyes a thousand miles away.

"Let's go," he said, and gestured down the hall.

She seemed to wake up, her eyes focusing on his face, and nodded quickly then started walking.

Ferris kept his light shining on the floor. It was thick with dust and scattered trash, evidence that no one had been here in a while, maybe years. Good. He wasn't following their script any more. 'Daisy's Gift Boutique' was stenciled on a filthy door. A quick look at the map and he was oriented. The stairs should be just ahead.

As quietly as he could, he pushed open the door to the stairs. Inside, it was just as filthy, just as abandoned. He headed up the stairs, and Rose followed him like a shadow, silent and close. He paused at the door at the top of the stairs, listening, then gently pushed it open.

The harlequin blindsided him with a steel pipe.

He had been waiting, still as death, just outside the fire stairs. Ferris caught a glimpse of red and black, but that was all. Before he could react, he was falling, his head feeling strangely numb, like it was some different head that had been stuck onto his neck by accident. From somewhere far away, he heard the sound of the impact.

His flashlight had rolled off someplace and was shining on a filthy white wall, which was a damned stupid thing for a flashlight to do. There was enough light reflected from the wall that he could see shadows moving, and he knew that he had to get to his feet and focus on what was going on. He got one leg under him and pushed himself up the wall. It wasn't exactly standing up, but it was close, which is why it felt so unfair when someone kicked his leg out from under him and he fell back to the concrete floor. He got a good look at a pair of boots. One was black and had red laces, the other one was red and had black laces. *I'm getting kicked around by somebody who doesn't even have shoes that match,* he thought.

It made him mad, mad enough to grab the offending boot and yank on it. *If I have to lie on the floor, then you have to lie on the floor, too.* That seemed fair.

There were altogether too many boots in this situation. Some red with black laces, some black with red laces. The ones kicking at his face were attached to skinny legs. He got his arm around them to stop them kicking. His head was starting to clear. The figure on the floor with him was female, he realized, a slim woman in red and black. The man who had hit him was dressed the same, both of them looking like animated checkerboards. The man was up against the door, struggling to pull his arm free. Rose must be holding the door closed on it from the other side. She wouldn't be able to do that for long.

The female harlequin under him jerked, and Ferris nearly lost his grip on her legs. First things first. He heaved himself to his feet, dragging her squirming body up with him.

"What is *wrong* with you people?" he shouted.

She swung a length of pipe awkwardly, and he stomped on it, wrenching it out of her grasp. Holding her upside-down he staggered into the wall, banging her as hard as he could against the concrete blocks.

"*Seriously!*" he yelled as she contorted her body to try to bite his leg, "You folks have some *real problems!*" He slammed her against the wall again, but she writhed and caught the impact on her shoulder, not her head. "I'm just trying to do *my job here*," again against the wall, and this time he heard her skull thunk on concrete, "and get *the hell out*," another blow against the wall. Her struggles were weaker now, "and you keep doing *this crazy shit*." He spun and swung her, saw her hit the wall face first and leave a splash of blood. "I am done *playing with you*." Her body hung limp in his arms, and he put his full weight into the swing, smashing her hard into the wall and then letting her fall to the ground. She lay in a crumpled heap on the floor.

Ferris turned and grabbed the pipe she had dropped. The male harlequin was still fighting against Rose, his attention focused on trying to force the door open and free his arm. Ferris swung the pipe like a bat and hit the struggling clown in the back of the head hard enough that he felt the shock of the impact to his shoulders.

The red and black figure dropped limply, hanging by the arm still trapped in the door.

"Rose," Ferris said, panting from his exertions, "you can let go now. He's down."

There was a pause, then the body slid the rest of the way down. Rose's wide eyes peered through the crack in the door. Satisfied that Ferris was standing and the other two were down, she opened the door the rest of the way.

As filthy as her clothes were, it took him a moment to realize she was spattered with blood across her chest and all down her right arm.

"Where are you hurt?" he asked quickly, bending to examine her arm.

She shook her head. "That's not my blood," she said softly.

Ferris looked down at the harlequin clown. The arm that Rose had pinned in the door was covered with gashes and blood. No wonder he'd been struggling so hard.

Rose paused to wipe the fresh blood from her machete on the male's clothes. She stepped deliberately towards where the female harlequin lay unmoving.

"Just leave her," Ferris said softly. "She won't be getting up any time soon."

Rose gave him a long, cold stare, and for a moment, Ferris was sure that she was going to rush past him to slice up the unconscious woman. Then Rose nodded sharply and turned away.

Ferris led the way down the hallway, wondering what on Earth they had done to her.

He wasn't sure he wanted to know.

Had they really just killed three people? It seemed so unreal. The woman harlequin might not die, but he'd given her at least a severe concussion, probably some broken bones. She needed medical attention. The two men? The first one, the one that was all in white, yeah—he was dead. Rose had damn near chopped his head off. The other one was probably dying right now, unconscious and bleeding to death from the gashes in his arm.

Unreal. Less than half a mile from here, traffic drove on a busy city street. They were in the suburbs, for Christ's sake. Thousands of commuters passed this building every day, glanced at the blank facade, and went on with their lives. While inside these walls—

Madness. Total insanity. Killer clowns and captives in cages and... what? What was that thing they had built in the food court? It looked like a commercial barbecue, the kind of setup used for roasting a side of beef or an entire hog or—

Ferris stopped in his tracks, his mind recoiling in horror. Had that been what they were keeping Rose caged for? Had there been others? Had she watched them do it?

No wonder the girl was ready to cut them to ribbons. He glanced back at her. She had stopped when he did and was looking off into space, her eyes as distant and cold as the dark side of the moon.

"Come on," he said, getting moving again. He held his flashlight in his left hand, the steel pipe in his right. He could take the service hallway all the way to the end of the concourse, then cross over and take the other service corridor back to the loading dock. It was longer this way, but it didn't look like they'd bothered to booby-trap the service areas. And this way they wouldn't have to pass by that damned food court again.

Dust. Broken pieces of shelving, flattened boxes, pallets leaning against the walls like drunks waiting for the bathroom, cables and cords left behind when the cash registers and closed circuit cameras were taken out, nametags and big, friendly "Ask Me!" buttons, all the rich and varied detritus left behind and rotting on the shore when the tide of the mercantile wonderland had rolled back out. The hallway was a dead place, a place of dreams gone stale and poured out like old beer. The inevitable tragedy of progress, written in formed plastic and cheap aluminum alloys. If the book of Ecclesiastes was a place, they had reached the heart of it.

And at the end of it all, past the shoe shops and game stores, the chocolate emporiums and the plus size clothing outlets, in the foul-smelling dimness of the authorized personnel only shipping and receiving area, Jack the stone cold joker was waiting for them.

His face was a white blur between his dark suit and hair dyed the orange of safety warnings. He stood leaning on a cane, perfectly at ease, between them and the only exit.

Ferris paused for only a moment. Then he continued, the pipe in his right hand, the flashlight in his left. Behind him, he heard Rose whimpering softly, and that just made him madder.

"We're leaving," Ferris said. "You're going to jail. You want to stop by the hospital first, that's fine with me."

The figure twirled his cane and said—his voice smooth and confident—"I'll make you a deal. Give me the bitch, and I'll let you go."

Ferris kept walking. The details of the man's appearance were growing clearer, white greasepaint and grotesque painted lips. "I've got a counter offer. How about I just bash your head in? Or you can run away. Your choice."

Jack stroked his chin as if considering the offer and Ferris noticed that he was wearing dark colored gloves.

"I think I'll eat your balls first," Jack said. "I'll roast them and let you watch me gobble them up."

Ferris handed the flashlight back, felt Rose take it in trembling hands. In the unsteady light he lifted the pipe to his shoulder, like a batter approaching the plate.

"Last chance, you sick fuck," Ferris said. "Stand aside."

Jack threw back his head and laughed, the mad comic book sound he'd made before, and Ferris was able to see the face clearly.

His face was chalk-white, and his skin a mass of scars. His eyes were wide, showing so much white that they were nearly lost against the surrounding painted skin. Only his mouth had any color, the lips full and wet, red as an open wound.

Ferris hesitated for only a moment, but in that precious moment Jack struck with his cane, a lightning blow that caught Ferris in the chest and drove the wind out of him.

Ferris managed to complete his swing, but the blow with the pipe was strengthless, and Jack batted it aside. Then the cane came around again, and Ferris tried to block it, but he was slow—too slow—and the pain in his hip was blinding. Jack kept laughing, the wide red mouth on that hideous face contorted with peals of black amusement. Ferris tried to rush him, to get close enough to bring him down to the concrete floor, but the nimble figure danced out of the way and delivered another brutal blow from the cane.

Ferris swung blindly and felt it connect. The unholy laughter came to a choking stop. He swung again but hit only air. He blinked tears out his eyes and tried to focus, to find the mad-eyed clown.

"That hurt." The voice came from behind Ferris. "You'll die slow for that. And you'll see her die first."

Ferris spun around, swinging, and managed to pull the pipe up just in time to keep from hitting Rose, who was held in front of Jack's lean body like a shield. Jack had produced a knife from somewhere, a long, thin blade that he held against Rose's face.

"Game over," Jack said, thick red lips smiling, "You took three of my pawns, but I have your queen."

Ferris stood and tried to get his breathing under control, the heavy steel pipe still in his hand. His flashlight was on the floor, shining at the wall, and beside it was the machete Rose had been carrying.

"I can taste your fear," Jack said. "You're all the same. Bluff and blustering and oh so full of yourselves until you encounter something truly extraordinary. And then—" he paused to lick the side of Rose's neck, his tongue glistening and squirming like an earthworm— "it's all over but the screaming."

Ferris took a step forward. Then another.

Jack pressed the knife hard against Rose's face. "Drop the pipe, or I'll cut out her eyes."

"You'd do that anyway," Ferris said and hurled the pipe to the side, diving forward when the clown turn his head to follow the pipe.

He hit them at the knees, and all three went down in a heap. Jack struggled to get back up, still gripping the knife. Before he could use it, Rose clamped her teeth on his wrist and held on. Ferris got a hand on Jack's head—the lank, greasy hair feeling like the fur of a dead animal—and slammed it into the concrete floor. Then again. And again. A growing slick red stain appeared under him.

The knife went flying, and Rose rolled away, gagging. Ferris held the clown down. The madman was laughing again, a screeching, inhuman sound.

Then he felt Rose return, close and warm beside him, and she pressed the machete into his free hand. He clenched the handle hard. "Shut up," he hissed. "Just shut up and lie still, God damn you!"

The clown kept laughing.

Ferris pulled back his arm. *I could do it*, he thought. *I could cut his fucking head off right here. He deserves to die.*

Ferris swung, but shifted his hand so that he struck with the handle instead of the blade, a hard blow to the temple. The body went limp.

Ferris stood slowly, watching the body for signs of movement.

Rose took his arm, pulling him towards the exit. "Let's go, Pete."

Once outside, Ferris pulled out his phone. Inside its rugged contractor case, the screen was lit and showing two bars of signal. That was enough.

"Nine One One, what is the emergency?"

"I want to report a... oh, Hell, I don't know. A murder. A bunch of murders. We got at least two dead people, maybe more. Maybe a lot more. You guys need to come clean this up."

Rose tugged on his arm, her eyes bright with wonder at the sky. The operator was still talking and Ferris gave him the address and his name and a bunch of other useless information. As he babbled into the phone, he followed Rose until they came around the edge of the mall and out into bright sunlight.

Rose stopped and stared, blinking away tears. Then she dropped the machete, and her arms came up around Pete's neck, pulling him close. The phone in his hand kept talking, but he ignored it, holding Rose close while she sobbed into his chest.

In the distance, sirens wailed a mournful symphony, drawing closer.

Look to the Skies

Look to the skies, the monsters cried loud
A warning will come from the sky
We waited for fire to fall from a cloud
Certain that we would soon die

Time is short, the end is near
The monsters cried out once more
We huddled together numb with fear
Sure that death stood at the door

This is it, the monsters announced
This time we mean it for sure
Rains of blood and dragons that pounced
Diseases that don't have a cure

Yet here we still are, and have been for so long
I'm beginning to think that the monsters are wrong.

The Old Covenant

Originally published in *Planetary Anthology: Neptune*, December 2020

> *"O fish, are you constant to the old covenant?*
> *Return, and we return.*
> *Keep faith, and so will we."*

Tim Powers, *Declare*

"Thank you for seeing me, Fyodor," Brother Vasili said.

"Tucker," I corrected him. "Not even my mother calls me Fyodor."

He conceded the point with a shrug of his broad shoulders. "Tucker. In any event, I appreciate you coming by. Won't you have a seat?"

The furniture in his office was very old, of very dark wood, and I sat gingerly in one of the chairs facing his desk. Like him, the desk was broad and squat. It was cluttered, with a coffee cup full of pens and stacks of papers. His computer, a slim laptop, looked out of place. It was probably the only thing in the room manufactured within a century.

"I had hoped to talk to you after services some week..." he cocked his shaven head and let the sentence trail off into an unspoken reproach.

I sighed. Aside from the Solstices, I hadn't attended services in years. It wasn't that I didn't believe, not exactly, it was more that it simply wasn't that important to me.

"I work outside of town," I pointed out. "It's difficult to get Fridays off."

I could see him deciding not to push the issue. Services began at sunset on Friday and lasted until midnight. He knew as well as I did that I could have gone straight to the temple after work and arrived only a little late.

He settled for saying, "You are welcome to visit the temple any time. There is always someone here."

I nodded without speaking. I knew why he had called me and wished that he would get to the point.

He did. "You're nearly thirty, Tucker. Your parents and I have been discussing your prospects."

"My mother told me," I admitted. I tried to have dinner with my parents a few times a month, usually at the Chinese restaurant on Clarke Street. Lately they had been hinting that since my career was going so well it was time for me to settle down and raise a family.

Brother Vasili smiled. It was meant to be a friendly smile, but his lips were just a little too thick and his neck a little too wide. His smile made him look like a toad. "There's a young lady that I believe would make a fine match for you," he said. "This Saturday we're having a chowder supper, I'm hoping that you'll attend so that we can make the introductions."

"I'll be there," I said quickly. It wasn't like a really had any choice. I'd always known this day was coming. And it wasn't that I was opposed to marriage or even an arranged marriage. The inevitability of it galled me, though.

"Excellent," he said, flashing his toad-like grin again. He stood.

I stood, too. "What's her name?"

"Nikki West. Her family is from up the coast a bit, near Norfolk."

I tried to smile back. "I'm looking forward to it."

I passed through the sanctuary on my way out. The choir was practicing.

"...our vigil we swear to keep
Until You waken from Your sleep
To look with favor on Your slaves
When all Earth is covered by the waves..."

On Saturday I drove to my parent's house. I wore a charcoal gray suit and a red silk tie. My mother fussed over me, my father curtly nodded his approval.

I left my truck parked in their driveway and drove my father's car, the two of them sitting together in the back. My parents don't drive anymore, since both of them have begun the change, but my father refuses to give up his old Mercedes sedan.

On the way to the temple, I picked up my sister Lana. She lived with a roommate in an apartment above the pizza place where she worked. It was a temporary arrangement. Somehow it had been quietly decided that Lana would get our parent's house when they moved out to the reefs.

That was fine with me. I rented a house on the inland side of town, in a new suburb—new for this town, meaning it had been built just after the Second World War.

Lana wore a deep green gown that made my suit look casual and a huge crockpot of chowder that I managed to wedge into the seat between us with a seatbelt to hold it in place.

Lana more than made up for my lack of zeal in theological matters. She was chapter president of the Young Lady's Oceanographic Association and taught the children's midweek classes at the temple.

"We're running late," Lana said petulantly.

I glanced at the dashboard clock. We weren't. The supper began at one, and it wasn't even noon yet.

"We'll probably have to park on the boardwalk," Lana went on. "Take Ocean Avenue."

"I remember," I told her, trying to keep my irritation out of my voice.

My sister's religious fervor wasn't the only reason that I'd stopped attending services, but it was definitely a factor. She was just so... *devout*. She hadn't gotten it from our parents—they'd taken us to services regularly but hadn't made a big deal of it. It was just part of life.

Father was a pharmacist, and while he'd been careful not to contradict the teachings of the temple, as I'd grown older, I'd gotten the distinct impression that he thought that the modern scientific world didn't have much room—or much use—for the Old Ones.

But for some reason, about the time that I was graduating from high school and my little sister was entering junior high, Lana had embraced the Faith. By the time that she was in high school and I had graduated with an electronics certificate from the technical college, Lana was a true believer.

She'd rode her bike to temple every day after school and made herself useful—I think that if the Order of Starry Wisdom had nuns, she would have taken vows as soon as she graduated.

Since they don't have sisters as well as brothers, though, she contented herself with joining every ladies' auxiliary that was open to single women. No doubt she was already eyeing the available young men in terms of which ones were properly devout.

Despite her apprehension, there were plenty of spots open close to the temple, and I parked and got our parent's walkers out of the trunk. Then I grabbed Lana's chowder, with her leading the way and opening doors to the gathering room. There were a dozen long tables set up, with tangles of extension cords for the crock pots. One of the brothers showed us where to set up.

Chowder suppers were an old tradition. Members of the congregation brought their pots, full of their concoctions, jealously guarded secret recipes handed down over the generations. Every pot was given a number and jar for donations. It was both a fundraiser and a competition, with the winner being the cook of the chowder that brought in the most donations.

My sister always entered, of course. She used a book called *One Dish Seafood Meals* that had been written by one of our people and published in 1980 or thereabouts, and Lana followed the recipe as scrupulously as if it had been handed to her by Obadiah Marsh himself.

It was okay, I guess, warm and filling, but rather bland.

Once I had her set up, I sat with my parents for a while and watched the throng assemble. This early, it was mostly older folks, those who had started the change or were getting close to it. As they came in, they shuffled around, on canes or walkers, a few in wheelchairs. Everybody had to make the circuit, checking in with everyone who was already there, saying *hello* and *how've you been* to the same people they had been saying it to two or three times a week for their entire lives.

And they all had to remark that they hadn't seen me since last Solstice, and they hoped that I had been well, and I had to reply that, yes, I was just fine, but work had been very busy.

And yes, I did still work for a company "in the west", which made it sound like I was commuting daily to Arizona or New Mexico instead of a couple of miles on the interstate.

This is what you have to look forward to, I thought to myself. *This... and then the sea.*

But what else could I do? I couldn't move inland—the sea, as the saying went, was in my blood. For the next twenty years or so, I would continue to look and feel as I did now, growing older, of course, but indistinguishable from inlanders.

Then, the change. I could see it in my parents, and I saw it in all of the older people who stopped by to pass the time with them. Their skin lost its color, growing pale and nearly translucent. They lost their hair—although most of the women wore wigs or scarfs. Their teeth fell out, and their gums grew hard ridges, making dentures both unnecessary and impossible. Their fingernails darkened, grew thick and hard and pointed, becoming claws.

They were becoming sea creatures. I'd seen it happen with my grandparents, was part of the crowd of well-wishers when they left dry land forever and slithered down the beach into the surf. Soon my own parents would make that same journey.

And my time was coming. Unless I died sometime over the next twenty years, got hit by a bus or struck by lightning, I would be joining them, out there in the lightless depths.

It was... inevitable.

And I had to admit, it didn't sound so bad. I'd felt the pull of the sea, one cool, early mornings, surfing with my friends from school. Out in the waves, the sun just painting the east with gray, shading to pink, the roll of the surf filling my ears, feeling the weight and force of all those millions of tons of water.

It had felt like it would be easy, shedding my wet suit and letting my board drift off and diving, down, down, down, naked and unashamed, losing myself in the dark stillness below. I already knew what it would feel like.

It would feel like coming home.

But... I thought, *not yet. Please, not just yet. Let me have a few years in the sun.*

"Tucker," my mother said, her voice full of bright cheer, "there's someone who wants to meet you."

I looked up, and my first thought was, *no she doesn't.*

My second was, *she looks like an inlander.*

She wasn't, of course. We can always tell, our people have an instinct that lets us recognize each other. But her hair was colored, with honey blonde streaks through the chestnut brown. She had makeup on—subtle, but I could tell. She wore little gold studs in her ears and her nails were covered in glittery purple polish.

Her dress was dark blue and floor-length—her one concession to what Lana would call "proper decorum."

I stood and bowed. "Fyodor Orlov," I said. "People call me Tucker."

She gave a little bow in return, looking as if she thought she should curtsy but didn't know how. "Nikki West." An uncertain grin. "People call me Nikki."

An Atlas of Bad Roads

"Harry West," said the big man behind her. He, too, looked like an inlander. A rich tan that had to be sprayed on, a full head of hair that was almost certainly a toupee. His suit was formal enough, but he wore it as if he'd rather be in a Hawaiian shirt and shorts. His hand came up, and I reached for it, but instead of a handshake he offered me a business card. "West Watercraft."

I took the card. Sure enough, it said West Watercraft, with an address a few towns north. "From Kayaks To Yachts," it promised.

"Pleased to meet you, sir," I said, sticking the card in my pocket.

"And this is the misses, Darla," Mr. West went on.

I bowed to her as well. She was younger than her husband, still a few years from the change, and dressed like a society matron, complete with a rope of huge pearls. She flashed me a tight smile, which I returned.

"Tucker builds computer networks," my mother said helpfully.

I suppressed an eye-roll. I worked for a company that installed mainframes, yes, as well as CCTV and alarm systems. What I did for them, mostly, was pull cable. My mother always wanted to make me out to be some computer specialist, when I was just a wire monkey. It was a good job, a union shop with excellent benefits, but I was no Bill Gates.

"A bright young man will always have a future in this country," Mr. West said.

Mrs. West turned to my mother. "That all smells so good," she said. "Let's get some, shall we?"

My father was blunter with Mr. West. "Let's give the young people time to get acquainted."

They shuffled off together, leaving me and Nikki alone at a table with a couple of styrofoam bowls of chowder and paper cups of sweet iced coffee.

We looked at each other a moment, then Nikki took a sip of her drink and her eyes got wide.

"That's not tea," she choked.

"Sorry," I said, starting to get up. "I think they've got lemonade, too."

She waved me back down, took another experimental sip. "No, this is fine. It's just not what I expected."

I shrugged. "We must seem very old fashioned to you."

"A little," she admitted. "But this is where the lighthouse is. This

131

is where it all started."

That was true.

Captain Obadiah Marsh had built that lighthouse on his return from his last voyage in 1685. It had been rebuilt twice since then, but it was on the very spot where he had first contacted the sea people in the new world. That lighthouse had been where the first services were held, and the first Solstice observances. For me, it was just part of the horizon—I'd grown up with it. But I could see where it could be significant to our people from other towns.

"Do you want to see it?" I asked.

She smiled, and this smile looked genuine, not forced. "Can we go inside? Is anything left from the old days?"

I shook my head. "Not much. What is left of Captain Marsh's things are here, actually, in the archives. The lighthouse is just a lighthouse now. I know the keepers if you want to go up inside it. There's a nice view from up there."

"Yeah," she said. "That sounds fun."

"How long will you be in town?" I asked.

She shrugged. "Maybe a week," she said. "It depends..."

She let it trail off.

Depends on whether or not I turn out to be an acceptable catch for Daddy's little girl, I thought. But neither of us wanted that to be said out loud.

Instead, she said brightly, "We're staying at Merchant Hotel, on the beach."

Of course they were. It was the closest thing to a luxury hotel we had—the only hotel in town proper, although there were a few tourist traps up and down the beach just outside city limits.

"What do you think of it?" I asked.

"I love it," she said, and her delight was genuine. "Have you been inside? It's like Captain Nemo's submarine."

I knew what she meant. The Merchant Hotel had been built right after the Civil War, and the furnishings ran heavily to polished brass and dark wood.

"All the history in this place," she said. "It's so fascinating."

I chuckled. "History is all we've got."

"Up the coast, it's different," she insisted. "Nobody cares about the past. They just knock it down and build something new. Everybody wants the latest thing. Daddy built us a new house, and it's just like every other house on the bay. There's like three floor plans for the whole town."

I knew what she meant. I'd installed alarm systems in new homes, and they all seemed the same. A nice enough place to live, I supposed, but no character.

Both of our bowls were empty. I gestured. "Want to try some more?"

She stood. "I was wondering how this works. Do you pay by the bowl, or what?"

"No," I explained, "you can just sample whatever you want. The jars are for voting."

We got up to try some of the other chowders, and of course I had to introduce Nikki to everyone I knew, which was everyone. More of the congregation had arrived, but they were still mostly middle aged and older.

Nikki smiled and explained to everyone that, no, she wasn't in school, that she was working for her father, selling pleasure boats, and yes, she thought this was a swell town, and this sure was tasty.

I could see she was probably really good in sales; she had an easy smile and a cheerful manner, but I could tell even on short acquaintance that it was starting to wear on her.

We don't get a lot of visitors here, and the attention could be a little overwhelming.

I saw Brother Vasili so I snagged his arm. "Nikki was asking about Captain Marsh's effects. Do you think you could open the archives and give her a tour?"

He seemed surprised and gave our bowls a sharp glance. "There's no food allowed in the archives, of course."

Nikki put her bowl down on the nearest table. I did likewise.

Brother Vasili, still looking skeptical, led us down the steps to the basement.

"Most of our collection is what survived the fire in 1821," he explained. "The archives had been stored in the lighthouse proper until then. Afterward, everything that could be salvaged was moved here for safekeeping, and the vault built. A bit like locking the barn door after the horses get out, of course."

It didn't take long for Nikki to win over Brother Vasili, though, with her obvious delight at seeing what relics remained from the founding of our people. There was the compass, big as a dinner plate,

The Old Covenant

from Captain Marsh's ship, the *Good Miss Browne*. Charts and maps of his voyages in the Caribbean, now carefully sealed in plastic. The captain's journals, written in a mixture of Dutch and English, with drawings of the island sea-folk, their features showing various stages of the change. And, of course, the wall-sized chart showing the family tree of our people, meticulously labeled with the date that each branch went into the sea to join their blood with that of the deep ones and beget a new line.

Nikki traced her family back to the 1830s. My own branch, the Orlovs, stemmed from Captain Marsh's third mate, Ivan Orlov, in 1693.

"Original stock," Nikki grinned at me.

I shrugged. I didn't consider my ancestry an achievement. I didn't have anything to do with it—it had all happened long before I was born.

Eventually my mother came shuffling down the stairs to find us. "*There* you are," she exclaimed. "Tucker, what on earth were you thinking? I am sure this young lady isn't interested in all these dusty old books."

"It was her idea," I pointed out, but we dutifully followed her back upstairs anyway.

There I ran into Karl, who was my age and worked for the fire department. We'd been friends in high school, but didn't see much of each other these days.

"Hey, Tucker," he said, "a bunch of us are hitting the point in the morning. You and Miss West should join us."

He had obviously been prompted, but his voice was warm and the offer genuine. I tried to remember the last time I'd taken my board out. Too long.

I glanced at Nikki, who looked back with polite confusion.

"Visverkoper point," I explained. "Where the lighthouse is. It's a good place for surfing."

"Oh," Nikki smiled. "I don't have my board."

"You can use mine," Lana said quickly. "And I think I have a suit that might fit you."

"I've got my wetsuit," Nikki said. "Thanks."

"We usually meet up at about five," I said. "That's when Lighthouse Donuts opens." I glanced at Karl, who nodded.

"Great," Nikki said, "I'll be there."

134

Her father swooped down then and said, "We're going to get back to the hotel now."

Nikki trailed after him, glancing back with a smile.

Okay, I thought, *I think that went well.*

The next morning, I was on the boardwalk by the point when Lighthouse Donuts opened. I had my board and Lana's in the back of my pickup. Lana used a short board, and I hoped that Nikki would be okay with it. I bought a large coffee and two dozen mixed doughnuts, handing them out as the other guys showed up. Kids I knew from high school, mostly. It was like a reunion of Marsh Consolidated, and when I thought about it, I realized that it had been ten years.

How had that happened?

Nikki showed up in a rental car. I waved her to a parking spot and watched as she got out.

She looked good in a wet suit, really good. I had been too nervous to pay much attention at the supper, but now I thought, *I could get used to sleeping next to that body.*

I grabbed the boards, and when I turned back I saw that she was giving me that same appraising look. I blushed a little and hoped that I was measuring up.

She accepted a doughnut with a smile and let me buy her a cup of coffee—hot, sweet, and light. We stood for a moment, leaning on the rail of the boardwalk, not talking, just watching the periwinkle sky grow red above the waves. The sound of the surf played in our ears, the slow ancient rhythm. The others were heading down the beach and into the water.

I nodded my head at the waves. She slammed the last of her coffee and grinned at me, and we hit the surf.

It wasn't a good day for surfing—too calm. Even on the north side of the point, where the bottom slopes up the most sharply, there were few decent waves. Nonetheless, it was a great way to spend the morning, bobbing and paddling next to Nikki.

"What are they doing?" she asked me suddenly.

I looked to where she was pointing. On the shore, the guys had assembled a mess of driftwood and old pallets and were lighting a bonfire on the beach.

"I don't know," I answered honestly, "let's go find out."

We struck out for shore. She was a strong swimmer, her slim body cutting through the waves like a fish. I had a sudden vision, watching her paddling on the borrowed board, of her going through the change, losing her pretty hair, her lovely skin turning leathery and pale, her eyes covered with an translucent film for seeing underwater.

It seemed to me just then a terrible shame that someone so pretty would become... one of *them.* One of the deep ones.

But then, I would be changing too, wouldn't I? Would my standards of beauty change with the rest of me? I suppose they must. My parents seemed to be dealing with the change together, still as affectionate towards each other as ever.

On the beach, they were wrapping corn and fish in foil to set in among the coals. I raised an eyebrow at that—this was suspiciously well-organized for an allegedly impromptu get-together. Someone—probably my mother—wanted to make sure that Nikki was charmed by our quiet seaside community.

She excused herself and headed to the boardwalk to use the bathroom in the doughnut shop.

Karl watched me watching her walk away and grinned at me.

"Lucky man," he said, punching my arm.

"She's lovely," I agreed.

"Rich, too."

I gave him a glance. "The boat business doing well?"

"Boats, hell," he snorted. "That's just a hobby for them. The Wests are old Boston money. Great-grandpa invented the iron lung or something. They are seriously loaded."

I gave him a skeptical look. Karl tended to jump to conclusions, and just because there was a family named West that was wealthy didn't mean that Nikki was heir to the fortune.

I didn't ask Nikki about her family finances when she got back—there didn't seem to be any polite way to raise the subject. Instead we took a walk up to the lighthouse while to fish was baking. The keeper on duty that morning was a guy I knew from school, and he let us climb the stairs to the top and go out on the circular balcony.

The view really was spectacular, the sun still low enough in the east that it painted the whole ocean shimmering gold.

After a while Nikki asked in a small voice, "Do you believe?"

I didn't have to ask what she meant. I replied honestly, "It does seem kind of far-fetched, when you think about it. A... *god,* sleeping on the bottom of the ocean for a million years or so, and someday

He'll wake up and take over the world?"

I sighed. "But then, there's us. The change."

"Lots of animals go through metamorphosis," she said. "Tadpoles and frogs, caterpillars and butterflies. It doesn't have to mean anything supernatural."

"There aren't any other mammals that become fish," I pointed out.

"That we know of," she argued. "Science doesn't know everything."

I nodded and looked past her to the vast expanse of the ocean. Most of the world lay under those waves. What did we really know of what was down there?

It could be anything. *Anything.*

"I guess we'll find out one day," I said, half to myself.

That was twenty-five years ago. Nikki and I got married in the summer of 1995, a few days after the Solstice. We bought a house in town and I kept working the same job, despite my father-in-law's generous offers of employment. I did let him buy us a cruise for a wedding present.

After Freddy was born the next spring, we started attending services regularly. The congregation was so generous with their time, offering to watch the baby, coming over to help Nikki with the housework, it seemed petty to stay away.

Then came Amanda, and the next year little Brian. I got promoted, and took some classes at the IBEW hall and somehow ended up as a master electrician. I started doing traveling for work.

When the Hurricanes got their new stadium, I was in charge of the crew that did the parking lot lighting. Ahead of schedule and under budget, as it turned out.

I never let them send me too far from home, though, and even when I was on the road, I spent most weekends at home.

The kids went to school in town and were initiated into the temple at 13, just as I had been. My parents had gone out to the reefs by the time that Freddy took the mysteries, but the ceremony was held on the beach in the dark of the moon, and I like to think my mother and father were out there, close by, watching their first grandson recite the old words.

The Old Covenant

Lana married a fisherman from down the coast and moved away. We ended up selling our parents' house and splitting the money. Nikki and I put our half into college funds for the kids.

The change began gradually, as it always does. Nikki's hair grew thin, and she started wearing a wig to go out. I started wearing my sunglasses indoors and ended up buying some safety glasses with mirror lenses, which Freddy said made me look like an evil robot.

One day, Brother Ivan, who had replaced Brother Vasili as first initiate, took me aside and told me, gently, but firmly, that I should put in notice at work. The change was becoming evident, and I shouldn't be around inlanders any more. I had a partial pension and investments, so I retired.

It's time.

I can feel the pull of the ocean. I find myself staring east, lost in thoughts that I can never quite remember. Freddy and Amanda have their own places now, and we signed the deed of the house over to Brian. We met with a lawyer to split up and transfer our bank accounts to the kids. Since most of our people don't ever officially die, it's more complicated than just writing a will, but there are attorneys in town who specialize in that paperwork.

We're going out together, Nikki and I. She has become even more beautiful over the years. Her body is lean and strong, lithe as a coral snake. Whatever waits for us in those cold depths we will face it together, a pair of pale shadows in the gloom, perfectly adapted for our new world.

Tonight is the new moon, and together we are going home.

As soon as it gets dark.

Dialectic Nocturne

Her heels tap slow down the hall past where I sit
Like the diktat of an autarch, or a deathwatch knell
And I look up from where I am face-deep in trivialities
Cigarette smoldering between my fingers, Do I know
what time it is getting to? I do not. And she passes by.

I get up and follow her not because she asked me to
—she didn't—but because that's the other half of this
Game we play, coy by turns, one to a side, and now
She stretches out full length on the bed and pretends
That there is something that she wants to talk about

Which there is, but her part of the conversation was
Walking slowly toward me and walking more slowly away
My answering argument was in following where she led
And once I'd reached her, leading her on to where she wants to go
Her eyes wide with counterfeit surprise and honest joy.

The Silk of Yesterday's Gown

Originally published in *All These Shiny Worlds II*, May 2017

L ook, I don't *have* to be here.

My lawyers don't want me to be here. I've got my own reasons for talking to you, and I'm going to make it quick, say what I have to say, and get out of here. Then I'm getting out of the country, going down to the Caymans for a while. A long, long while. I've got a jet waiting.

What I say doesn't leave this room.

I mean that. You don't tell your wife, you don't tell your partner, you don't tell your god damned cat. *One word* of this gets out, and I am going to have this department in litigation for the next hundred years. You're going to be selling your guns for court costs. And I will see you, personally, in the most brutal jail in the state, in the general population. Is that clear?

No questions. I am going to tell my story and get out.

That's not negotiable. *None of this is negotiable.*

I've got the Governor's private cell number in my phone. Last week I had margaritas with three US congressmen. I am not somebody that you can mess with.

Are we clear? Absolutely, crystal clear?

Good.

You're not going to find Marci.

I know you're looking for her. It's on the front page of the god damned paper—my wife is missing and the cops are looking for her. What I'm here to tell you is that you're not going to find her, and you need to stop looking before you find... something else.

I'm not saying that she's dead. I don't know that. I think she is— hell, I *hope* she's dead. I loved her more than I've ever loved anyone. More than I ever will love anyone again. And every night I pray to God that she's dead.

But I don't know. I didn't see her die.

I saw enough to know that you'll never find her. She's... gone.

I don't expect you to believe me, and I don't care. Like I said, I'm going to speak my piece and get out. After that, whatever happens is on your head.

You've been poking around in my personal life enough that you know about the Storyville Club, and I'm going to assume that you've been warned off doing any digging there. That's okay, because it's got nothing to do with what happened to Marci. Well, maybe not nothing, but it's a dead end as far as her... *disappearance* is concerned. All asking questions about Storyville is going to do is kill your career. It's a place for public personalities to do private things, and there is some serious leverage to keep it private. Swingers, mostly, very, very exclusive—I'm sure you've figured out that much.

I met Marci there, okay? She was someone else's guest, and she left with me. We started hooking up regularly. We had... similar tastes. Complimentary, I guess you'd say.

We got close enough that I married her. I—

I loved her. Not just her body, not just her style, but *her.*

She's an artist—*was* an artist. I set her up with the gallery. It lost money, of course, those places always do. But it made her so happy. It wasn't just something to keep her busy when I was out of town— she *worked* that gallery. She had a real eye for talent and signed the best local artists. It was a career to her, not just a hobby.

That's where she met them, at the gallery.

It was an opening, the usual wine and cheese bash. I wasn't there that night, I was in LA signing papers. But I heard all about it.

Ta—*Christ,* I can hardly say their names.

Tam and Robin. Linn. Married couple. Swedish papers, although Tam was Welsh originally and Robin was Scottish. Or so we thought at the time.

Beautiful couple. Breathtaking. Tam was the woman, Robin the man. Same coloring, black hair, pale skin, green eyes—they had the same eyes. They looked more like brother and sister than man and wife.

Maybe—

It doesn't matter anyway.

She made sure that I met them as soon as I was back in town. We had a champagne brunch. They were in banking—well, that's what he told me, and he knew the business, seemed to know all the right people. A man in my position has to develop an instinct for when he's being played, and these two gave every indication of being the genuine article. Marci was smitten with them—that's the only word for it. I knew what she wanted, and, yeah, I wanted it too.

The Silk of Yesterday's Gown

And them? They had a kind of... *chemistry*. That's all I can call it. Robin had this way of dominating any conversation without being pushy about it. Trust me, on the level I work, you meet some outrageous egos. Any time you sit down to negotiate a serious deal, you have to spend the first day cat-fighting over who's got the biggest dick in the room.

Robin wasn't like that. He just had this charisma, I guess you'd call it. I've met movie stars, I've met kings—I sat in a meeting with Sultan of Brunei once.

I never met anyone like Robin.

Knowing what I know now, I hope I never do again.

Tam had the same thing, but it was different. Robin was commanding, Tam was... *captivating*.

It wasn't just that she was the most beautiful woman I've ever seen. She had sex appeal, sure, enough to cause traffic jams when she crossed the street. But she was charming. Warm, friendly. Most women that sexy push men away—they have to, or else they get swarmed. Tam didn't. She always talked to you like you were the one who was fascinating.

We spent a couple of hours together the first day, talking, getting to know each other. Marci was all ready to get to know them a lot better, but I was going to take things slow. We made plans to meet later in the week.

Now, despite what you may have read in the Wall Street Journal, I am not a stupid man. I have some discrete researchers on my staff, and I ordered up a background on the Linns.

And it came back clean. *Clean.*

Robin Taliesan Linn and Tamera Alice O'Shann-Linn were exactly who they said that they were. It was perfect in that it wasn't *too* perfect, it was just messy enough to convince me that it was real. Evidence of a scandal in Manchester that was covered up, a couple of questionable deals—I've read a lot of dossiers in my time. You can't fake a real identity, not to the depth I could dig.

So we did a couple of dinners, and I took them to a party at friend's house, and they were always lovely. Discrete. There was an undercurrent, but nothing untoward—I mean, nothing that would cause talk. We all wanted the same thing, but they weren't being... blatant about it.

Marci was the one I had to watch. She was ready to get on her knees under the table for either or both of them—preferably both. I had to caution her to remember we were in public.

So we took the next step.

There's a hotel—I'm not going to tell you which one, but you'd know the name. The owner and I have an arrangement. There are two rooms—not suites, just rooms—that aren't ever rented to anyone else.

The mirror facing the bed is only a mirror from one side. On the other side, it's a window.

Marci took men there sometimes. Women, a couple of times.

What I said about complementary tastes? That was it. Marci liked to play the field. I like to watch. Usually she'd text me when she was on her way, and if I was free I'd make my way to the other room without Marci's friend being wise to it.

The Linns knew I was there. Marci insisted. I... well, I wasn't happy about it, but I couldn't deny Marci what she wanted. Privately, I had my reservations.

We met for drinks in the hotel bar.

I wasn't comfortable being there. This was Marci's place. I had always come in the loading dock and up the service elevator. I didn't like being exposed like this, and I damned sure didn't like sitting down in a booth with a man who knew he was about to get lucky with my wife.

If Robin had so much as smirked at me, I would have called the whole thing off. If he—if either one of them—had played the bull and started talking down to me, I would have walked, and Marci would have walked with me. I would have made sure of that.

I enjoy my wife's pleasure. That doesn't make me a cuckold.

They were late. Late enough that I ordered Marci and I a second round, and I started to think that they wouldn't show.

Then they came hurrying in, and Robin's suit was rumpled. He had black smudges on his hands and started apologizing before they had even sat down. His car—a vintage jag in pristine condition—had a blowout on the highway. Tam followed him, not quite rolling her eyes as he detailed how he had to change a tire in the breakdown lane. He was still obviously rattled from the experience and—

Damn it! I just now realized that was all an act.

I was such an idiot. I bought it, signed a twenty year note without reading the fine print.

The Silk of Yesterday's Gown

Of course he knew what I was feeling, what I didn't want, and he gave me just the opposite. He made sure I saw him looking vulnerable and scared just when I was feeling that way myself.

I needed something to feel superior to him about, and he hand-fed it to me.

Tam ordered some bar food and we had a couple of more rounds. The tension drained away from the evening, and it became comfortable. I had been thinking about how to break things off from them, to tell Marci not to see them again in a way that would stick, but I found myself enjoying their company.

Tam even flirted with me, let me know that it was my choice not to get involved. She made me feel like I was in control, or at least not a passive participant.

Bullshit. All bullshit. Those two monsters played me like a violin, without breaking a sweat and making me think it was all my idea.

I left first, through the kitchen and up to the service elevator. I got to my room and sat on the bed, looking through the window into Marci's room. I got undressed and folded my clothes.

I waited.

The three of them came through the door laughing. Tam had her arm around Marci's shoulders, and Robin followed them, shutting the door behind them.

And then—

You don't need to know. I'm not going to give you a play by play, every kiss, every caress, who undressed whom and where the clothes got dropped on the way to the neatly-made king sized bed. That's mine, no matter what else they have taken from me, that first night is mine and mine alone.

They worshiped her.

I saw the love of my life, the bright morning star of my night sky, the woman of my dreams being adored. I don't expect you to understand. I buy and sell a dozen men like you before breakfast every morning, and you are sitting there thinking that you are superior to me because you lock your woman in some eighty-thousand dollar cracker-box condominium and never let her out.

Fine. Laugh at me all you want.

They gave me heaven. They showed me what true love looks like, just so that they could take it away from me in the end.

I left first, as I always did, dressed in the darkness and left Marci lying between the two of them, her tanned skin glowing beside their pale bodies. I went home to sleep alone, confident that she would spend the night in that room that didn't exist on any official record.

Marci crawled into bed with me about dawn, warm and wet from them. She told me that they were waiting outside and that they wanted to go to breakfast.

I had never been friends with any of Marci's lovers before. My impulse was to turn away, to tell her to tell them to get lost, but something in her eyes made me agree.

Robin drove us to some dive on the riverfront, a 24-hour place frequented by truckers and longshoremen, and he ordered absurdly complicated omelets all around. Robin made me laugh and Tam made me feel like a man, and both of them made Marci so very, very happy.

That was how it started. Again, I don't expect you to understand, but they seduced us both. Marci was the one they had sex with, held in the night when she cried out in burning, murderous ecstasy, but they knew that Marci was mine and they had to win my heart to take her. It wasn't about sex; sex was the tool they used, but I am sure now that it meant nothing to them. It was about control, and never letting me know how much I had given up.

After that, Marci saw them when she could, when they were in town. Their schedule was chaotic and always changing. It was, I am now sure, a carefully calculated random, designed to leave both of us always wanting more.

We went out together, to dinner, or for drinks. If they were in town when I was traveling, they took Marci out. They spoiled her, pampered her, bought her exotic gifts, strange handcrafted jewelry, and clothing tailored to her curves in rich fabrics. They were beautiful things, in a style that seemed Celtic but more intricate than I had ever seen before.

They took her for a long weekend out of town, driving up to the wine country to a farm owned by some friends. Marci loved it there, and she talked about it at great length when they got back. I wish that I had listened more closely to her descriptions of the trip, because I can't find the place on any map. I somehow doubt that it is on any map.

She said they raised pigs and grew grapes, and she came back with bottles of wine, home-brewed and unlabeled, deep, rich red and delicious. She said that she loved it there and that she wanted to go back and live there forever.

She also came back with a necklace made from carved wood. It was a chain, the kind that you see in craft shows, but it was continuous. Carved from a single block, unbroken, but somehow they had fitted it tight around her throat. She claimed that she didn't remember how Robin had put it around her neck, and I believed her.

I was too cynical. I assumed that there was some kind of trick to it, that given time I would discover how it was done and be able to undo it. I saw magic, saw it wrapped tight around the face I woke up to every morning, and I didn't recognize it for what it was.

Things in the hotel room, though, were getting more... *intense.*

Marci had always liked it rough, rougher than I wanted, and I accepted that she got that from her other lovers. With Robin and Tam, though, she took it to a whole new level. She urged them to cruelty, begged them for it. And they gave her what she needed, defiling her, working together, one causing her pain while she pleasured the other, humiliating her, abusing her, and always driving her to greater heights of desire and fulfillment, with me always watching silently from behind the glass.

I didn't like it, didn't like at all how they talked to her, how they used her. I couldn't deny how she responded to it, though. Seeing her exquisite body jerk and thrust in abandon was worth whatever it took to get her there, or so I thought then.

I know better now.

It was always both of them. I never saw one without the other, which should have given me pause. I was frequently out of town myself—DC, New York, LA, London—and Marci stayed here. But Robin never left town without Tam by his side. If I had ever gotten Tam alone, I thought in those days, and imagined... well, it doesn't matter. I wasn't what Tam wanted.

Or was I? Not my body, certainly. Her flirtation was just a mask, as unconsciously deceptive as a chameleon's coloration. But in the end, she and Robin cut into my soul and harvested all that mattered to me. Was that what they were after all that time? Was Marci their prize or just a means to an end? In my better moments, I believe that I meant nothing to them. In the dark nights of my soul, I am sure that I meant everything.

Hell isn't another world. Hell is when we see this world as it truly is.

I saw that the night that Marci disappeared.

I was supposed to be in DC that weekend. I was testifying—well, if you want to know you can look it up in the papers. It was all part of the media smokescreen. That's how the game is played, you give the politicians the soundbites they need to wave in front of the voters, and they give you the elbow room to do your job.

My particular sideshow got canceled because one group of idiots in some desert hellhole killed another group of idiots. Again, you can look it up if you care.

I jetted back home late afternoon. I didn't tell Marci that my trip had been canceled. She said that she would be meeting Robin and Tam at the hotel. I wanted to watch them without them knowing I was there.

I went to my room and ordered a meal and a bottle of wine.

It was late when they came into the other room.

I was dozing on the cheap double bed, thinking that the Linns were out of town and I should just go home. Then the door in the other room banged open, and I started awake.

They were cruel. More than rough, they were brutal. Robin held her Marci down while Tam used her teeth and nails, leaving trails of blood on my love's perfect skin. I would have done something—crashed into the room, called 911, something—except that Marci was craving the abuse, loving it, needing it, begging for more.

And then Tam produced the skin.

I watched. To my eternal damnation, I watched the king and queen of Hell take my beloved, and I did nothing.

Tam was nearly naked by then, dressed only in an unbuttoned blouse. Marci was entirely naked, and Robin wore one sock, a gray knitted sock that had somehow remained in place.

Yet Tam produced a hide from somewhere. It was raw, still bleeding, freshly flensed. She laid it on Marci's body, the dark side upwards, brownish pink, the side oozing blood against her skin.

Marci changed.

Her belly swelled, and her legs contracted, and she threw back her head and howled, a sound that I will take to my grave. Robin took one arm and forced it under the skin. I could hear her bones pop and her muscles pull in, and Tam pushed the skin over Marci's face.

The Silk of Yesterday's Gown

The howls grew deeper, altered from human cries into deep guttural grunts.

I see it now, every time I close my eyes. I tell myself that I didn't know what I was seeing, that I didn't believe it. That's a lie. I knew, and I believed. I saw what they were doing. I didn't understand how it was possible, but I saw it with my own eyes.

I did nothing because I was afraid.

I was a coward. My beloved was suffering. I couldn't imagine the horror that she was experiencing. They were remaking her, turning her beauty and her creativity and her laughter into a thing, a fat sow, a helpless creature for their bloody-handed amusement. I watched, and I did nothing because I lacked the courage to act.

But that's not the worst of it.

That's not the thing that broke me.

It *excited* me.

I was sick with fear, numb with horror, but at the same time, I was horribly, painfully erect. Despite having pleasured myself watching their earlier performance, this ultimate degradation, this impossible dehumanizing transformation aroused me past anything I had ever felt before.

The bloody skin filled out, and the slack pig's face grew mobile, the snout twitching, the eyes opening. Eyes that were not pig's eyes, but Marci's own beautiful blue.

Tam bent her head and brought her mouth, open-lipped, to the blood and snot smeared snout of the pig. Her pink tongue lapped at the pig's blunt one and the pig grunted, a sound unmistakably of deep, unreasoning pleasure.

Helplessly, I ejaculated into my lap.

Tam grasped the wooden chain still binding Marci's altered neck and dragged her sow's body from the bed. Nearly naked, she led her away. Robin stood to follow them.

Before he did, he turned, and he looked at me. Through the mirrored glass he faced me, his eyes meeting mine, like he'd known I was there all along, and he smiled at me.

Then they left the room.

I don't suppose I have to tell you that no one saw a naked man and woman leading a pig through the halls of a five-star downtown hotel.

And I don't suppose that it will come as a surprise to you that

Robin and Tam Linn are gone. More than gone, they never were. There is no record that they ever existed. Every mention of their names has been erased, all over the world.

I looked at the files that I had been given those months ago, and the pages are all blank. The man whom I'd asked to prepare the report doesn't remember me asking him. I've talked to the people at the parties that I took them to, and every one swears that Marci and I came alone.

The jewelry, the clothing, all the gifts they had given Marci are gone. I've torn her closets apart, looking for some evidence, some proof. Nothing.

All I have is a green glass bottle without a label and a hand carved wooden stopper. What's left of the wine inside it has gone rancid.

I'm leaving now. You're not going to stop me. You're not going to try to contact me. You are going to close down this investigation. Marci will be recorded as an unsolved missing person.

I am going to the Caymans, and then I don't know what I am going to do. I don't know if there is anything I can do, anything left for me.

Maybe I'll just sit on the beach and drink myself to death. I have a lot of money—it won't take long.

Goodbye.

The King of the Robot Men

On Space Station Zero the Robot Men waited
Assembled in ranks to honor their king
Their armor was freshly titanium plated
Their voices were ready their anthem to sing

But the waiting went on and there was no king
"Why isn't he coming? What has gone wrong?"
The Monkey Musicians could not play a thing
The Dinosaurs asked what was taking so long

"Is not everything ready?" wondered the team
"The Giants with trumpets, the Dwarfs with their drums?
The Atomic Electric Butterfly Beam?
Who shall we serve if our king never comes?"

On Space Station Zero no music will play
One of the mighty has fallen today

The Darkest Hour of the Night
Previously unpublished

"Have you ever done anything really bad?" asked the man with the gun.

He reached and touched the keys hanging from the ignition, then dropped his hand away without starting the motor.

The thief, wide-eyed, shook his head.

The man with the gun didn't seem to notice. He looked through the windshield at the closed garage door. "Have you ever done something so bad that God Himself couldn't forgive you? Not wouldn't—*couldn't.* Some sin of action or omission so evil that eternal, almighty God was powerless to wash the stain away?"

The thief sat on the bench seat beside the man with the gun, in a car in a closed garage. He didn't try to speak. He felt like he was about to piss his pants.

The man held the gun easily in his right hand. It was a big hand, and it looked used to holding guns. The man turned his head, but his eyes didn't quite focus on the thief. He seemed to be looking past him—*through* him, as if the thief weren't even there, weren't trapped in a car with a madman, the place he most of all did not want to be.

"What's your name, stranger?" the man asked, softly, almost kindly, still looking through him at the wall of the garage.

The thief shook his head. He didn't want to tell this stranger his name. It was important not to say his name, not to... *confess* it.

"Your name?" the man repeated. "Tell me."

"I..." the thief was so scared that he wasn't sure he remembered his name.

The man lifted the gun until it was pointed at the thief, pointed right at his chest. "Speak your name."

"Pete," the thief gasped out. He was scared to death. Absolutely to death.

"Peter," the man nodded and lowered the gun. "That's a good name, Peter. It means rock. That's what Christ named His favorite disciple, you know. Peter the rock."

The man lifted the gun and set it on the dashboard of the car. He started to take his hand away, then rested it protectively over the

151

heavy pistol.

"You wouldn't be thinking about trying to take this, would you, Peter?" the man asked. "Snatching up my gun and putting a bullet through my head, splattering my brains all over the inside of my car? That thought wouldn't be crossing your mind, would it?"

Pete swallowed hard. "No," he whispered, then added, because the moment seem to call for it, "No, sir."

The man nodded, and he took his hand away, leaving the gun on the dash. "I didn't think so, but it's always good to ask."

He dropped his hand to the keys in the ignition again, and seemed about to turn them, but stopped. There was a cracked leather disk attached the keys, decorated with daubs of peeling paint. It looked like something a kid might have made some summer at vacation bible school, may years ago. It was funny, the things you noticed at a time like this.

"Do you know why you are here, Peter?" he asked. "Here in this particular car, at this particular time, with me?"

"I'm sorry," Pete gasped. "I'll pay for the window, just please don't hurt me."

"Hush," said the man. "You're not here because of the window. You're not here because you tried to steal a car. You're here because you tried to steal a car and failed. Remember that fact. Focus your mind on it. It will be very important to you in the near future."

"I wasn't going to steal anything," Pete sobbed. "I just wanted to look at it, that's all. You can call the police, I'll go with them."

"The police would be a very little use," the man said absently. Then, "How old are you, Peter?"

"I'm sixteen," Pete whispered.

"Yes, of course you are," the man agreed. "And how long have you been sixteen?"

Pete opened his mouth, but couldn't find the words to answer the man.

He was sixteen. His birthday had been... earlier. In the summer. After the end of the school year. In the summer he had turned sixteen. Other kids had gotten cars for their sixteenth birthday. Kids who didn't live in trailer parks. Kids with parents who had jobs.

For Pete's sixteenth birthday, his parents had given him a bicycle. A second hand bicycle, painted a flat dull red to hide the places where the frame had been welded back together. He tried not to be disappointed. It was a good bicycle, better than his old one, which was quietly handed down to a cousin. It wasn't a car, but it was a big boy bike at least, and he could take it all over the county on the hot, empty days of summer.

It wasn't summer now. It was cold. It was always cold.

What had the man asked? How long have I been sixteen? A long time. Pete shook his head. He couldn't remember.

"It doesn't matter," the man said. "You're sixteen now, and that's what counts. Am I right?"

Pete nodded. The man seemed to be talking to himself as much, or maybe more, than he was talking to Pete. He was crazy. He was very dangerously crazy.

The man touched the keys and turned them suddenly. Not far enough to trigger the starter, just to the accessory position. The dash lights came on, and the radio played softly.

"Peter," the man said, "I shouldn't turn the motor on. One should never run a gasoline engine in an enclosed space like this. It isn't safe. In fact, people die that way. But we can listen to the music on the radio."

Pete nodded, not sure if the man even noticed.

"You like music," the man went on. "Of course you do. And you liked the radio in this car—that's part of why you wanted it. For the radio."

"I didn't—" Pete started to say.

The man just talked over him. "A very good radio. Let me know if it plays any songs that you remember."

I'm being kidnapped, and this crazy man wants to talk about songs on the radio. What does that have to do with anything?

Pete took a deep breath and tried to keep his voice level, "Mister, you can't just keep me here like this. It's against the law, even if I did break into your garage."

"So, you're sixteen, and you want a car," the man said, as if Pete hadn't spoken. "That's the most natural thing in the world. Nothing wrong with wanting a car. Other boys had cars. And you weren't going to steal it, not really, just take it for a drive. Am I right?"

Pete nodded. He wanted to talk, wanted to find the right words that would make this madman let him go, but his mind was blank. He just wanted to go home. As bad as it was at home, it was better than this. Anything was better than being in a place you could never leave.

"This car," the man tapped the steering wheel. "This exact car."

"I'm sorry," Pete said. It was all he could think of to say.

"I don't want you to be sorry, Peter," the man said, "I want you to think. Do you recognize the song on the radio? This song, the one that is playing now?"

Pete tried to listen; the radio was playing so softly that he couldn't make out the song, but he was afraid to ask the man to turn it up. He was crazy, who knew what he would do?

Pete shook his head. "I don't know the song."

"That's okay," the man said. "Remembering things is hard. Do you remember how you got in here? Into the garage?"

Involuntarily, Pete looked through the side widow of the car, up to a high, narrow window in the garage. "Through there."

"That's right," the man agreed, smiling. "You climbed in through the window. Broke it, too."

"I'll pay for it," Pete said, "I promise."

"Oh, let's not worry about a broken window, Peter," the man said. "Let's talk about why you went in that way."

Why had he come in through the window? He remembered breaking the window. He hadn't wanted to, he thought that he could just push the window up with his screwdriver, but it had been latched and the glass cracked. Then he'd reached through and worked the latch until he could push the broken window up and out of the way.

He was good at that kind of thing. Someday he'd be a mechanic like his uncle.

By why had come through the window at all?

Pete glared out the windshield of the car at the wooden garage door.

The man nodded as if reading his thoughts. "The overhead door was padlocked, wasn't it? And the side door was locked. The window was the only way in. For you, anyway. You're a skinny kid. A guy my size would never fit through there."

The man was looking away from Pete, up at the high window. Pete put his hand on the door handle. Maybe now he'd have a chance...

Quickly the man snatched up the gun from the dashboard and swung it around to point at Pete's forehead. "You're not going anywhere, are you, Peter?"

Pete raised both hands quickly. "No, sir!" he almost shouted.

"Good." The man put the gun back. "Because we're not finished with our conversation. We haven't gotten to the important part yet."

Pete let out a long ragged breath. His heart was pounding. He wanted to go home, back to the little bunk in the laundry room, back to his mom and dad always arguing about whose fault it was that they were poor. Anywhere. Pete would even go willingly back to school if it got him out of here. He'd go back to school and kiss Miss Butler on the lips, sit in the front row, and write down every word she said, if it got him out of this place.

Anything was better than being in a place you could never leave.

"Let's talk about what happened next," the man said. "After you got into this garage."

Pete looked down sullenly. "You kidnapped me," he said, as angrily as he dared. The anger almost drove out the fear. It wasn't right, being kept here against his will. It wasn't fair. He hadn't done anything bad enough to be trapped in this cold dark garage in this cold dark car with a crazy man.

The man smiled broadly. "Oh, I think you're leaving a few very important things out," he said gently. "But I'll let it pass for now. Why do you think I did that?"

Pete looked at the man. Such a big man, solid with muscle. Pete felt like a little kid next to him. A baby.

"Because I tried to steal your car," he admitted, looking away. There were shelves built into the wall of the garage, homemade from uneven, splintery planks. There were jars on the shelves, furred with dust.

The man raised his finger. "No, Peter, remember what I said. It wasn't that you tried to steal this car, it was because you tried to steal this car and failed. I told you that was important."

"Okay," Pete agreed. "I failed."

Failed at being a car thief, just like he'd failed at everything else he tried to do. But he wasn't a thief. He didn't steal anything. Thieves go to Hell.

"You failed to steal this car," the man said again. "This precise car that you wanted so much."

The man seemed to be waiting for something, so Pete said, "Yes, sir."

"It's not my car, you know," the man said. "I'm just renting it for

155

the night."

Pete frowned at that. At some level, he knew, the man's story didn't make sense. Of course it didn't make sense. He was a crazy man. Only a crazy man would pull a gun on a kid just for breaking a window.

But he was still talking.

"We have—as they say—placed you inside the garage, by way of a broken window. Then what happened, Peter? Do you remember that? Before I... kidnapped you, I mean."

"I—" Pete broke off, confused. "I just want to go home, mister. Please just let me go home."

Home. Sun-faded green paint and aluminum trim, with two lawn chairs outside the front door that were always surrounded by drifts of cigarette butts. Peeling dark paneling inside, and windows that let in air, sticky in the summer, icy in the winter. Waking up in the night to the barking of dogs throughout the park whenever a car went by the old county road. He didn't have an address, not a real address like Maple Street or Broadway. His address was just a bunch of numbers, like the numbers you held up in front of you when they took your picture in jail.

Home smelled like cigarettes and beer and casseroles donated by the Hope Lutheran Church. Home sounded like other people's TVs and radios coming through the thin walls. Home looked like an old box leftover from some Christmas years ago, thrown out and faded by the sun at the side of the road.

Home was the most beautiful thing in the world. He would do anything to go there.

"All in good time, young man. Believe me, I want you to go home, too. But you can't. Not just yet."

"What do you want from me?" Pete asked miserably.

"Do you recognize the song on the radio?" the man asked.

"Shut up about the radio!" Pete snapped. "I can't hear the radio."

The man reached down and turned the knob. "Can you hear it now?"

There was nothing but a crackle, like a broken speaker or distant lightning. "It's broken."

The man shook his head. "No, it's not broken. I can hear it just fine."

"You're crazy," Pete said, then clenched his jaws, trying to take

156

back the words. Crazy people never wanted to hear that they were crazy. It made them violent, on the TV shows that mom like to watch.

But the man just smiled. "You're not the first person to tell me that," he said. "But let's not talk about me. Let's talk about you. You remember breaking the window to get into the garage, don't you?"

"Yes," Pete whispered. "I remember."

He'd dragged a trash can over to the window to stand on. It wobbled, and he had to hold on to the windowsill to keep from falling. He'd gotten a splinter in his finger. Idly he sucked the finger, felt the tiny sliver of wood under his skin. He wished he could dig it out, be rid of it.

The man looked kindly at the boy. "Tell me what happened next. It's important."

"I don't know what you're talking about," Pete said. The man was crazy. He was trapped in a car with a lunatic and he had to get out. Even if the man shot him. Anything was better than being in a place you could never leave.

"I think you do, Peter," the man insisted. He reached up and reclaimed the gun from the dashboard. "And I think you remember what happened after you climbed through that window."

"I didn't do anything wrong," Pete shouted, knowing in his heart that was a lie. Breaking windows was wrong. It was wrong to go into other people's property without permission. It was wrong to...

The man's voice was low and calm. "I didn't say that you did. Not really. Nothing that God can't forgive you for."

"Why do you keep talking about God?" Peter asked. The words just kind of slipped out. He hadn't intended to say anything of the kind. All of sudden, though, it seemed to be the most important question. More than, *Why did you kidnap me?* Pete wanted know, *Why do you talk to me about God? Who is He to you?*

"Because God is in the forgiveness business," the crazy man said, sounding calm and reasonable, just like crazy killers always sounded on TV shows. "I'd like to forgive you myself, Peter, believe me that I would. But I can't. Only God can forgive."

"*Let me go!*" Pete cried.

"Only you can do that."

"*What do you want from me?*"

"First you have to tell me what happened when you got into the garage. Did you go for a drive?"

The Darkest Hour of the Night

Suddenly, the fear of the man's questions was worse than the fear of the gun, and Pete lunged at the door handle, yanking up with all his strength. It didn't budge. He couldn't escape, couldn't get out of the car, out of the garage, away from this madman and his madman's questions. Questions that Pete was afraid to answer.

"The door was padlocked from the outside, Peter," the man said. "Remember that?"

Pete stopped yanking on the door handle and looked out the windshield. The heavy wooden door was down, and he remembered the big padlock holding it closed. He could see it in his mind's eye, red with rust, the hasp screwed clumsily into the wood. The original lock on the door was broken, and somebody had added a hardware store padlock to keep the door closed. To keep out bad people. Guilty people. Car thieves.

"I remember," he breathed. The memory felt heavy, like a cannonball on his chest.

"You couldn't go anywhere," the man said. "I don't even think you know how to drive, do you, Peter?"

Pete shook his head, more confused than ever. Could he drive? They didn't offer driver's ed at the county school, just at the Catholic school that was much too expensive for him to go to. His father didn't even have a car. Sometimes he borrowed a truck from his brother, Pete's uncle. The mechanic. Pete's uncle had a lot of cars and trucks in his yard. Had Pete's father ever borrowed one to teach Pete how to drive?

That wasn't something he could imagine his father doing.

Had he ever driven? He couldn't remember. Did he have any friends with cars that they would let him drive? Did he even have any friends? Surely he did, other kids he rode bikes with, other kids he played with on long summer evenings. Where were they now? Summer, the summer he'd turned sixteen, seemed so very long ago now.

"You just sat in the car, isn't that right, Peter," the man asked kindly. "You listened to the radio. And after a while you got cold."

"Shut up!" Pete shouted at the man. "Just shut up! Let me out of here!"

How long had he been in this car? Why hadn't anyone come looking for him? Didn't they care? Didn't anybody wonder where he was? Why didn't someone come looking for him?

"I can't do that, Peter," the man said sadly. "I can't let you out. Only you can do that."

"*Leave me alone!*" Pete screamed. "*Please, God, just leave me alone! I'm not hurting you!*"

"You've been left alone too long already, Peter," the man's voice was low and calm. "Far too long."

"*Why are you doing this to me?*"

The man didn't seem to hear the question. "You know what happened that night. You got cold and you turned on the car. So you could run the heater. Just for a little while, right? Just until you got warm."

"*Go away!*" Pete shouted. "*You don't have any right to be here! This isn't your car!*"

The man nodded. "You're right, this isn't my car. Like I said, I'm just renting it for the night. But it is the car you tried to steal. I tracked it down, and I brought it back here, to this garage, so that we could have this talk."

The man lifted the gun, pointed it at Pete's head. "Tell me what happened. You sat in the car. With the motor running. In a locked garage. Tell me what happened next."

Pete howled. It felt like he was sicking up his guts, like everything inside him was running out his nose and mouth.

Still speaking softly and calmly, the man repeated. "You know what happened, Peter. I know you remember it now. Say it."

"*I died!*" shrieked the ghost.

"That's right, Peter. You died. Eleven years ago." said the man, putting down the gun on the empty passenger seat. "Now you can go home."

Helping Her Move

Forever, in this case, lasted five weeks
I remember a lopsided smile on her face
Speaking the same words that she always speaks
Of how she had found at long last her place

I thought then, perhaps, and I still think it now
Not so much a thought that it wouldn't last
But a wearisome thought considering how
Surprised she would be it unfolded so fast

It isn't so much that she didn't know
Her history, I think, must provide her some clue
The way that these things invariably go
The things that these men invariably do

She's packing right now, as fast as she can
In boxes she's saved from the last perfect man

What Lola Wants

Originally published in *Switchblade Magazine #11*, October 2019

M y wife and I once had sex in the shower stall of a stranger's apartment while a party was going on outside the bathroom. We had been married for six months and had already found ourselves drifting away from the old crowd, isolated by the sense that we had done something irrevocably adult. The party had been thrown by some friend of a friend, and we both found it dull, and quite suddenly she took me by the hand and led me down the hallway, and there in the bathroom she backed me up against the wall and unzipped my pants.

We leaned against the wall, and she was shockingly wet, her hands gripping me, and I was hard and inside her before I could quite believe that she was doing this, surrounded by stained green tile, her grin speaking silent volumes, and it was over so quick, but she didn't mind, just rearranged her clothes and led me out again.

We left shortly after that, and we never spoke of it, but sometimes I would catch her eye and be certain that she was thinking of that moment and her sudden and absolute conquest of me.

Some mornings I wake up in my bed, that used to be our bed, and I see her twisted between the rails of her own bed, and before I am fully awake and beginning the day's chores, I remember that moment and I think of what I would give to have that again, just one last time.

But this is how we live now.

I wake up before the alarm, every day, and I slip out of my bed to make coffee and light the day's first cigarette. I have few precious minutes, maybe as long as a half hour, to organize the day in my mind. On weekdays I make us some breakfast before I go off to work. While I'm in the kitchen, I hear her waking and getting out of bed. I stay in the kitchen, even though I hate to hear her struggling and I want to help her.

She doesn't want me to help, though, not with that. She's told me that she has to be able to transfer from her bed to her chair by herself, she has to know that she can do that much. As long as she can get to the chair, she's not helpless.

I respect that. I listen hard, in case she really does need me and calls my name, but I let her do that by herself.

She rolls out, and we have breakfast together. I wash the dishes and put them away while she rolls into the living room to log into her computer for the day. She does medical billing, working remotely, and it doesn't pay much, but the hospital has good health benefits. We need those.

Then I go off to work. I sell plumbing fittings, wholesale. I used to be a plumber, back before my wife's accident, so I know my product line. I don't make as much with this job, but I don't have to go out at night any more. I don't like leaving her alone after dark.

Sometimes I do go out, though, in the evenings, for a couple of hours. I'll go out to a bar, have a few drinks. My wife tells me to go out and have a good time, that she'll be fine.

It was a Wednesday in April, one of those raw, cold days that feels like a flashback to February, and I was leaving work for lunch when I saw the kid leaning against my car. He was skinny, in a ratty coat too big for him. I figured he was waiting for the bus, and I was about to ask him politely to move along, when he gave me a big grin.

"Hey, honey," he said. "Miss me?"

I frowned at him, trying to place his face.

His smile was replaced by a theatrical pout. "You don't recognize me, do you?"

And then I did. I'd never seen him dressed as a man before.

"Hi, Lola," I said. "It's been a while."

"Ninety days," he said. "Shoplifting."

"You were in jail?" I asked. I did not like him hanging around my car. I wasn't even sure how he'd found out where I worked.

"Total bullshit," he said. "I didn't do a damn thing. But the idiot PD they gave me told me to plead."

"What are you doing here?" I asked pointedly.

"You know it's cold as shit out here, right?" he shot back. "You wanna maybe get in the car? We could go get a burger or something. You know, for old times' sake?"

"Why are you here?" I repeated, making no move to my car.

He leaned forward. "What's the problem, honey? Scared your buddies might see you with me?"

"I just want to know your business," I said, not wanting to admit how right he was.

I had met him—as Lola—on one of my nights out. We had

162

worked out an arrangement. A strictly business arrangement. I wasn't proud of it, and I had been relieved and disappointed in equal measure when he'd dropped out of sight.

He dropped his voice into the husky whisper he'd used as Lola. "Maybe I just want to suck that fat cock of yours one more time."

"Get out of here," I told him, keeping my voice down with effort. "We're done."

He laughed then, a faggy falsetto laugh. "Or maybe I want to go home with you and meet the wife. We could have such a nice talk, her and I. Girl talk, you know?"

I took a step towards him and my hands made fists before I could stop them. "You leave her out of this."

"Or what?" he asked. "You gonna get all manly and kick my ass? You big butch bruiser, you."

I took a deep breath. "Just tell me what you want."

"I want to get out of this fucking wind," he said. "Come on, man, let's go get a burger. We can talk in the car."

I clicked the fob to unlock the doors. I knew I was making a mistake when I did it, but I gestured for him to get in.

As I pulled out of the lot and turned on the heater he said, "Hey, got a cigarette?"

I handed over my pack. There was a drive-thru a couple of blocks away, and headed that direction.

"My cheerleader uniform got ruined," Lola said in a plume of smoke. "When I got sent up, this fat-ass queen where I was staying decided to go through my shit and ripped the seams trying to stuff into it. Can you believe that shit? And my silver wig is gone. Just gone. Faggots, man, they'll steal anything."

"You got a new place to stay?" I asked. I didn't care, I was just trying to make conversation.

"Yeah, I'm at this lame halfway house. All kinds of rules in that place. I got to get a straight job so they'll let me move out," he said.

Despite myself, I had a sudden and uncomfortably vivid memory of his mouth on me. When dressed up Lola didn't look like a woman, not exactly, he was too exaggerated, too much a caricature. His face was painted almost clown-like, eyelashes a half inch long, powdered cheeks, lips painted fire engine red. I remembered him on his knees, applying lipstick before he... did what I paid him for.

"Is that what you need?" I asked. "A job?"

"I need to get my life together, man," He stubbed out his cigarette and lit another from my pack. "I don't want to end up like those old queens, turning tricks in bus station toilets. I'm off the weed, I'm gonna get my GED. I just need, you know, a little hand up."

"You can use me as a reference," I said, "to get a job."

We reached the drive-thru, and I ordered us two meals. I didn't bother asking him for money for his, I just paid for both.

He attacked his burger and fries like he thought I'd take it away from him if he didn't eat it fast enough. I pulled into a spot at the back of the lot and ate mine a little more leisurely.

He wiped ketchup off his lips with his thumb and again I remembered his mouth. I looked out the window.

"I can ask around," I offered. "See if anyone is hiring."

"I got a gig lined up," he said. "This guy I met inside offered me a job. Installing vinyl floors. You know that stuff that looks like wood, but it's really just plastic strips? He pays by the job, and I could make decent money."

"That sounds good." I finished up my burger and wadded up the paper. I hadn't turned off the car, so I just put it in reverse and pulled out.

"You gonna eat your fries?" he asked.

I handed them over.

"The thing is," he said, mouth full, "I need six hundred bucks. Like, for tools and this class and shit."

"Oh." I should have seen it coming.

"So I was thinking maybe you could loan me the money and I'll pay you back once I'm working," he said, his tone deliberately casual, like six hundred dollars was no big deal.

"I haven't got that kind of money," I said bluntly. "I sell faucets, okay? My wife is paralyzed. We're just barely scraping by."

"I could be really nice to you." In Lola's voice. I hated myself for the thrill that sent down my spine.

We were back at the warehouse. I slammed my car into a parking space. By the dashboard clock, my lunch was over in four minutes.

"I haven't got it," I said.

He looked at me.

"So get it," he smiled at me. "Or I have a chat with your wife."

There was something cold and primal in his eyes, something I had never seen before.

I had known Lola was a mask, a false face he'd put on to fool the world into thinking he was something alluring and harmless, but I saw now that the scrawny kid whom I'd seen leaning on my car was a mask, too. I caught a glimpse of the predator underneath all the masks, the real man behind the lipstick and powder.

It scared me.

"Think about it, okay?" he said. "I'll be in touch."

And he was out the door.

I made it back inside in time, but just barely.

When I got home that night my wife apologized for not having dinner ready, Her hips had been bothering her, and she hadn't felt up to it. I told her not to worry about it and started some ground turkey browning on the stove.

"Is something wrong?" my wife asked.

"Just work," I told her. "Nothing important."

Lola let me stew for five days.

Over the weekend I took my wife to the mall, pushing her chair through the weekend crowds to the multiplex where we saw some movie I don't remember at all and after that to dinner that was pricier than I was comfortable with. I smiled, though, and I did what I could to make her happy. That was what was important, making her happy.

No matter what it cost.

On Monday, Lola was back, leaning on my car again at lunch time. This day was warm, spring having returned with a vengeance. He was in a sleeveless T-shirt and skinny jeans.

"Well?" he asked airily, "Can you help me or do I go talk to the missus?"

"I can help you," I said, "But I want you to do something for me."

"Sure, honey," he smiled. His lips weren't as pretty without paint. "Anything you like."

"I want the usual, and I want Lola," I said. I lowered my voice. "Understand? I want you to be my girl. You still got your red dress, or did they take that, too?"

"I still got my red dress," he purred, "and for six hundred you get the royal treatment. When do you want it?"

"Tomorrow night," I said. "After work. Six o'clock at the Harvest Inn. I'll meet you in the bar. This is the last time. After this, we're done."

"If that's the way you feel about it, baby." he said in Lola's voice.

165

Whatever Lola Wants

My wife had dinner ready when I got home, lasagna and peas, both microwaved. I told her that I was going out with friends from work the next evening and that I wouldn't be home for dinner.

She agreed to that easily, as I knew she would, and suggested going for a drive that weekend, and seeing some local wineries. We hadn't done that since her accident, but she said that she'd checked on-line and had a list of places that said they were wheelchair accessible. The weather was supposed to be beautiful.

I told her that it sounded like fun, and she smiled like Christmas morning.

I had problems sleeping that night.

Lola. I didn't even know his real goddamned name. He'd been named that by some older queen. He hadn't even known about the Kinks song until I told him. Increasingly, though, it hadn't been Ray Davies I had heard when I thought that name, but Gwen Verdon's song in *Damn Yankees*.

"Whatever Lola wants
Lola gets..."

I had never tried to pretend that I thought he was a real girl. He never tried to pass, not seriously. He was a walking pinup, a parody of a woman, a pose that concealed—not very convincingly—a contempt for actual females.

It was that artifice that I had found irresistible. It was like... it was like I wasn't cheating, because Lola wasn't a real person. In fishnets and paint and ridiculous falsies, he'd made himself into a cartoon.

The only part of him that was real was the hot, wet cavern of his mouth. I'd look down past the wig and eyelashes and lipstick to where I was entering that mouth.

"You can't get that from your wife," he always said, afterwards, not knowing how true, in my case, that was. I'd never told him anything personal about myself, but somehow he'd found out where I worked, and probably where I lived.

Even if I'd had six hundred dollars to give him, I knew it wouldn't stop there. Once he knew I'd pay, he'd find something else to ask me for, some other "loan." I had to stop him, and I had to stop him now.

Make up your mind to have no regrets, I told myself, and at last I was able to sleep.

The next day I was in the bar at the Harvest Inn, at a back corner table, by five-thirty, nursing a beer. Lola came in at ten minutes after six, making a splash as he always did. He really had pulled out all the stops tonight, a blonde wig that looked new, the red dress I remembered, bodice bulging with stuffing, high heeled boots, fishnets.

Everybody stared as he made his way across the bar to my table.

Good. They were staring at him. Nobody was going to be able to remember what I looked like.

"Don't sit down," I said softly. "Room sixteen. Head on down there, I'll follow you in a minute."

The painted face pouted. "Oh, are you shy?" He extended a red-nailed hand. "I need the key."

I shook my head. "It's open."

It would be, too. I'd taped the latch after I climbed in through the window. Rooms at the Harvest Inn had doors that opened into the parking lot, not an internal hallway. Number sixteen was at the far end of the lot, and there weren't any cars parked close to it.

Hotel records would show that room as vacant, and the only camera in the whole place was in the lobby, over the cash register. I hadn't been near the lobby.

I gave Lola ten minutes by the clock over the bar. I finished my beer and left the empty glass and a dollar tip on the table. On the way across the lot, I pulled on my gloves. Mechanics gloves, heavy and waterproof.

He was sitting on the bed when I walked in, demurely, knees together and skirt pulled down. The drapes were closed and the only light was from the bathroom.

I closed the door behind me and took two steps, half crossing the tiny room.

"Got my money?" He asked in his Lola voice.

"You first," I said. "You know what I want."

He slid gracefully off the bed and onto his knees. "You got a lollipop for Lola?"

As his red nails touched my , I reached up for the pipe I'd laid on top of the TV when I'd broken into the room.

Three quarter inch black iron by thirteen inches long. A piece of scrap left over from a customer's custom cut order. No one would miss it, and there was no way to trace it back to me.

Lola never had the chance to scream. My first blow knocked his blonde wig off and tumbled him against the bed. I hit him again on the side of the head, and he fell limp as a rag doll.

I followed him down to the floor and made sure of the job. My first blows had the strength of fear and rage behind them. Now I worked methodically, like I hammering an inlet valve free of a rusted-out boiler. His head was pulp when I was done. There was no movement in his chest, no pulse in his wrists.

No more Lola.

I shoved the body under the bed and tossed the pipe in after it. In the bathroom mirror I checked myself and washed the blood off, then wiped the sink clean.

There was a wet stain by the foot of the bed, but it would dry and the carpet was one of those splotchy brown and green patterns designed to hide stains. With luck it, would be days before someone rented this room and found the body.

On the way home, I changed my shirt and threw my gloves and shirt away in a dumpster behind a Chinese restaurant.

That weekend I took my wife on a long drive through the country. We found a winery up on the bluffs that could accommodate her chair and took the tour. She had some samples and got flushed, her eyes shining like they used to, so long ago.

They had outside seating for lunch, and we sat together on a deck high above the river, in the sunlight and the open air.

She reached across and took my hand. "Thank you," she said, "this is lovely."

"Anything for you," I told her.

And I meant it.

Sunrise Is Another Country

Sunrise is another country
A place I've heard of, but not been
Beyond the sky, beyond the sea
Inhabited by different men

They don't speak my language there
A dialect of future tense
Their words are made for different air
The things they say there don't make sense

In their land they know things unknown
They see things that here are out of sight
What's living here over there is bone
Beyond the borderland of night

And yet, each day, despite all pains
They invade, and drag us there in chains

A Cup of Kindness

Originally published in *Haunted Yuletide*, December 2020

K arin had broken up with him a week before Christmas.

At that moment, full of sick anger and pain, he had thrown the bracelet he had bought for her, which had cost him more than he could comfortably afford, at her before he had stormed out.

Later he regretted that. He could have returned it. Later still he accused her, in his mind, of timing the breakup with the expectation that he would make such a grand—and expensive—gesture.

He wouldn't ask for it back. He knew it, and he knew that she knew it. By the time the wounds she'd made in his soul had scabbed over enough to brave that conversation, she would have sold it, he was sure. It was gone, gone like everything else he had given her, the money, the gifts, the last year of his life.

All gone.

And yet Christmas, truth to tell, hadn't been *that* bad. He'd driven up to see his parents and their response to Karin's conspicuous absence had been gentle sympathy and—he suspected—a bit of relief. They'd never liked her much.

His kid sister had been too focused on her pregnancy to comment on Karin's absence or even notice it. She had her new husband in tow, a burly former football player turned boat salesman, and every topic of conversation had to be turned to how it would affect the baby, as if anyone could forget that she held in her belly the winning ticket in the first grandchild sweepstakes.

The day had been surprisingly relaxing. The boat salesman—not a bad guy, all things considered—had talked football with father, and kid sister had talked prenatal vitamins with mother. He ate too much and let the familiar surroundings lull him back in time to a place where Karin had never existed.

So that was Christmas, and he got through it okay, just fine, no problem.

But now it was New Year's Eve.

He had made reservations for the *best* party, the one that all Karin's friends would be attending. More money he'd never get back. Of course he wouldn't go there. Even if Karin weren't there, all her friends would be—rich kids comparing vacation tans and graduation present BMWs. But she *would* be there, he was sure, wearing that electric blue dress that clung to her body like a coat of enamel and made her look too perfect to be real. She would be there, dancing with the boys and chatting up her next sucker.

He hadn't made any plans, thinking, hey, *I'm twenty-six, that's practically thirty years old. I don't have to prove I'm old enough to drink anymore. I'm a grownup, I can stay home and go to bed early. I've seen clocks hit midnight before, it's no big deal.*

And that worked up until 8pm on the 31st of December. Then, sitting alone in his apartment—it had always been *his* place, never *their* place; they had talked about moving in together, but had never been able to find a place that she could accept and he could afford—he knew that if he didn't get out of there something bad was going to happen.

Not front page of the newspaper bad, just painfully humiliating bad, involving calling Karin and leaving messages either begging her to take him back or screaming at her that she was a horrible bitch, or most likely both.

It was his fear that he was turning into *that* guy—worse, his horror at the thought that Karin had *turned him into that guy*—that forced him out into the brutal cold in search of escape.

He could have gone looking for people he knew, but he frankly wasn't up to explaining that no, Karin isn't with me, and yes, we broke up, and no, I didn't break up with her, she broke up with me, and yes, you were right along, the bitch was poison...

Nope, not going to go there. He lived in a major metropolitan area, home to millions of people, and it was the busiest party night of the year, so surely there would be some place he could go that would be full of lights and music and friendly people and booze...

You'd think so, anyway.

Mile after mile of packed parking lots guarded by men in layers of coats and cardboard signs. Parking 5$. Parking 10$. Others where the men had fled inside, leaving bigger signs saying LOT FULL.

And the bars with lines outside, people shivering in the cold.

He ended up in an American Legion hall, lured in by the promise of NO COVER and CHAMPANE TOAST.

He parked in the lot—three pickup trucks and two motorcycles that must belong to yetis, since surely nothing human could be riding

A Cup of Kindness

a bike in this weather—and went inside. The front hall was wide and empty. He shook the salt off his shoes. Snow had been threatened all week, but never materialized. It was too cold for snow.

A broad curving staircase took up most of the entrance. He went around it and saw a pair of double doors with plastic sheeting taped over them and a hand-lettered sign that said, "Closed for renovation."

Up the stairs, then.

At the top of the staircase was a big open space that looked kind of like a high school gym. A half-dozen folding tables ringed by folding chairs had been set up randomly in the space, each with a cluster of balloons. Against one wall was a raised stage area, empty. Music played through the space, that Madonna song that was everywhere. Thankfully at low volume.

A big man in biker leathers sat on a folding chair at the doorway to the big open area, reading a battered paperback book. The biker glanced up with a face that was massively scarred by an old burn. An equally scarred hand waved towards the open area, and without speaking the ravaged face bent back to the book.

At first, the big space looked empty. It wasn't, not quite; there was a bar in one corner of the room with some figures clustered around it.

He walked over, feeling awkward and out of his element. The girl at the end of the bar was slim and blonde and looked too young to be in a bar. He hoped that the plastic cup in front of her just held soda. Her hair was so pale that it was almost white and hung straight as a ruler around her face.

Next to her was a woman of maybe thirty, her hair the same white-blonde color as the girl's, but wild and curly. She was voluptuously curved and packed into jeans and a T-shirt just a little too tight to contain her body's generous curves.

Past her was an old woman, stooped and wrinkled, her hair in a bone-white braid down her back. She was knitting, something long and tangled, made of bright red yarn that sparkled like it was sprinkled with glitter.

"Hi," he said. Nervously he added, "This isn't a private party, is it?"

The old woman cackled at that. "Hardly," she said.

"Open to everyone," the woman in the middle said, her voice low and with a seductive edge to it.

The girl just ducked her head, a shy smile on her face.

"So... how do I get a drink?"

The girl gestured at the bar. "Help yourself."

Sitting on the bar were several bottles of booze and soda and a bucket of ice.

Moving cautiously, in case the offer had been a joke, he mixed a drink—plastic cup, a couple of ice cubes, a splash of some obscure store brand whiskey, and the rest from a bottle marked simply, Cola.

"Thanks," he said. He looked around for a jar for tips or donations, didn't see one.

As if reading his mind, the woman in the middle said, "Your money's no good here. Drink up."

He raised the cup to his lips and took a sip. Not bad. He suddenly realized that all three women were watching him intently, identical smiles on their faces. They looked like they were waiting for him to notice the plastic bug frozen in one of the ice cubes or something.

He finished his swallow and smiled back, a little uncertainly. "Thanks," he repeated.

"We dance at midnight," the girl said brightly.

"Sounds like fun."

A laugh from the woman in the middle, deep and erotic. "Oh... you have no idea." At that, the old woman cackled again. "Perhaps you'll dance with me," she said.

He took another sip of the drink, feeling even more uncomfortable. "Sure," he said. "I'm not much of a dancer, though."

"You will be," the old woman said, suddenly looking very seriously. "When the time comes. You were born to dance with me... but not now. Not this year."

"I'll just, uh..." He waved at one of the empty tables.

Smiling and nodding, he took his cup to the table and had a seat, making a show of looking around the nearly empty ballroom. An effort had been made to decorate it, paper streamers and balloons were taped to the walls. A banner read, "Happy New Year," all the vowels wearing top hats.

Better than drinking alone in his apartment? It was was a tough call. But maybe more people would show up—people who weren't quite so... odd. It was still early.

He sipped his drink, and it was suddenly empty, just amber ice cubes. Just as suddenly, he realized that he didn't want another bad enough to brave the trio at the bar. He shook an ice cube into his mouth to chew on, and—

Someone was sitting across from him at the table.

It was that quick. Nobody there, a glance at the bar, and then somebody was. An older man, a buzzcut of gray hair, unhealthy looking, too thin.

He sputtered, started to say something.

"Shut up," the old man said. "I haven't got much time."

What the hell? Was the American Legion hosting a New Year's Eve party for some mental institution?

"Ya gotta leave Karin alone," the old man said.

"*What?*"

"Leave her alone. Don't call her, don't go by her place, do everything you can to avoid crossing paths with her—*ever.* You got that?"

"Who are you?"

"Who the hell do you think I am? Listen to me—I just *died.* Went code blue and flatlined. In about five minutes, some prison doctor is going to be cracking open my ribs to fondle my heart. I'm staring down the barrel of eternity here, and I went all in to come back and talk to you, so you better listen up."

"Uh..."

The face across the table from him was disturbingly familiar. Older, yes, much older. Maybe sixty? The skin was a sickly jaundiced color, dry patches around the mouth cracked and raw. He was in a gray uniform of some kind that hung on him like a sack.

"You can't let her screw up your life, boy," the old man went on, his voice quivering with intensity. "This is the time, right now, when you can change things. You can avoid making my mistake."

"Which was...?" He took a long drink from the plastic cup, not even registering that it had been empty a moment ago.

"*Karin!*" the old man shouted. "She was my mistake. Walk away, man, just walk away. You see her coming, you cross the street to get away from her. I..." his voice broke. "I didn't do that. But you gotta. Promise me, man."

"Wait... prison?"

"You picked up on that, huh?" A wry grin that showed gums devoid of any teeth. "Yeah, prison. It all started with her. Violating a restraining order, yeah, I'll cop to that. But the rest of it was

174

bullshit. The assault was just her word against mine, and the judge was golf buddies with Karin's dad. Didn't even look at the evidence."

The old man looked away, sighed. "Then... more shit inside. Stupid shit. I figured I could make some money, you know, for when I got out. Only I never got out." The eyes tracked back to his face, the stare piercing. "I *died* in there. Just now. Or... maybe thirty years from now. Depends on where you're sitting, I guess."

"Thirty years?" It seemed like all he could do was repeat random words from the old man's ravings.

"Thirty years. Life, as it turned out."

He took another long drink, the plastic cup full again, and looked at the old man across the table from him. That gray outfit could be a prison uniform, he supposed. "So... I'm supposed to believe that you're me? My... *ghost*? From thirty years in the future?"

"Yeah, you wanna put it like that," a dry chuckle. "*Ghost.* Yeah, I guess that's the word. Don't got a bedsheet—they don't give us sheets in max."

"Because of Karin?"

"Because *I wouldn't stay away* from Karin," another sigh, this one like air escaping a slashed tire. "You know, I can't even remember her face now. But when I was your age—hell, when I was *you*—I kept after her. I got stupid. And she screwed me. She screwed me good."

"So... what, you're from the year 2020?"

"Not quite. 2019. Missed 2020 by a couple hours. But, yeah, that's when I died."

"What's it like?"

A bark of bitter laughter. "Not that great a view from the exercise yard, you know?" A sigh. "Hell, the world was supposed to end a couple of times, but it didn't. Right at the turn of the century there was a big computer glitch that was supposed to shut down civilization. Then some Arab assholes flew a couple of planes into the twin towers in New York. Bunch of wars. Lots of new computer stuff, video games and shit, but we're not living on Mars or anything. When you're inside, man, nothing really changes."

"But..."

"You want me to tell you what stocks to buy, boy? I got one thing to say, man. *One thing.* You got that? Stay away from Karin—stay right the hell away from her. The rest of the shit, you can figure that out for yourself."

The old woman from the bar touched the old man on the shoulder and said, "It's time."

Without a backward glance the old man got up from the table and took her in his arms and there was music playing, an old, old song...

"For auld lang syne, my dearest,
for auld lang syne,
we'll drink a cup of kindness yet,
for auld lang syne."

They danced slow, the old woman's long braid swaying gently down her back, and she was in gown that brushed the floor and shimmered like water in sunlight, and then a bell was ringing, a church bell, the sound deep and somehow heavy, the weight of the world tolling, *one* and *two* and *three* and somewhere far beyond the ringing of that great bell there were shouts and car horns honking.

His eyes snapped open. He'd fallen asleep on his couch, a half-full bottle of whiskey on the floor beside him, the TV chattering something over a video a balloons sailing fuzzily into the night, and outside his neighbors were whooping and hollering.

Midnight. January 1st, 1990. A new decade. A new start.

He got up and stretched, picked up the bottle and carried it into the kitchen, put it firmly away in the cupboard above the stove. The commotion outside was dying down, the drunks running out of steam and the realization settling in that it was too damned cold to be outside yelling like a lunatic.

In the kitchen, he took down his old calendar and put up the new one—helpfully provided by the gas company. In the kitchen drawer, he found a thick marker and wrote across the map of January in big letters.

RESOLVED: Never see Karin again.

And he never did.

Drive In Movie

Look, just don't near that place
I don't care if there's holes in the fence
It's the scene of a horrible murder case
Still unsolved—what are you, dense?

Did you notice the row of dolls on the shelf?
They're all looking at you with ominous eyes
Fine, I'm leaving, stay here by yourself
What happens next can't be a surprise

What part of "haunted" don't you apprehend?
For Christ's sake, the walls are starting to bleed
Believe me, I'm telling you this as a friend
Forget the mystery, it's an exit you need

Okay, if you're staying I'll stick to you like glue
But don't say I didn't warn you

We Pass From View

Originally published in *Sins Of The Past*, October 2014

Josef Naamaire directed 47 films, beginning with *The Congo Gunman* in 1955 and ending with *Mission: Asteroid* in 1974. All of his films were made for B-movie mill Spectacular Studios, mostly produced by Hymie Greenbaum. While several of his movies—notably *Hellcats In High Heels* (1964), and *The Room Without A Door* (1966)—enjoyed a brief cult status for what were, for the time, shockingly explicit scenes of lesbianism, Naamaire is best known for a film that, it is said, no living person has ever seen.

We Pass From View was filmed in July and August of 1963, with principal photography on location in what is now Wildwood Canyon Park, outside of Burbank, CA. The script was based on the book of the same name, written by a young man named Michael Chase, who would go on to found the cult Clear Vision World. Chase and his followers—including four children—were brutally murdered on April 23, 1982, by persons unknown.

How Chase's book became the basis of a Spectacular film is an interesting story in itself. In 1961, Robert Sterling, at the time the chairman of the studio's board of directors, made arrangements to purchase the film rights for the entire catalog of the paperback original publisher Cupid's Bow Press. As a condition of the purchase, Spectacular was required to film *We Pass From View*. It is believed that this unusual clause was made a condition of the deal by Cubid's Bow publisher Sabrina Erikovitch, who went on to join Michael Chase's organization and eventually die with him.

Since Cupid's Bow owned the rights to the popular *Code Name: Hangman* spy thriller series, Sterling agreed to the terms, and gave studio staff writer Robin Wilde the task of converting Chase's book into a screenplay. (Spectacular went on to film six *Code Name: Hangman* movies, which were among the studio's most lucrative films.)

No known copies of Michael Chase's original book exist. By all accounts, it did not sell—only one edition was printed, and the majority of it was likely sent back to be pulped. Robin Wilde, in a letter to his longtime companion actress Ellie Vance called it "this unreadable pile of shit."

An Atlas of Bad Roads

Even Cupid's Bow catalog is uncharacteristically terse. *We Pass From View* appears in only one edition, Fall, 1960. The entry reads: "A fascinating look at the myths and realities surrounding death and dying, by professor of philosophy Dr. Michael Chase." Michael Chase, it should be noted, often claimed a doctorate, sometimes in physics, sometimes in philosophy, however there are no records of him completing an advanced degree at any of the schools that he claimed to have attended.

Faced with the daunting task of transforming a "look at the myths and realities surrounding death and dying," fascinating or otherwise, into a screenplay suitable for the drive-in movie market, Wilde chose to pen a tale of a group of college students who go camping in the woods and die from mysterious causes, one by one. (It will be remembered that Wilde is also responsible for the screenplay of Spectacular's "adaptation" of Baudelaire's *Flowers Of Evil* that contained, among other things, vegetable creatures from Venus who had come to Earth to harvest human males' "vital fluids.")

Since neither the book nor the screenplay is available for comparison, the question of how faithful the latter is to the former must remain unanswered. Given what we do know of both works, however, the probable answer is "not very."

There is, however, one section of the screenplay that seems to have been lifted directly from Chase's book. Shortly before her death from bone cancer in 1987, Bette Blowe (born Elizabeth Tucker), the lead actress in *We Pass From View* and Josef Naamaire's wife, was interviewed in Playboy magazine. While most of the article is concerned with her claims that she carried on numerous homosexual affairs with various female celebrities, towards the end of the interview she was asked about *We Pass From View* and the film's alleged effect on the test audiences. Her reply follows:

"It was that fucking Appendix B. They made me read the whole thing aloud. Robin refused to transcribe it—he just told me to read it out of the book. He said Bob [Sterling] told him that had to be in the movie. That's the part that made everybody go apeshit. It was bad. I don't remember what it said—I don't remember reading it at all. It was like I was in a trance. But I know it was some serious bad shit. Joe didn't let anybody watch the dailies of that scene, he just shipped it straight off."

We Pass From View

It was a very small crew who traveled to the campsite north of Burbank to film *We Pass From View*. Most accounts report that Naamaire operated the cameras himself (he had begun his film career as a camera operator and frequently chose to run the cameras, both to keep costs low and to control the specifics of his shots.) The sound technician was one Greg Donnely, who committed suicide in May of 1970. It is likely, although employment records are unclear, that Alice Monroe served as assistant director on the film. She worked with Naamaire on many of his other films, and at least one account of the location shooting refers to "Alice" setting marks during the shoot. Alice Monroe died in September of 1968, also a suicide. Although there were almost certainly other crew members, no one else associated with the location shooting has been identified.

The cast was also small. In addition to Bette Blowe (first billed on the released material), Ellie Vance (billed as Esther Vance for contractual reasons), Eve Eden, Neville Brook, and Hank Renck comprised the company. Bette Blowe's sole published remarks regarding the film are referenced above. Neville Brook is on record threatening the life of a reporter who asked him about the film. None of the other cast members are believed to have commented about the film in print at all.

Eve Eden vanished without a trace in late 1965. She had reportedly incurred very large debts to Las Vegas casinos, and it is believed that she either vanished to avoid her creditors or was murdered by them and her body hidden. Rumors have circulated regarding her reappearance since then, but none have been confirmed.

All of the other cast members are now dead.

Ellie Vance was murdered in February of 1972 by Robin Wilde, who then killed himself.

Hank Renck died of complications from syphilis in November of 1975.

Neville Brook was found in a hotel room in Tijuana, in June of 1980, shot in the head. The case is still unsolved.

At the time that the following interview was conducted, January 17th, 2014, Josef Naamaire was the only living person who could be reliably placed at the campsite north of Burbank during the filming of *We Pass From View*. He was 83 years old, and had recently been diagnosed with late stage pancreatic cancer. He would die within the month, on February 12th.

The interview was conducted by Aaron Tellman, a graduate student in film history at UCLA. Naamaire was residing at the time in a managed care facility in Anaheim, CA. Tellman contacted the notoriously reclusive Naamaire without much hope that permission for an interview would be granted. The director agreed to talk, however. It is likely that news of his impending death induced him to tell his story.

The transcript that follows is unedited:

Aaron Tellman: I really can't tell you how much this means to me, Mr. Naamaire. I am a huge fan of your body of work, and—

Josef Naamaire: Save the bullshit, son. I'm a dead man, I don't have time for it.

AT: Okay, let's get to the point. Your career includes—

JN: I said save the bullshit. I've waited fifty years to tell this story. Are you going to record it or not?

AT: I am recording, sir. See?

JN: That's a recorder? Damn, and we used to lug around those monster reel-to-reels. That little thing's going to get all this?

AT: Every word.

JN: It better. I'm not saying this twice.

AT: I can play it back and show you.

JN: Naw, you say it's working, it's on your head. Now, tell me what you think you know about *We Pass From View*.

AT: It was your nineteenth film for Spectacular. It had a very limited release in the winter of 1963, and no copies are believed to exist.

JN: That's it? I thought you were a movie guy.

AT: That's all that's known for sure.

JN: But they still talk about it, right? What happened in Topeka and St. Louis?

AT: There are rumors.

JN: So spill, already. I don't want to waste time with shit you already know. Give me the Weekly World version. What do you think you know?

AT: Rumors are that the film had a bad effect on the audiences who saw it. There were riots at the theaters, and Spectacular had the film destroyed.

JN: Riots? Son, in St. Louis a man ate his little girl. Clawed her chest open and swallowed her heart. His own daughter. Because of a movie I made.

AT: That's... extreme.

JN: You don't believe me. This was the sixties, boy. No internet. No Twitter, no cell phones with cameras. In those days, you had the money, you got things silenced. Heck, St. Louis was the easy one. Old mob town, you know? They're used to making things go away. Topeka was something else... Hymie had to sell his soul to get that one squashed. That's the whole reason we started doing the skin flicks, to pay back favors.

AT: How does watching a movie make someone do... something like that?

JN: Damned if I know, son. Damned if I know. Something in that book. Some kind of evil magic spell. That picture was cursed, you could feel it.

AT: You knew there was something wrong when you made it?

JN: Not at first. Oh, there were problems from the get-go. But they were the usual problems. The script was crap. Robin could do good work—he could do damn fine work when he was sober. But he wasn't ever sober. This one was worse than usual. Neville was a problem, but he was always a problem. Reefer and opium mixed, and I never did find his stash. We're living in tents, and he figured out someplace to hide his dope where I couldn't find it. You seen those zombie movies everybody's making now? That was Neville after noon, the walking goddamned dead. Hank, God bless the man, big, pretty, dumb as a box of rocks, all the heart in the world, but he couldn't remember two words in a row if they weren't written on his hand. And then there was Bette and Eve.

AT: Bette and Eve?

JN: They had just... become an item. Hooked up. Whatever you want to call it. Those kids were all over each other, and we didn't have a lot of privacy, you know?

We Pass From View

Hell, even Hank picked up on it.

AT: So you knew?

JN: Of course I knew. I knew she was a dyke
when I married her. Sorry, ain't supposed
to say "dyke" any more. Lesbian. Person of
woman-identifiedness. Whatever. She never
lied to me, we were always honest with
each other. Back then, it was all about
keeping up appearances. Out in public, we
were the perfect couple. After hours, she
had her girls, and I had mine. That's why
she wanted to do all those "girls behind
bars" pictures, you know? It let her be
herself on film. Everybody in the industry
knew, we just kept it out of the papers.
Like I say, keeping things out of the
papers was a lot easier back then.

AT: Drugs, sex, those were the usual problems?

JN: The movie business is as crazy as roller
skates for snakes, always has been, ever
since Tesla invented the damned thing. Too
much pressure, too much money, everybody's
a prima donna, and you're all working way
too many hours in a day. Shit that'd get
you fired from any other job is just
business as usual in Hollywood. These days
are just the same, take my word for it.
Folks just had to learn to be more
discrete.

AT: But you said that picture was cursed. More
than just the usual problems.

JN: Yeah. Yeah, it was. I don't know... it was
fifty years ago. I don't remember all that
clearly any more, what I knew at the time,

184

what I figured out later. Hell, some of it I maybe made up over the years. Some things, son, they give you nightmares for the rest of your life. After awhile, you can't tell the difference between the nightmare and what really happened.

AT: What do you remember?

JN: At first, it was just a monster movie. Robin's script didn't ever show a monster, everything happened off-screen. Kids around a campfire, one of them goes off to piss, you hear a scream, then you find a body. Shot it with a day for night filter so we didn't need to rig lights. Hot as hell with that campfire. August in the desert, you know. I don't think Hank even packed a shirt. I'd get Neville's dialog in the morning, because I knew he'd be nodding off all afternoon. Trying to keep the girls separated. All the time, I got to keep to the schedule. That space-woman movie, *Gravity*, they said he took three years to make it. In my day, three weeks was a long shoot.

AT: A lot of stress.

JN: That's the business. You work your ass off and then you blow off steam and then you go back and do it again. Anyway, we'd send off the dailies, and most of the time that was it. They only said something if there was a problem.

AT: And there was a problem?

JN: Yeah. Got a message from Hymie to make sure that the crew was staying out of the way, because there was a strange shadow in a couple of the shots. Now, remember, we're shooting day for night in August, in the woods. The whole frame is nothing but shadows. I've got the two darkest filters we own stuck on with gaffer's tape, and I'm trusting the lab to make it work. If there's a shadow that shouldn't be there, it's on their end. Besides, all the crew I've got is me, Alice, and some union putz running sound.

AT: Alice Monroe was there, then.

JN: Of course she was there. She was my AD on every picture I made, up until she died. God, that hit me harder than when Bette died. Alice was... well, she should have been listed as director on half of my pictures. More. But in those days, girls didn't direct. Hell, even now there ain't many, and they're all indies. The old boys club never dies. Equal rights is for on the screen, not behind the camera.

AT: You, Alice Monroe, and Greg Donnely. That was the crew?

JN: Greg Donnely? Was that his name? I don't know, maybe. I just called him dickhead. He thought he needed an air-conditioned trailer and a twenty minute break after every shot. He knew how to run a boom, though, I'll give him that. Never saw him or his shadow through the viewfinder. Alice, of course, she was always right behind me.

AT: But the shadow?

JN: I told Hymie that it wasn't on my end, check with the lab. He sent me a still. It was a shot of Bette, Neville, Eve, and Hank. Ellie was out of the picture by then, she did her death scene and went back home. Anyway, you got the four of them sitting on this log by the campfire. Eve's talking, she's got her mouth open. And standing behind them there's this... shadow. It's like a man all in black, just standing there, looking down at them. You can see he's got his arm's crossed, and you can almost see his face. It's like he's listening to what Eve is saying.

AT: What did you think?

JN: First off I thought, that man is standing on my grave. That picture bothered me in a way I can't explain. Knowing what I know now, just thinking about it makes my blood run cold. At the time, though, I figured it was a double exposure. Spectacular bought film as cheap as possible, and some of it was spoiled. I knew that figure wasn't anything that I had shot, so I guessed the last can I'd used had been partially exposed before it got to me. Either that, or the lab was dicking around. This was before photoshop, remember, everything we did on film had to be done optically.

AT: What did you do?

JN: I asked Hymie if he wanted me to reshoot those scenes. He said no, of course. Reshooting costs money. So we kept going.

AT: You kept on schedule.

JN: Heh. Beat the schedule. If I remember right, we had thirteen days, and we did it in eleven. Maybe ten. We were supposed to go home Sunday afternoon, and we packed it in Friday night. All of us just wanted to get gone from there. The mood at that campsite... it got ugly. Everybody was on edge. The heat, the bugs, eating box lunches three meals a day. We hated that mountain, and we started to hate each other. Neville just about tore Hank's head off one day, over nothing, I can't even remember what started the fight. Punching Hank was like kicking a puppy, the kid was a big old teddy bear. There was just so much tension out there. And things kept moving around.

AT: What kind of things?

JN: Personal things. Neville was reading a book, I think it was Jack Kerouac. One morning it wasn't where he left it, and we find it later that day stuck in a tree. The girl's clothes... Bette had this blouse, it was blue silk. She looked dynamite in it. I got it for her in Mexico. She loved that blouse. Anyway, it goes missing, and she thought Eve took it—which was nuts, they shared a tent, so where was Eve going to try to hide it? We found it on the ground a couple of days later, covered in the most revolting slime you can imagine. Like... goose shit or something. Only there weren't any geese up there. Wasn't much of anything up there. I remember that. I mean, sure it's the desert, you don't expect Bambi and Thumper. Still, it was way too quiet on that mountain. I don't remember seeing a single bird, or a lizard, or anything. Alice made jokes about camping on an old Indian burial ground, but she wasn't really joking. The place felt wrong, and it got worse the longer we were there. When I said I wanted to wrap up early, everybody was on board with it.

AT: What happened when you got back?

JN: I went to Mexico. Bob Sterling had a house in Vera Cruz. I think it was his brother's or his cousin's or something. I took this dancer who was between shows, and we sat on the beach and drank rum for a week.

AT: You didn't edit *We Pass From View*?

JN: Never even saw it.

AT: You directed it. You shot it.

JN: Yeah, but I never watched it straight through.

AT: You never watched your own movie?

JN: Never seen most of them. Do I look like Steve Spielberg to you? Spec made movies the way Ford makes cars—on an assembly line. No such thing as creative control at a place like that. They give me a list of shots, I shoot 'em, wrap 'em up, give 'em to the gofer to drive back to the studio.

AT: And at the studio?

JN: They splice 'em together. Shot one, shot two, shot three, all the way to the closing credits.

AT: So nobody ever watched the movie straight through before it was released?

JN: I didn't say that.

AT: Then who saw it?... Who—

JN: I heard you the first time, boy. You got anything to drink on you?

AT: Drink?

JN: Booze, boy. You got a bottle stashed in that snazzy coat?

AT: Uh... no. Sorry.

JN: Didn't think so. You know you look queer, son? That's a good thing, these days. To get anywhere in the industry these, days you gotta be queer or at least look queer. It used to be all showgirls, now it's those muscle boys with their silly-assed hair.

AT: That's interesting. Do you remember—

JN: Dave Cohen and Sharri Long. It had to be them, on account of what happened later.

AT: What happened?

JN: It didn't happen right away. Not like the other screenings. They waited to the weekend. They were married, not to each other, to other people. I don't know if they had a thing going first or it was all from... what they saw.

AT: What happened?

JN: Maybe if you shut up for a second I'll tell you. Damn, I need a drink. You can't get a drink in this damned place. You can get morphine but no whiskey. How does that make sense?

AT: ...

JN: You figured out how to shut up. Smart boy. They went to Dave's house first. Killed Peggy, Dave's wife. Took her body over to Sharri's house and killed Tom, Sharri's husband. Cut up both of the bodies, cooked them. Then they ate themselves to death. Didn't know a person could do that, did you? Shove so much meat down your own throat that your stomach bursts.

AT: I never heard about that.

JN: Nobody ever did. By the time we found them, we already knew about Topeka and St. Louis, and we were ready. Made them disappear, too.

AT: I see.

JN: You don't see shit, but that's okay. It's nice of you to say so. Don't lie to me, you don't believe a word of this. I don't care, I gotta tell it no matter what, and I don't have much time. I wish I knew why they didn't go bugfuck right away. Maybe because they watched movies for a living, they were, I don't know, habituated or something. It took a while to work. Maybe because it was just the two of them, that it worked faster with a crowd, all those

people feeding off each other, like a mob.
I hope that's it. Or else...

AT: Or else?

JN: It *knew*. It knew that if it took them right
away, the picture wouldn't get released,
and that means that it's smart. Smart
enough to know where it wanted to be.

AT: It? What is it?

JN: I don't know. I don't know, and I don't
want to know. Ever since Auschwitz, I
didn't believe in God, and I didn't
believe in the devil. I still don't
believe in God, but now I know the devil's
real. I know it for a fact.

AT: The devil. Is that what you shot out there
in the woods?

JN: I don't know what else to call it.

AT: And the film?

JN: Burned every print and made damn sure we
got *every* print. The work prints, the
dailies, the test shots, we even cleaned
out the cutting room. There ain't one
single frame of that damned thing left. No
stills, nothing. Burned every copy of the
script, and every copy of that damned book
we could find.

AT: You're sure it's all been destroyed?

JN: I told you I was sure. Back then, movies
were big, a half-dozen reels. You couldn't
copy a movie on a flash drive like you can

today. We knew how many prints we paid for, and we burned that many. End of story.

AT: End of story. Why are you telling that story now, if it's over?

JN: 'Cause I'm dying, son. Parts of me are already dead—I'm all rotted inside. If that thing, that shadow that got into my film and killed all those people, if it really is the devil, then that's what waiting for me when I go. And that's not the worst of it. They'll be waiting, too.

AT: They?

JN: Bette, Alice, Neville, Hank, Eve... all of them. Ellie and Robin. They all died first, that means they've been waiting down there, in whatever hell that thing calls home. They're waiting for me, and they're going to be hungry.

Interview ends.

Insomnia

I am no more than a clever hand
Finger-walking around a quiet house
About the time that midnight
Turns the corner into morning

It's a nailed down fact that the sun
Is only on vacation, not retired or fired
I know it to be true, I'm sure of it
Fairly sure, or at least I was

If I were gripped by ruminations
On some dire catastrophe
Inescapable, Hamlet-like, brooding
Then I might style myself tormented

But no, not bedeviled, but be-imped
Mosquito-stung, more or less
Mostly less. Has the milk turned?
Will I need to buy more stamps next week?

Is that place in the yard where the grass died
Something that needs immediate concern?
Why can't I remember where I left my lighter?
I've got others, but where did that one get to?

I will not look at the clock, I won't
I refuse, and now it is 3:14 and now
It is still 3:14 and I could swear
That those numbers will never change

Like some mediocre circle of some mediocre hell
Cut from the Inferno by Dante's publisher
The Pit of Non-returners Of Overdue Library Books
Condemned to meander through an endless night.

Everyone Knows This Is the End of the Line
Previously unpublished

The deck chairs had been placed at wide intervals along the boardwalk so that the old woman, when at last she spoke, had to raise her weak voice to be heard by the old man.

"How do you think they'll do it?" she asked.

"Do what?" The old man was staring out to sea, watching the sun and the surf and the gulls wheeling.

"Kill me."

The old man looked over. "Eh? Why, I don't think they'll do it at all. Isn't that the point of this place? To let nature take its course?"

The old woman raised a hand—thin and pale, but not shaking. Not shaking at all. She pointed to one of the red boxes that looked like vending machines scattered along the boardwalk. "That's not nature taking its course."

The old man considered. "That's different. No one is going to make you use it. They just make it available. A convenience, like."

"A murder machine."

"It's not murder if you do it to yourself."

"They used to call it that," the woman countered. "Self-murder. It's a sin. A terrible sin."

"If you believe in sin," the man agreed.

"Don't you?"

There was a long pause. Then the man said, "It's been a long time since I've thought about it. I haven't had many opportunities for sin in my life, recently."

"One can sin in thought as well as deed."

"What am I going to think about? Sneaking an extra piece of key lime pie with dinner?"

"You could think about murder," she said, her voice lowered. "I do. A lot."

"Self-murder?" the man asked.

"No, the other kind."

"Anyone in particular?"

"The guards."

"We don't have guards. We have nurses."

"Pfui!" The old woman nearly spat her contempt. "They don't do

195

any medicine, and they keep us from leaving. Just because they wear white uniforms doesn't make them nurses."

"They don't carry weapons."

"They don't need them. Not with a bunch of old, sick people to guard."

"So..." the old man considered. "You think about murdering them?"

"All of them," the old woman's voice was harsh with emotion. "Lining them all up and machine gunning them. Don't you?"

The old man closed his eyes. The sun was warm on his face. Beyond the boardwalk, the sea rolled gently in. "There's no point. I don't have a machine gun."

"But if you did?" the old woman prompted.

"It wouldn't help." The old man sighed. "I'm eighty-one years old, and I'm dying anyway. My stomach is bad, my liver is all but shut down, I've got spots on my lungs. I'd be dying no matter what—even if there wasn't this place."

"Well, I'm not dying," the old woman said fiercely. "I'm here because I'm old and my grandchildren don't want me around anymore."

The old man opened his eyes and looked over at her curiously. "You didn't sign the release?"

The old woman scowled. "Of course I signed it—it wasn't like I had any choice."

"Well of course you had a choice," the old man said. "They can't make anyone come here. That's the law."

"The Hell they can't," the old woman shot back. "They keep working on you day and night, telling you what a burden you are to your family and how much better off everyone would be if you just... went away. It's inhuman. Using my own flesh and blood against me. Teaching a little girl to say, 'I can't afford to go to summer camp because my grandma won't go to the island.' It's cruel."

The old man turned back to watch the sunlight dancing on the sea. "It's not so bad here," he said at last.

"Everyone here is just waiting to die."

"Better than waiting to die in a hospital," the old man said contemplatively. "At least here there's a view."

"Well, I'm not going to do it," the old woman said resolutely.

"Not going to die?"

"No. I am healthy, and I am going to stay that way."

A bitter laugh. "Let me know how that works out for you."

"I'm just afraid," she dropped her voice again so that the man had to strain to hear her, "that they'll get impatient."

"The nurses?"

"The guards!"

"Whatever. You think they'll... take matters into their own hands?"

"Why wouldn't they?"

"Well, it is against the law."

"The law!" the old woman's voice was contemptuous. "Do you see any policemen here? We're outside the law."

The old man pursed his lips, giving the question serious consideration. "I don't see them doing that, honestly. This place can't cost much to run, not compared to a hospital. I expect they'll just leave you alone and see what happens."

"I'll outlive them all," the old woman announced defiantly. "I'll live forever, just out of spite."

The old man laughed, and then coughed. The coughing turned to choking, and his face was red by the time he got his breathing under control.

The old woman looked concerned and started to get out of her chair, but the old man waved her back. "I like that idea," he said at last, his voice weak but a smile on his wrinkled face. "I think you should. Will you dance at my wake?"

"Are you going to...?" she nodded her head in the direction of the red dispenser.

He shook his head. "Not like that." He looked out to sea. "If the pain gets too bad, I'll just walk out there and let the waves carry me away. I don't expect they'll bother looking for my body."

"Is the pain bad?"

"Not too bad," the man sighed. "Not yet."

"I'm glad," the old woman said. "I don't want you to go. No one else will talk to me."

"I can't imagine why not," he said dryly. "You're so cheerful."

She looked offended, then chuckled. "I suppose you have a point. But what else is there to talk about here?"

The man looked over at her. "I am going to get up," he said, "and go to the bar and have one pina colada, which will make me very drunk. Care to join me?"

Her face wrinkled into a wry grin. "I shouldn't go drinking with strange men."

"A good policy," he agreed straight-faced. "I might take advantage of you."

"Would you?" she asked. "Would you really?"

"Probably not," he said. "But we could think about it."

The woman began the slow process of getting to her feet. "Yes, let's," she said. "Let's go to that den of inequity and sin in thought."

Eyes

It's about making a connection
Between the west horizon and the corner of your eye
Sketch a line and intuit its direction
Along the transit of the sun across the sky
Where the vultures circle and wait for you to die

An exercise in expanding your perception
Details noticed never seen before
Adding objects to your mind's collection
The sunlight on the wood grain of your door
Rusty nails dripping with bright gore

You learn to see things that don't get seen
Pieces of a world not far from here
Beyond, behind, inside, or in between
A world a little odd, a little queer
A world that runs with terror, screams with fear

Once seen, of course, it cannot be ignored
Although you close your eyes and turn your head
The hollow center like an apple cored
You had to follow where the pattern led
And learned that Hell is not just for the dead

The Lord of Slow Candles

Originally published in *Sins Of The Fae*, November 2019

Thered was a fingerer clinging to the outside of the Kum & Go, just above the front door.

"Fingerer" wasn't the real name for the thing, of course, not a name by which it could be called and to which it would answer. Those kinds of names couldn't be spoken, or even thought. They had to be written down, written just right and in the right color. Grace had notebooks full of their real and proper names, the names of power. She carried them with her, carefully wrapped in plastic bags. You couldn't be too careful with that kind of thing.

But she also made up her own words to describe the things she saw and had to deal with, things that other people didn't know were there. She had to call them something, even if she was just talking to herself.

Another person would have walked right past the fingerer—the little knot of flesh with five hands radiating out from it like arms on a starfish, each with long, long, fingers—without noticing it at all.

Unless it decided to drop on them. Then it would cling to the person's head and stick those long fingers into their brain and make them *do* things.

Usually, fingerers made people eat things that weren't food. Keys and coins and little bits of gravel. They didn't usually kill the people they rode, at least not in any obvious way, not like headsnatchers or fiddlers or carpet lurks, but they made people very sick. And still no one would notice the creature. No one except Grace.

But fingerers were easy. They hated nines. So Grace tapped the door of the Kum & Go, nine times, counting each tap in a whisper. Numbers didn't have power unless you counted them.

And it had to be out loud. Counting just in your head didn't work.

When Grace reached "nine" and stopped there, the fingerer ran off, scurrying up over the roof on all those long, long fingers like a big spider. Then she was able to go into the store.

There were two clerks in the store, one she knew and one she didn't. The people who owned the Kum & Go stores had just hired a lot of new clerks because the bad store, the one out by the highway, had gotten robbed and the clerk was shot, and they decided they should always have two people working at night in all of their stores.

Grace waved at the clerk she knew, and he waved back. His name was Tom, and Grace's hidden name for him was Thomas Aquinas Spiderman, because the first time she saw him, he had a crucifix around his neck and had been wearing red and black.

He thought she was crazy, of course. Everyone thought that she was crazy. The Lord Of Left Handed Threads had told her they would when He gave her the power to hunt and fight the things that had killed her mother.

Grace accepted that. She was a practical woman. You had to practical when you fought things that no one else could see.

Grace walked the perimeter of the store, counterclockwise, turning to the right once she was through the door. At the revolving display of sunglasses, she paused to turn it and check each of the three mirrors for mouseroot, which grew on mirrors and could get into people's eyes and make them see movement in the corner of their eyes when there was nothing there. The mirrors were clean.

Then past the bags of charcoal briquettes—carefully, because there had been a carpet lurk under there once and she wasn't entirely sure she had completely killed it. Sometimes the things she fought only seemed to be dead and would come back to life later. Particularly the powerful ones, and carpet lurks were very powerful.

Then past all the car stuff—oil and brake fluid and air fresheners. She'd woven a bounceback around the display because a lot of cab drivers got stuff there and cab drivers were particularly vulnerable, since they spent so much time dealing with numbers—addresses, credit card numbers, fare amounts, times. Numbers worked both ways; they could drive things away, but they could also attract them. If a cab driver had been exposed to unlucky numbers, he might be a magnet to unseen things and not know it.

So Grace renewed the bounceback, walking back and forth six times and touching each end of the display with a different number each time. All odd numbers, and never fifteen or seven. You don't want to have fifteens or sevens anchoring a spell. Those were slippery numbers.

Then on to the drinks station, which was big and clean and neat, with different kinds of coffee and different kinds of soda and cups and straws. It was also infected. It usually was—people used it a lot at sunrise and also at noon. The four compass points of the clock—

sunrise, sunset, noon, and midnight—were when an infection was most prone to breed. There were eggs on the drinks station, fingerer eggs, eyeworm eggs, elbowtongue eggs. Grace set to cleaning them all up, tapping and counting quickly.

There were seven places in the town that the Lord Of Soft Radios had instructed her to protect, and this Kum & Go store was one of them. Grace took her duties very seriously.

"Hey!" said a voice. An unpleasant, unnecessarily loud voice. "Are you gonna buy something?"

Grace turned and was face to face with the other clerk, the one she didn't know.

"I'm gonna buy something," she muttered automatically, then recoiled.

There was a grue inside him.

Grues were the worst. The absolute worst. Grues made people *murder*.

Grace hated grues even more than she hated eyeball-butterers, and it had been an eyeball-butterer that had killed her mother.

The grue inside the clerk had gotten big and fat from eating the clerk's food. The man's stomach bulged, and anyone else would think that *he* was fat, but he was really just skin and bones, stretched over the bloated body of the grue. Grace could see the parasite through the man's skin, coiled up and squirming.

The man was frowning at Grace, looking like he hated her, looking like he wanted to murder her right now, but that was the grue looking through the man's face. The man was still inside there, but by this point, there wouldn't be much of him left. His thoughts and memories were all smooshed into a corner of his head to make room for the grue's murder-thoughts.

Grace kept tapping and counting. You didn't stop cleaning when there were still eggs left, or they'd come rushing back, and it'd be like you'd never started at all.

"Well then buy something and get out," the clerk said in his mean voice.

"Leave her alone," Tom called from up by the register. "She's a customer like anybody else."

The fat clerk looked at Tom like he wanted to murder him, too, but just for a second, and then he went off to the other end of the store to fill a mop bucket.

An Atlas of Bad Roads

It must be very late, Grace thought. She didn't sleep any more, and she never looked at clock if she could help it, so she didn't always know when it was very late. It was after midnight, of course—she always knew when it was midnight—but now it was in the silent hours, when nobody was awake except for policemen and all-night store clerks. That's when they mopped the floors at the Kum & Go.

Grace finished cleaning up all the eggs, then took a cup and filled it with coffee. As it was pouring, she felt the jingle of coins in her pockets. Then she went down the third aisle in the little store and took things off the shelves. A bag of pork rinds. A can of tiny sausages, the kind of can that didn't need a can opener. A box of donuts covered in white powdered sugar.

As she picked up each item, she felt her pockets get heavier with change. She had a lot of pockets, and the money just appeared in one or another. She always had exactly the money she needed to buy things. The Lord Of Backwards Chalkboards provided for her.

She had a lot of pockets because she wore a lot of clothes. She wore them in layers, pants and shirts and skirts, all in different colors. That was her armor—not the layers of fabric, but the layers of *color.* The unseen things were unseen because they were a different sort of matter than strictly Earthly things. Light didn't bounce off those things, it went through them. You could see them, if you had special eyes that didn't just use light, and Grace's eyes were very special.

But the business with light going through the unseen things worked both ways. They didn't see with light—how could they, when the light just passed through them?—but they could hear the vibrations of colors. Every color had a different frequency. When you wore a lot of different colors in layers, it made you hard for the unseen things to hear; you turned into a kind of blur to them.

That kind of advantage was important.

So Grace had to reach into one pocket and pull out the coins that were in there, then feel for another pocket and get those coins, and so on, laying them out on the counter in neat little gleaming piles.

Tom rang up her purchases and watched as she dug into her pockets to dump change on the counter. He sorted it into stacks, pennies, nickels, dimes, quarters, half-dollars, dollar coins. Tom was quick and good with change, and he never mixed up the quarters and the dollar coins, even though a lot of other clerks did. Sometimes you had to tell them to look again.

As Tom was sorting the change, Grace looked over at the other clerk, the one who was just a man-shaped sack full of grue.

"What's his name?" she asked.

"That's Kevin," Tom said without looking up. "He's new."

Kevin, Kevin, Bo-Bevin, Fee, Fi, Foe, Fevin, Grace thought. *Kevin*.

It didn't help. She needed a hidden name for him. That was the best way—the only sure way—to get a grue out of someone. You needed to be able to call the person by their hidden name in order to make the spell work. Otherwise the grue would come back.

But hidden names had to fit the person. You had to be able to see the person's inside face and pick the name that would make the inside face smile. Kevin's inside face was covered up by the grue. Somehow she had to get him to shake off the grue's hold long enough to see his inside face, and then she could make a spell to get the grue out of him altogether.

And she had to do it quickly. The grue was almost full grown. Soon it would make Kevin kill somebody. Maybe tonight. And the only people around were her and Tom, and she didn't want either of them to get murdered.

Especially not her.

"What's he like?" Grace asked quietly.

Tom looked over at Kevin briefly.

"He's okay," Tom said, but he didn't mean it. He couldn't see the grue inside his coworker, but he could feel that there was something wrong. "He's just in a bad mood."

"Do his socks match?" Grace asked.

Tom gave her a sharp look, then laughed. "You noticed that, too?" He lowered his voice. "I think he can't see his feet past his belly."

Grace nodded gravely. As grues got closer to fully controlling their host, they were less and less mindful of keeping up the illusion of being human. Mismatched socks was one of the signs that Kevin's parasite was ready to make its move.

But he must have been human enough to get this job, and even a store manager desperate to fill shifts would have noticed something seriously wrong with the man. He must have been okay when he had the interview.

That meant the grue had grown fast—faster than they usually do.

Of course, if Kevin worked nights and kept his windows covered during the day, he didn't get much sunlight. Still, there had to be more. He probably had 1111 in a number he used a lot—a phone number or credit card number or something.

Tom was looking at her kindly. "Are you okay, Grace?" he asked. "You need anything else?"

Grace shook her head and took her bag out into the parking lot. She had to figure out what to do, and she did her best thinking under the stars.

She walked to her usual corner by the air pumps. She began counting steps—four, stop, six, stop, two, stop—to shoo away the tanglers that infested the air pumps, then paused.

The air hoses hung neatly coiled on pumps. There was no sign of the tanglers.

Tanglers didn't live inside people; they infested places and just influenced humans who were in the area. Grace had kept them away from the gas pumps, for the most part, but she'd never been able to clear out the nest by the air hoses.

Something else had.

It must have been the grue. Kevin had gone out by the air hoses, probably to smoke, and the grue had reached out and snatched up the tanglers. Eaten them.

It must be very strong. The strongest grue Grace had ever seen.

Grace looked around the air pumps. There were cigarette butts all around the ground. Menthol ones. She looked inside the trash can. It was full of snack bags. Salty chips.

She could imagine Kevin out here by the air pumps, smoking and eating chips, his mind filled with thoughts of killing, while the grue inside him snacked on the tanglers and grew fatter and stronger...

"Get off our property!" The voice quivered with barely controlled rage.

Grace spun to face clerk. He was advancing on her, a box-cutter knife held comfortably in one hand. Not that he would need it against her, not with his bulk and her slender frailty.

Grace dashed six steps to the left, singing, "*Where* the *hot springs bub*ble and the *cold* winds *blow*," then hopped in the air and dashed five steps backwards, "I *know* some *place you can't go!*"

Then she ran into the street, thinking furiously. Behind her, Kevin was looking around in confusion, but the little charm wouldn't last

205

long. Not long enough to weave a really solid spell of invisibility.

Grace could get away, though, because even stuffed with grue, Kevin wouldn't venture far off the property while he was on the clock. That would mean abandoning Tom, though.

And the Lord Of Brass Springs had entrusted this place to Grace. She had to go back to the Kum & Go and save Tom. To save Kevin, too, if she could. It wasn't his fault he'd become infected with something he couldn't even see.

Grace ran lightly across the parking lot to the glass doors of the store. She felt her charm fading, knew that the grue would be after her in seconds. She needed to weave the exorcism quickly and have it ready to go. She went through the doors and skipped down the first aisle, counting steps.

When she got to thirty-five, she slowed to a walk and started tapping the shelves as she passed them. Twenty-one on the left side. Seventeen on the right side.

The fat clerk burst through the doors, slamming one back so hard that the glass cracked.

Grace's heart jumped, but she didn't lose count. Exorcisms were long, complicated rituals, and this one had to be perfect. If it wasn't...

"I'm going to kill you!" the grue roared through Kevin's mouth.

At the counter, Tom was moving his head back and forth, gaping at both of them. "Jesus, man," he breathed. "What happened?"

Grace reversed directions and kept counting. If she could keep the aisles between her and it long enough to finish the spell, she might have a chance.

The grue ran Kevin's body through a display of chips, scattering bags as it ran after her. Tom was coming out from behind the counter, saying loudly, "Calm down, Kevin!"

Thirty-seven taps on the left, then back to counting steps. Fortunately, the direction of the steps didn't matter, not with an exorcism, so she was able to keep ahead of the grue.

But then it lunged into a section of shelves and knocked them over into Grace's path. She hopped over it without losing count, but he was right behind her now, and his beefy hand grabbed the collar of one of her many-colored shirts.

His other hand came up with the knife.

Grace kept her feet and lips moving. *"Seventeen, eighteen, nineteen,"* she muttered.

Tom was there, and he grabbed Kevin's arm. "What the *hell,* man? If she did something, we can call the cops. What is wrong with you?"

Grace started to tap her fingers together, but Kevin's arm was around her neck, choking her. She kicked back and felt the arm loosen just a bit as Kevin grunted in her ear.

"*Thomas Aquinas Spiderman,*" Grace gasped out. "*Count to fifty-one. Now! Out loud.*"

Tom's eyes grew wide as he felt his mouth open and heard himself begin to count, his body obedient to the compulsion she had laid on him with his hidden name.

"One, two, three, four, five, six...."

The grue paused for a moment, torn between a choice of targets, and Grace drew in another ragged breath. She was stronger than she looked, but that still wasn't very strong. She prayed to the Lord Of Reversible Umbrellas for the strength to keep fighting the grue for just a little bit longer, then ducked her head and tried to bite Kevin's arm. She couldn't reach it.

"Twenty-four, twenty-five, twenty-six, twenty-seven..." Tom's voice was regular as a metronome as he struggled to pull the pair of them apart.

Kevin's hand came up with the knife, and Grace jerked with all the power in her spindly limbs and managed to get her teeth on the hand, biting hard. The knife went clattering off somewhere, and the arm around her throat loosened enough that she could draw a deep breath.

"Forty-seven, forty-eight, forty-nine, fifty, fifty-one," Tom chanted.

"*Kevin Kool Kat Rancher!*" Grace cried, "*I declare you clean of all infestations and possessions!*"

Kevin's vast bulk spasmed, and Grace was thrown against a rack of shelves which started to totter, spilling cans of chunky soup in all directions. Behind her, she heard Kevin hit the floor.

Gasping, black spots dancing before her eyes, Grace turned. Kevin's body was vomiting up the grue, convulsing. Tom knelt beside him, trying to hold the big man's head steady without getting spattered with what he would see as thick, almost clear fluid.

The grue was crawling away like a huge worm. Grace followed it. It was as badly hurt as Kevin by the violent separation. It would die without a human host. All Grace had to do now was make sure

207

it didn't find one in time.

"Hey," Tom shouted. *"What the fuck just happened?"*

Grace kept her eyes on the grue. "It's better you don't know," she said wearily. "Call an ambulance. He's gonna need a doctor."

Grace hurried up and wove a circle around the grue, tapping out all the sacred numbers she knew to keep it contained.

While she was working, the ambulance showed up and turned the parking lot into a kaleidoscope of red and blue light. They put Kevin on a rolling stretcher and wheeled him out the cracked glass door.

He'd be okay now. Probably. At least he wouldn't be a killer.

One of the paramedics came up and wanted to look at the bruises on Grace's neck. She told him to go away and kept walking circles and counting.

Eventually he did.

The grue turned gray and started to melt, turning into a pale liquid that steamed and bubbled for a while and then evaporated, leaving the tile floor clean. Grace did one more circle, just in case.

There were men up at the front of the store, talking to Tom in voices of strong, quiet concern. Grace listened as Tom told them that Kevin had some kind of attack, and that Grace had helped hold Kevin still so he didn't hurt himself.

Grace walked out towards the door, very aware of Tom's eyes on her. But nobody tried to stop her.

It wasn't very late any more. It was very early, and the sun was coming up.

The dawn was green with heavy clouds, and the wind as hot and wet as the breath of an amorous giant. As Grace stepped out into the parking lot, the cars of early morning commuters avoiding her without the drivers quite seeing her there striding away in triumph, the clouds opened with a thunder crack, and the rain came down.

It was warm and fragrant, and Grace turned her face to the sky.

The rain was cheese soup, with onion and pepper. Grace drank it in, feeling warmth through her and a distant memory, before the bad times, of her mother making her this very same soup when she was a sick little girl.

No one else could taste the soup, to them it was just rain. The Wednesday morning people kept their heads down and cursed the weather.

Grace alone felt and tasted the feast the poured down from the sky, and reveled in it, turning her body as she walked down the middle of the street, all the cars too obedient to the arcane mathematics of the rules behind the rules to come near to hitting her.

The Lord Of Slow Candles was pleased with His chosen servant.

End Notes

"Mystery Train" I wanted to write a Western and I wanted to write a Catholic Fantasy, and somehow those ended up being the same story. I, myself, am not Catholic, but I did have several friends who are read it over and made changes based on their suggestions. I flatter myself that G K Chesterton would approve of this one.

"The Summer Of Love" This story grew out of a discussion regarding Communism and Fascism during the second world war. It occurred to me that Hitler and the National Socialist Party might have been the only thing keeping Germany from becoming a Soviet Bloc nation, and a Russian-German alliance could have actually taken over the world. From there, I came up with the idea of a time traveler who goes back to kill Hitler and returns to find that he's made things worse.

"Burn Silent, Burn Bright" This is an intensely personal story. My own upbringing was not so bizarre (or quite so interesting) as Michael's, but casting off an old belief system isn't easy, even when you intellectually know it to be false. In some ways, there is a deep part of us that never quite escapes where we grew up.

"Dead Man's Chest" I wrote this for an anthology of "Pizza Horror". It was rejected there, but accepted by a publisher who now, sadly, seems to have dropped out of the business. I have never trusted the frozen pizzas sold in bars, and you shouldn't either. You are what you eat, indeed.

"Black Dog" I love this story. I originally wrote it for a collection called *Sins Of The Gods,* and in case it isn't perfectly clear, the black dog of the title is Anubis. The main character is a composite of myself and a long time co-worker. Both of us had messy divorces, and honestly, this is more a story about men recovering from a divorce than it is about death.

"227 Progress Loop" I wanted to write an "unfinished business" style ghost story, and I'm not entirely sure I succeeded. I probably should have expanded on the relationship between Michael and Mistress Paradox, but there didn't seem to be any way to do that. Eddie is peripheral to what happened between Hecate, her boy, and Paradox, so I left it there, with the main character never finding out the whole story.

"Epilogue" is a retelling of a classic fairy tale. I leave it as an exercise for the reader to figure out which one.

"The Blacklight Ballet" I wrote this one for a project that ended up folding before it began, and I can't complain because it was my project. I had the idea of doing a collection of 21st Century Pulp stories—classic Pulp adventures that weren't historical fiction, but set in the current day. I got a lot of really good material and had made a deal with a publisher. Then the publisher went under. Fortunately, most, if not all, of the stories written for the project found other homes.

"The Old Covenant" I don't tend to write a lot of pastiches of other author's work, but it should be obvious that this is Lovecraft's "The Shadow Over Innsmouth" from the perspective of the deep ones. I never liked the ending of the original story, with the military moving in with explosives to destroy Devil's Reef. Why? The folks in Innsmouth weren't hurting anyone. So I decided to write my own ending, and feature a main character who accepts his nature and eventual transformation.

"The Silk Of Yesterday's Gown" I'm not entirely sure where this story came from, except for a vague dissatisfaction with how The Fair Folk tend to be portrayed in Urban Fantasy. Fairies are not the good guys. They are wicked and evil and seductive and not to be trusted. The title is a kind of sideways paraphrase of the lyrics of The Velvet Underground's song "All Tomorrow's Parties".

"The Darkest Hour Of The Night" Another ghost story. This one was originally written for a collection of ghost stories that all took place in the same house, with each author taking one room. I took the garage, and this is what came out. I like the Twilight Zone conceit of the story told from the ghost's perspective, with the exorcist as the antagonist. The Haunted House project never got off the ground, so I'm glad I was finally able to find a home for it here.

"What Lola Wants" I wrote this one for Switchblade Magazine, and they bought it. I deliberately mimicked the style of old True Crime magazines, with an unnamed first person narrator who does a very bad thing for the very best of reasons.

"A Cup Of Kindness" I wrote this for a collection called *Yuletide Horror*. The stories were supposed to be about Christmas, but I'm not good at following instructions and went with New Years Eve instead. This is kind of "A Christmas Carol" if the young Scrooge had been confronted with the ghost of the old Scrooge.

"We Pass From View" This is one of the fastest stories I ever wrote. I basically just sat down and typed it straight out, just as you see it here. The backstory refers to my first novel, *Catskinner's Book*, but it's not necessary to have read the novel to appreciate the short story. I love movie gossip, and I always wanted to write a story about The Film That Was Too Terrible To Be Shown. This is it.

"Everyone Knows This Is The End Of The Line" I try to avoid politics in my work, but this is an unapologetically political story. If you think that legalizing assisted suicide is compassionate then you need to brush up on your history.

"The Lord Of Slow Candles" This is my attempt to write a Tim Powers kind of piece. If you're not familiar with his work (and you should be, he is one the giants of Fantasy fiction), what he does is take real historical events that don't make sense and invents a supernatural rationale for them. I used to be a night clerk at a convenience store, and we'd get customers like Grace. So I started with the question, "What if everything that a so-called 'street crazy' does is actually a perfectly rational response to something that I can't see?"

www.ingramcontent.com/pod-product-compliance
Lightning Source LLC
Chambersburg PA
CBHW051133020726
47501CB00005B/1491